MATT RUBINSTEIN was born in 1974 in Sydney, Australia,
lived in Adelaide for fifteen years before returning to Sydney in
1997. He practised law for five years and now writes full-time.
He is currently working on a new novel, a feature film script
and several short film projects. He is Gillian Rubinstein's (aka
Lian Hearn) son.

0

VELLUM

Matt Rubinstein

Quercus

First published in Great Britain in 2007 by Quercus
This paperback edition published in 2008 by

Quercus
21 Bloomsbury Square
London
WC1A 2NS

A CIP catalogue reference for this book is available
from the British Library

ISBN-13 978 1 84724 293 8

10 9 8 7 6 5 4 3 2 1

Typeset by e-type, Aintree, Liverpool
Printed and bound in Great Britain by Clays Ltd, St Ives plc.

ᎣᎾᏩᏂ· ᏳᏲᏣᏆᏩᏁᏏ

SOUTH TYNESIDE	
38664	
Bertrams	19.01.08
CNL	£7.99

ℊℂⱲ∩∩

The sea had been here, years ago. There was still a slipway for raising and lowering boats, an old wharf, a tangle of cranes and gantries. The concrete tables of a picnic ground overlooked the beach. But the beach went on forever, now: the old seabed was desert sand to the horizon. Soviet agricultural policies had diverted the rivers that fed the inland sea. The fishermen had all left; the cannery had survived on fish trucked from the Baltic, but not for long. The village was sinking into the poisoned sand.

Zhenshchina wandered the seabed as the sun began to set. Rusting ships lay in the sand, casting long shadows back towards the village. She was old; perhaps she had lived here as a girl before the sea went away. The shadows gathered in the lines of her face as she pressed her cheek to the hull of an old fishing boat. Flakes of rust came away at her fingers. The sun glowed in the crusts of salt the sea had left behind. It was a beautiful and terrible scene, perfectly composed, slightly grainy with the high-speed film.

There was something heartbreaking in her expression, and Jack leaned closer to make it out. She was looking for something; she had lost something among the graveyard ships. Perhaps long ago, when the boats were still afloat, the sea deep with mysteries, when she and her friends had played at the beach. Jack didn't know what it was, but her hand kept rising to her left breast, or her heart, and he thought she might have lost a lover or even a child. He shifted in his chair.

A stocky man stepped out from behind a half-sunk dredger: Chelovek. He wore jeans and a baseball jacket. He stuck his hands into his pockets and looked around like a tourist. He stopped beside Zhenshchina and neither of them spoke. There was no music on the soundtrack, only the sound of the wind. It made Jack shiver. But he liked the falling light, the hulks in the desert, the two of them.

The woman said, 'After it rains a little on Thursday.'

Jack eased the brake pedal and her lips paused, slightly apart. He rubbed his forehead and reached for the script. Photocopied many times, fastened with industry brads: half a page of stage directions, then a little rain on Thursday. He'd never seen a Cyrillic typewriter, but he could imagine its mirrored letters and extra keys. And the phrase intrigued him. Only a little rain, and why on Thursday? There must have been complex Slavic reasons: the pale midnight steppes, the tundras and taigas – and the course of some historic Thursday altered forever, and all because of the rain.

It wasn't a common idiom, even in Russian, but he knew what it meant. It meant never. When hell freezes over, when pigs fly. But none of those sayings had the yearning, the poetry. They weren't even close.

He pulled the keyboard closer and the computer woke. The cursor blinked at him. He saw his reflection in both screens, his sandy hair, his grey eyes staring through his glasses. He was thirty-two years old, and he didn't know how to subtitle the line. *Never? On a cold day in hell? After a shower or two on Thursday, which as everyone knows is very unlikely?*

The man and the woman in the desert, the ships looming over them, the salt and the sand – they needed the right subtitle. But he wasn't even sure what Zhenshchina meant. Was she refusing to give up her search, or resigning herself to failure? Was she thinking about the phrase itself, as Jack was? A little rain, there in the desert, the fishing village a hundred miles from water – did she finally understand what it meant?

2

He typed in a few alternatives, but none of them fitted. Perhaps he was wrong about the idiom. Was *chetverg* really Thursday? He felt a gathering panic. He wondered when Beth would be home.

The film was called *Kino*. It was notorious in certain circles, and there had been some doubt that it could ever be subtitled. Polish maybe, Czech, but never English. His colleagues had warned him when he'd first heard about the job, and their doubts had made him bold. But he had been arrogant, foolhardy. The panic gave way to dread.

He switched to the reverse pedal and rewound to the beginning of the film. He must have missed something in the desert and the setting sun, the staring and the sound of the wind. There had to be something. There had to be a perfect translation.

The temperature was dropping; the air held the promise of winter. Beyond the light of the screens, the church felt sanctified and cold, still like the church it had been for more than a century. Its ceiling was too high, its roofbeams lost in shadow. Through the tall windows – the squints – the sky was low and overcast, and gnarled trees stood by the churchyard's only headstone. Jack left his desk and padded through the nave, looking for a warmer jacket. Behind the raised and railinged chancel, a series of stone cells or oratories led into the vestry, the linoleum kitchen and bathroom. Stone walls, stone in the ceiling, stained glass in the windows. It lay a few kilometres from the city centre, in the eastern suburbs of Sydney. It was the eleventh stone church built in New South Wales.

Beth's father, Frank, had preached here for fifteen years – long ago, before Jack had known him. He had been a young and enthusiastic minister, but his congregation had dwindled, the building had run down and the diocese wouldn't repair it. Frank had bought it for a psalm and spent years fixing it up, mostly by himself. But its doors had never reopened, and his flock had never returned.

He had been dead for a month. Beth had looked at the floor when the executor read out Frank's codicil, listening for his voice through the lawyer's talk. She was surprised by her father's wishes. But she and Jack had been renting an apartment full of mould and whistling edges and the smell of week-long stocks and sauces, and they couldn't wait to leave. And Frank had wanted it, after all; it was his will and testament, and that was enough.

The nave had been dusty as the moon when they'd moved in, and scuffed with Frank's footprints. Beth had wanted to keep the dust and the footprints to remember him by. But they'd opened the heavy doors and all the squints, and the wind had eased in and worn down the footprints like the tide. There were piles of magazines in the oratories, some theological, some scientific, all stiff with age.

Jack had unpacked his video equipment and hung the posters of films he'd subtitled, Russian and German. Beth was taking care of the last of the legalities. Their moving boxes stood among the pews and pulpits. He picked his way through them as he returned to the desk. Clothes and photographs and many hundreds of books, boxes everywhere.

He was still circling the film when Beth came home. He heard the heavy door, her footsteps knocking through the porch. He swivelled and left his chair to meet her.

She was covered in rain. He had pressed so close to the screen that he hadn't noticed the storm worsening. Now brackets of rain lashed the windows, and the jacarandas snapped in the lightning. The wind howled, and Beth was soaked through. Her hair fell over her face and ran into her mascara. She stood in the middle of the nave and dripped onto the floorboards.

'Sorry, I'm so late. I had to—'

After hours in other languages he often felt his English had atrophied. He wanted to reassure her, but all he could do was draw her in and muffle her with his shoulder. He held her as tightly as he could, hoping she would understand. She leaned back and kissed him on the mouth, cold with rain, warm with everything else.

'I had to make sure Mum was all right.'

'Is she?'

'I don't know. She kept – she's got this teapot full of whisky, and she kept pouring herself cups of it. I mean, Delft teacups of whisky. I don't know who she thinks she's fooling.'

'That's—' He paused. 'That's not a bad idea.'

She smiled. 'I guess she was all right. They're not so big, are they? Those cups. And she just sipped at them. She blew on them, and took little sips.'

Beth held an imaginary cup in the okay of her fingers, blew through her pursed lips and made a pleased drunk face. She returned to herself and shook her head.

'She's all right.'

He persuaded a slick of hair from her forehead. 'How about you?'

'I'm all right too. Thanks.'

He saw that she'd been crying, unless it was the rain. She saw him looking and took a few steps into the nave. When she reached the shrouded altar she brushed her fingers against it. She looked like she was dusting for fingerprints.

'I mean, it was complicated,' she said. 'There were lots of things to sign. I wasn't really listening, it's all so – I can't believe it's mine, it seems too strange. Ours, I mean.'

'It's yours, of course it is. Your church.'

'I'm not so sure I want it, all by myself. I don't know if I can handle it.'

'Of course you can. That's what Frank wanted.'

'He seems to have, doesn't he?'

She pulled her mouth to one side, the way she did when she couldn't quite smile. Her shoulders felt like sponges in his hands.

'You're all wet,' he said.

She let him unwrap her coat, roll the turtleneck over her

5

head, unbutton her shirt. She kicked her boots and socks off and followed him to the corner they had called their bedroom, over on the gospel side; she left her jeans twisting on the floor. She sat on the bed and raised the quilt to her shoulders with a shiver.

'Thanks, Jack.'

She was tall and slender and had astonishing skin. In the autumn it was fading to paper-white. It was paled by her dark eyes, her hair almost black when dry, now black with rain. In the summer it tanned to a comprehensive brown, which suited her better. But Jack liked her winter skin, goosepimpling at his touch, stretched over her chest's blue veins. It was barely there at all.

He sat beside her and stroked her shoulder. She felt soft and uncertain. She dripped into his arms, and despite himself he watched her breasts pressing at the quilt. He tried to shunt away from her, embarrassed – but she always knew. He felt her smile at his throat and she leaned up to kiss him on the jaw and reached for the tight part of his jeans, then stood up and wrapped the quilt around her body and returned to wander the church. She felt the stone's corners, stared along its planes and angles.

'You know it was ten years ago, when he bought this. I thought I was remembering wrong, but it said so on the thing, on the title. Ten years.' She scratched at the sandstone with her fingernail and rolled the loose grains against her thumb. 'He was meant to fix it and get everybody back, that was the whole idea. That's why he bought it in the first place.'

'That's what I thought.'

'But look, it's fixed.' She glanced up at the ceiling, jutting her bottom lip. 'It's all done. There aren't any nails to bang in, there's no chalk marks or sawdust, there's nothing even to file back or spack over.'

The only way to light the whole church involved the fluorescent strips in the roof. Jack and Beth had resorted to the floorlamps, which spilled bright disconnected circles and left giant shadows. But Jack looked around the nave and knew she was right.

'So how come—'

She gave a series of small, quick nods. 'How come he just left it, how come it was never a church again?'

'Right.'

'Exactly. I don't know.'

She slipped from one island of lamplight and washed up on another. She had the beginning of a tattoo on her left shoulder: two intersecting lines in a deep black, one of them curved. She'd been drunk on her eighteenth birthday, but not too drunk to change her mind. Now she couldn't remember what sort of tattoo she'd asked for, ten years ago. It could have been the first two lines of anything.

'But the funeral was weird, don't you think? There was something weird about it.'

She climbed the chancel steps; she felt the door with her thumb and shuffled into the oratories. Between the bouts of rain Jack could hear her footsteps and the hollow sound of boxes. The noise kept fading, as if the oratories went on forever.

ᚢ丿

'The joy of our heart is ceased; our dance is turned into mourning. The crown is fallen from our head.'

Jack had never belonged to a church or known any holy men, but Frank had looked the way he thought a Protestant minister should. He was a tall, pokerbacked man with a square head and a proud chest, both tanned to leather and thick with white hair, and a broken nose like the boxer-priests from movies. He never wore his dog collar, but you could tell that he once had: the skin of his neck, the way he held his chin. He was softly spoken for a preacher, but otherwise he seemed thoroughly clerical. He was serious, helpful, and unnerving, with something unshakeable inside him.

'I went mourning without the sun. I stood up and cried in the congregation. I am a brother to dragons and a companion to owls. My skin is black upon me, and my bones are burned with heat. My harp, also, is turned to mourning, and my organ into the voice of them that weep.'

The bishop conducting the funeral looked more like a casino boss, with his ashtray sunglasses and his prow of silver hair. There was something unconvincing in his posture or his voice. The cemetery beetled over the Tasman Sea, tucked between the city's famous beaches. Whitecaps swept below them, and the hills bristled with stone angels.

'But it is better to go to the house of mourning than to go to the house of feasting. Sorrow is better than laughter: for by the sadness of the countenance the heart is made better. The heart of the wise man is in the house of mourning.'

Frank had been a wise man, said the bishop, or at least he'd always tried. He was famous at the seminary for his match-winning hook shot and his impersonations of the Three Stooges. But those who knew him better were struck by his battles with the scripture and his appetite for learning, from biblical archaeology to quantum mechanics. His sermons were often long, rarely orthodox, always worth hearing.

'Wisdom – she crieth at the gates, at the entry of the city, at the coming in at the doors. Hear; for I will speak of excellent things. I am understanding; I have strength. I love them that love me; and those that seek me early shall find me.'

Beth was almost monochrome in her dark suit and her pale skin, until she took off her sunglasses. She squeezed Jack's hand. Her mother, Judy, stood with her head bowed beneath a flat black boater and a fishnet veil, an obsidian expression masking her face. And their friends were there, Thorn and Peter, Sandy and baby Dev. They smiled and blinked away tears, though they'd only met the dead man two or three times – and Dev never had, and he cried harder than anyone.

'We commit his body to the ground: earth to earth, ashes to ashes, dust to dust.'

Beth had pointed out some of Frank's old congregation; they shifted their weight and looked guilty. There were priests and deacons in cassocks and stoles. Frank had died from a heart attack, but at the funeral it had seemed more like a suicide, an unsanctifiable death. Nobody mentioned heaven, or the life to come, or God.

5

Beth emerged from the oratories carrying a cardboard box. It wasn't one of theirs; with her hair still wet and the quilt left behind it looked like she'd rescued it from a shipwreck. The glass in the squints flowed with waterfalls, and thunder rattled the churchstone. She sat on the floorboards in her underwear and showed him her hoard.

'Look, I noticed this yesterday, I thought I recognised it. It was behind the magazines, it must have been here the whole time.'

She reached into the box and held it all out to him. Old albums and wallets of photos: toddler Beth and toothless beaming Beth. Plastic cans of Super-8 film, a cartridge of slides. And handfuls of childhood drawings, a game of cricket, a day at the beach, dedicated in crayon or rainbow pencil to Mum and Dad from Beth or else Beht. He watched her as she unfolded the pages and looked for herself in the photos.

'He said he was fixing the church, but he was here by himself, here with all this stuff. He could have opened the doors and asked everybody back, but he sat here by himself – and looked at these pictures, he must have. Every day.'

She twisted towards him, near-naked in the church, the old promises all fulfilled, and he swallowed. She pushed the drawings back into the box.

'I hate that, I hate to imagine him here all alone.'

He soothed the side of her neck and didn't know what to say. She leaned into his hand and he felt the blood sailing through her.

'What was he doing?' she said.

Jack looked around the church. A siren moaned along the street. The rain on the stone made everything seem distant. He shrugged.

'It seems like a good place to think.'

'About what?'

'I don't know. I would have said God. But maybe it was the Three Stooges.'

She smiled at him. 'Maybe.'

He stroked her eyelids with the first two fingers of his hand, barely touching: a tender version of the trademark poke. She let him close her eyes and tilted her face into his palm. After a moment she looked crookedly at him.

'Was that – did you just do Moe?'

'I think so,' he said. 'It might have been Shemp.'

'That's – a bit off, isn't it?'

'Probably. Sorry.'

'Do it again.'

He went for her again, and she raised her hand like a blade against her nose and forehead, trapping his Stoogefingers. She grinned, and her eyes filled with tears as she pulled his hand from her face.

'That's what we used to do. He was so embarrassing. Not only a minister but with that sense of humour, I couldn't stand it. God, this is so wrong.'

'It's all right.'

She looked shyly at him. 'What else have you got?'

He leaned in and bit her gently on the nose, still Moe; her face wrinkled. She stroked his cheek and he stroked hers, a gentle slapstick. She took his nose between her knuckles and twisted it for him, nyucking away.

There were different moods of passion, he thought. Maybe sorrow was better than laughter after all. He reached for her as the rain sharpened against the roof. The windows rattled in their stone frames.

He folded his jaw around the Brooklyn vowels. 'Why, I oughta …'

She led his hand over her body, the corrugations of her ribs, a palmful of breast, the ridge and descent of her hipbone and thigh. Lightning flashed and she glowed. 'Maybe you oughta.'

He found his fingers slipping beneath her elastic; he felt her warmth and the wet scratch of her hair. The trees were epileptic, tearing at themselves, and an unattended door banged through the neighbourhood. She bit her lip and stared and blinked and stared again, and he leaned in to kiss her and stopped.

It sounded like artillery on the roof.

And the church was suddenly full of shingles and moss, mud and broken wood, shimmering water and ice hanging in the air for a long second, reflecting streetlight and lightning and appearing to circle, glittering – until an immense dark shape fell like a winged creature through the carousel of debris and splintered into the chancel floor, and the whole sky of the church cascaded around them.

Beth shrieked and hid her head in her forearms as the night opened above them. A tranche of roof tiles teetered and fell. They both leapt up and slipped on drifts of hailstones. A jagged chunk the size of Jack's fist landed, spinning, on the floor. Beth picked up the box of photographs and ran into the oratories. Jack heaved the desk into a corner, away from the rain. The hail kept pelting, stinging his skin. Beth was screaming or laughing; he couldn't hear her over the din.

They saved what they could and hurried to the bathroom. Jack lit candles and Beth filled the bathtub with warm water. They lay together and felt the heat soaking into their bodies.

Ripples spread across the surface as the taps dripped out of time. The tub was huge and old, with clawed feet that seemed profane in the church. The hail had melted to rain and it was quiet outside: only the steady sound of runoff from the roof. Jack reached for the hot tap with his toes.

Beth sank her hands, tiny whirlpools. 'Do you think God's mad at us?'

'For defiling His house, you mean?'

'Or trying to. I did go to this church for twelve years. Something like that. It feels a bit weird to be messing around in it.'

'We got it deconsecrated, didn't we?'

'Maybe it didn't take.'

'That guy – he was a bishop?'

She considered her wrinkled fingertips. 'He might have come around for dinner, at least once. I remember him arguing with Dad.'

'He almost seemed eager to do it,' Jack said. 'What did he say? To appropriate it to other worldly purposes.'

'I'm not sure this is what he had in mind.'

'It's just and right and not displeasing to Almighty God.'

Beth smiled. 'It's not too bad.'

She leaned back into him and tilted her head against his chin. Her breasts nudged the surface of the water, foamed with soap, and her legs rose glistening to the edge of the tub. His sudden hard-on urged the smooth skin of her back, and she shuffled backwards into the tangle of his arms and legs.

The water had calmed them. It felt like the safest place to be. Every time he thought about the nave he saw the chancel's wedged stone and broken woodteeth, the spreading mess of the floor, and he had to think about something else.

He herded bubbles across her chest. 'Or do you think Frank's mad at us?'

'You want to talk about Frank?'

'I don't mind.'

The water had reached the bathtub's rim. He searched for the plug and sent waves to the floor. She leaned forward and spoke to him over her shoulder.

'I never told him I'd stopped believing, I was just busy every Sunday until I moved out. And he didn't want to ask, but he must have known.'

'Or else he would have asked.'

'I think so,' she said. 'And I certainly didn't tell him about going to see cover bands and smoking cigarettes with boys even I didn't approve of, but he must have known that too. He was a lot smarter than me.'

'When you were fifteen.'

'Especially. But maybe he didn't, maybe he had his own – if there were things about him, stuff I didn't know. Not opening the church, giving *me* the church. I hid things from him but I thought we had enough. I didn't realise he was holding back too.'

Jack shrugged. 'I never understood anything about my parents. I thought I would, after they died. I was waiting for some kind of flash, at the funerals, or the next day. But it's been years.'

'What did you want to know?'

'A lot of things. What they thought of each other, how come after the divorce they hardly spoke but kept moving to the same cities, all over the world. Were they ever really happy, and when.'

'Maybe there's still time, somehow.'

She raised her knees and rested her cheek against them, looking out into the gloom. The rain had stopped, and the air was cool and easy to breathe. He wiped soapsuds from her back, uncovering her tattoo. He brushed it with his thumb.

'Maybe it was a mermaid.'

'What was?'

'Here.' He traced flowing hair and breasts and a tail into her back. 'Or an anchor, or maybe a lighthouse. Here.' He drew a great beam across the rocks of her spine.

She looked over her shoulder. 'What made you think of that?'

'I don't know.'

'Maybe it was going to say *Jack*, maybe I knew all along.'

'Then how come you didn't go through with it?'

'Tom would have killed me.'

He splashed water into her face, and she laughed.

'Harry wouldn't have liked it either.'

'All right.'

He slid his hand down her side and into the bathwater. She backed into him, nudging his cock with the cleft of her buttocks, full of otherworldly purpose. She flexed her body, as if testing it – then lifted herself on the bathtub's rim and slid onto her knees.

He grinned. 'What are you doing?'

'Hold still.'

She found him with one submerged hand and lowered herself precisely. The tub filled with currents as Jack held her hips and reached for her breasts and she rocked into persuasive angles. She filled the air with slow panting, and he felt the first tilt of his descent, the steepening, and muttered to himself, *a little rain on Thursday, on Thursday*. They settled into a slower rhythm, an unrhythm that made them laugh as if sharing a joke – until he felt her muscles clenching and the room swam with all of the sea gods and goddesses. Beth made a noise that could have been laughter and shook, perhaps with tears, and wouldn't show him her face until she'd caught her breath and he'd imagined all of her expressions converging into a kind of lost sadness, which surprised him.

The church looked worse in the daylight. The chancel a landslide of splinters and stone, the sky through the roof. The furniture sprawled across the nave, boxes piled against the walls and stacked on pews. The bed and the floorboards were steaming already.

Beth stood and stared at the mess. 'Jack, look at all this.'

'I know. It's not finished now, is it?'

She rolled her eyes. 'No, this is much better.'

Branches and trees had been blown or smashed down all along the street. Every car was dented, every windscreen starred or shattered. Neighbours in pyjamas wandered through their shredded gardens, shaking their heads. The storm had battered most of the suburbs between the city and the eastern sea, lifting only when it reached the harbour. Hail the size of cricket balls, the size of half-bricks.

An efficient team from the Emergency Service arrived to bandage the street with blue plastic sheeting. The church took half an hour of ladders and guy lines to secure. The rigger swore at his hitches, then remembered where he was. He wiped his forehead. 'You two live here?'

Beth nodded. 'We just moved in.'

'Power'll be back on in a couple of hours. Hope you're insured.'

'It's a church, it must be an Act of God.'

The rigger raised his eyebrows and put his shoulder into the knots. Misty clouds drifted away in the brightening sky. The forecast was for a little rain later in the day.

*

15

The tarpaulin admitted a blue light to the church, and the stained glass had survived to smear the rubble with colours. The heaviest roofstone had fallen into the raised floor of the chancel and broken through to the older floor a foot below. Jack caught a pale glimpse of the original floorboards – and something else, a glint of gold as the sun moved over the roof.

'I think this could be okay,' Beth said.

She was lifting the movie posters from the computer and the television, where the rain had plastered them. A Japanese cartoon full of bright disembowellings, an erotic history of Gutenberg. Some were laminated and seemed to have deflected the downpour; the rest left offset colours and came apart in her fingers.

'It might need the hairdryer, that's all. And this stuff in boxes should be all right. It's lucky we're so hopeless.'

She probably got her pragmatism from Frank, who was always turning up with something useful: fuse wire, a newspaper clipping. He'd taught her how to tie knots and talk about sport, and how to get on without him. She tried to prise open a swollen book, then consulted the cover and wrinkled her nose and threw it away.

Jack turned and stepped into the ruin of the chancel.

There was a hollow sound at his feet, a wrong echo as the light glanced again off a brass ring set into the old floor. He knelt and swept the silt from a furrow between the boards. He traced it into a right angle. He tipped the heaviest stone away to reveal a perfect square. A flush square rounding at the corners, a tarnished ring – a trapdoor at his feet.

'Look at this.'

She looked up from her pile of books. 'What is it?'

He lifted the ring and showed it to her, stomping his feet. The echo sounded like caverns beneath them.

'Did you know this was here?'

She shook her head, and the muscles in her face shifted into an arrangement of doubt. 'Are you going to open it?'

He tilted the ring towards her. 'You should do it.'

She shrank back. 'It's – maybe it's not a good idea.'

'Because of Frank?'

She nodded, and for a moment he thought he saw it – beneath her resilience, the cost of her father's death and their move to the church, the storm and collapse. For a moment she looked tiny and the church huge.

'No, let's open it,' she said.

'We don't have to.'

'Go on.'

He saw that she meant it; he reached and pulled at the trapdoor. It was heavier than he'd thought. He staggered sideways and it opened to a gust of stale air. Beth stood a few paces back, and he saw the smell sweep across her face.

'Oh, what—'

'It's just air. I think.'

She wasn't convinced. 'All right.'

Steep stone steps retreated from the trap, turning as they disappeared into the darkness – and Jack had the feeling that the darkness down there was occupied, it was somehow full. Even Beth felt it; he could tell by the lean of her body. All the church's lines had pointed to the altar. Now they drew the eye to this gap.

'Do we have a torch?' he said.

'I'll get a candle.'

Angular shadows loomed in the candlelight as they felt their way down. The walls were rough and dry, the air hollow. There were ten or a dozen steps. He coughed, and the darkness held his cough as he swept the candle and the flame dipped and guttered in what was clearly a crypt.

'Jack?'

'Yes.'

It was three or four metres long, slightly less wide, slightly taller than he was, carved from the natural rock and finished with the same stone as the church. The chisel marks joined and separated in the shifting flamelight. Recesses cut into two walls at knee and shoulder height, each wide and deep as a man laid out. It was cold, and a soft whisper seemed to issue from the rock.

He kept expecting the light to flare into sudden horrors. But there were no skeletons, no suspended knuckles. Nothing but old dust rising in the new air. Jack ran his fingers along the recesses, swept the candle into the corners. The crypt was empty, but he couldn't stop looking. He felt his skin goosepimple, as if the rock had sighed on him. He couldn't tell whether it was the memory of corpses, the bonedust joining the rest of the dust, or just the emptiness. Beth shivered at the same time.

The porch door closed heavily, and although it sent vibrations through the crypt it seemed to have happened in another church far away. Footsteps clocked across the floorboards, and for a moment Jack felt that they'd been caught in an elaborate trap: the will, the hailstorm, all contrived by enemies. But it was only Beth's mother, who had let herself in.

'What in – what on earth's happened here?'

They looked at each other in the flickering light. He almost put his finger to Beth's lips: they'd hide down here until the coast was clear. She saw the temptation in his eyes and smiled at him, and for a moment it seemed like a warm place, a place without secrets, and he was sorry to leave it.

Judy had grown up in a bad neighbourhood and had escaped it through hard work and grammar. She never mentioned the suburbs of her childhood, and had screamed at Beth for saying *haitch* or *somethink*. She was always well dressed and carefully made up, but somehow brittle. She struck Jack as a kind woman unsure of her place, as if she had never decided whether Frank was more or less than she deserved. Jack had often wondered what they were doing together, the way he wondered about most people.

'I knew something like this would happen. That man and his projects.'

Beth kissed her. 'It was the storm, it happened to everyone.'

Judy stepped over the chancel's remains and frowned up at the tarpaulin. 'It can't all have been the storm.'

Jack didn't know when she had last been to the church. She was wandering through it uncertainly, as if it had been years. She didn't seem to want to touch anything.

'It was all fine when we got here,' Beth said.

Judy only looked slightly surprised. 'It was finished?'

'He didn't tell you?'

She shook her head. 'He must have just finished.'

Beth gave him a look. He could see her trying to decide how much she could ask Judy. 'Was he still coming here, every day?'

'He said so. He left every morning and came back at night. I'd ask him how it was and he'd say it was coming along.'

'You never came down?'

Judy sat on one of the covered pews and surveyed the tiles and planks where the chancel had been. She looked like she wanted to drag on a cigarette, though Jack had never seen her smoke.

'We were married here, did you know? It was the first thing he did after they ordained him and assigned him: he arranged our wedding here.'

'I knew you were married here.'

'There wasn't much of a congregation. They were all off making vegetarian quiche for the markets. But it was a beautiful – well, a picturesque building, and his own ministry. The things he was going to do.'

'Didn't you wonder how it could take him ten years to fix it?'

Judy looked up at the stained glass: an open Bible surrounded by rays of light, grimy with dust and city rain. 'It was a big job, it was completely dilapidated. And then there were only two of them. I suppose I wasn't surprised that it should take so long.'

'There were two of them?'

'He had his friend, the one he used to take running. He was a proper tradesman, even a mason. He had a Catholic name.'

'Like Pope?'

Judy looked pained. 'No, O'Something. O'Rourke. You might get him to come back and see to this, if he's still working.'

'We might. We will.'

Judy ashed her invisible cigarette and felt the dropsheet between her thumb and fingers. 'I wonder if I'll ever see it finished. The way it was.'

'We'll be done in no time.'

'That's what your father said.'

Beth's eyes were filming. 'Why don't you stay here for a while?'

Judy looked around. 'Where?'

'We can sleep in the bathtub. It's huge.'

'Don't be silly. I'm all right.'

'You're sure?'

Judy nodded. 'Are you?'

They were all nodding, all blinking. Jack didn't know what else anyone could do.

ʊ)

He knew that when people died you had to do things you couldn't explain: particular, crucial things. His own father had given up fishing after the divorce and the Buddhism, but he'd taken Jack to a long jetty, creaky with salt and gullshit, and sat with him all night as the tide heaved at the piles. He'd said almost nothing, just wanted to spend the night there with his twelve-year-old son. It was only once, but Jack had driven the five hours from his father's funeral to sit by himself on the jetty. He'd had to do it. A couple of fishermen had caught a decent yellowtail; Jack watched it somersaulting on the deck, then bent and threw it back in. The one in the flannel hat stood and asked what the fuck, but the other one had seen Jack's black suit and tired eyes and held his friend back with a small firm gesture. He'd known what Jack now knew, about the specific things.

The power flickered back on towards the end of the afternoon. Beth chose an old reel from the box in the oratories, and Jack unrolled the screen and threaded the projector. The film was from the silent, eight-millimetre seventies. Frank had chestnut hair and sideburns and looked almost superhumanly vital. Judy looked like Farrah Fawcett, silently teaching her four-year-old to say *th*. There was always water: the beach, the backyard pool, the garden hose. Beth had thick blonde hair and brown skin; she looked like a negative of her older self, the Beth who sat on the pew and watched the unfolding light. There was something ancient about the movie, its faded colours, the jittering scratches and stains.

She turned to him, gathering the old lights on her skin. 'Look, there we are. That's exactly how I remember it.'

'It's great. It's exactly right.'

'Isn't it? It's ideal. Every time I saw anyone's home movies I thought they were ours. I'd always be waiting for the camera to find us.'

'You had a home-movie childhood.'

They were all at the beach, building sandcastles, burying each other in sand. Shallow waves swept in and out of the frame too quickly. He couldn't tell which beach it was; the background didn't have enough focus.

'Mum and Dad and little Beff. Look at them. Aren't they in love? They must have been, with all that hair.'

'You can't argue with that hair.'

'They're younger there than we are now.'

Jack peered closer, and she was right. Judy could have been Beth's little sister; they had the same jaw, the same shoulders. Frank wore a blue singlet bursting with chest hair. He bent to Beff and jabbed two fingers at her eyes; she mashed at her forehead with one curled hand and fell into giggles.

'Was that—'

'Don't get any ideas.'

The camera lifted to the sun and the beach disappeared. The screen darkened and Jack thought the bulb had gone, but he looked again and saw faint stars sprinkled against the night, orange sparks helixing skyward. The film wasn't quite up to it, and the church wasn't dark enough, but it looked like they'd shifted to a park for a barbecue, all silhouettes and coals.

Beth squinted at the shadows. 'He always made us stay until the sun went down and everyone had left, and we'd have chops and he'd show us the stars and tell us everything he knew about them.'

Jack thought he could see Frank kneeling by Beff and pointing dark things out to her. The clicking of the sprockets seemed louder. There was something timeless about the scene, the gentle hand Frank rested on Beff's shoulder, the rapt angle of her head.

'He told me about this theory that right at the beginning the universe blew out to a gazillion times its size – *whoomf*, like that – much faster than light. And although that only made it about the size of a cricket ball, it was enough to explain everything.'

'Cosmic inflation? Or something.'

She nodded. 'I asked him if God made the *whoomf*. And he wouldn't answer me, he just looked at the sky, and then a week later he came back and said he didn't know.'

A faint beam rolled across the screen, stretched and returned. Judy must have been filming; she moved in on the barbecue, its glowing worlds. Beth's face flickered red and orange as she watched from the pew.

'He never said anything different, even in church. He never read anything from Genesis, or any miracles. There were great chunks of the Bible he wouldn't go near.'

'Strange, for a minister.'

'He got into all kinds of trouble. But he wouldn't believe

in impossible things. He had to find other explanations, or just ignore those parts.'

'There must have been a lot of them.'

'There were.' She looked up at him as the film ended. 'Maybe, in the end, he ran out altogether.'

'Maybe.'

The screen flared and the reels rattled, whipping the air, but Frank was still with them, alone in the church, pitting his Bible against stacks of journals, painfully bracketing verse after verse. Like an Antarctic castaway forced to burn his raft for its lifewarmth, plank by plank.

Beth had taken a day off work to help mop up the church and clear the rubble; now she was back at the library on an extended shift. Jack had spent the morning tidying the boxes away. Some of the pews and floorboards had warped as they dried, but the church was in reasonable shape. He hadn't yet tested the video or the computer with the Russian film.

He had swept the crypt's corners with a lamp on an extension cord but found no more than he had with the candle, nothing to explain his first feeling. Now the lamp stood in one of the recesses, letterboxing the crypt with shadows. Small sounds echoed through the stone, voices from far away. They only made the crypt seem more desolate. He'd be glad to fill it with wine.

The recesses were the perfect size. He loaded a case of Hunter reds he'd bought with Beth. They hadn't been impressed by the tasting but had been allowed to stomp grapes in a wooden tub, the pulp between their toes, the blood-purple up to her shins. Then a cabernet from the Coonawarra. He remembered touring through the gnarled parallels, picking handfuls.

He stooped and hefted a box of semillons and verdelhos bought with an old girlfriend, feeling abstractly unfaithful. They'd promised the case would age and mellow, but he was certain it would be sour by now. He didn't know why he kept it.

The wine resisted when he tried to slide it in beside the others. It stuck out halfway, stubborn as the ex-girlfriend.

He pushed it harder, and the case wedged into the recess but wouldn't sit flat.

He pulled it out. The recesses had been finished with shallow flagstones, fitting together into smooth slabs. The flag behind the sour case jutted above the others. He tried to push it down but couldn't. He tried to lift it and broke a fingernail. He cursed and tried again, and the crypt seemed to shake with his effort – but it lifted.

The stone fell heavily to the floor, and he pulled at the lamp and shone it into the recess. He half-expected to find a secret passage, a cathedral of stalactites stretching beneath the suburbs. There was nothing like that, just a dent in the rock. But in an instant he realised why the crypt had never felt empty.

It was almost an inch thick, the size of a thick comic book. Its pages were irregular; its edges bristled. A grimy cover wrapped around the outer leaf, folded over like a dustjacket. Apart from its smudges, the cover was blank. He sat with it on the nave floor, thinking that he should wait for Beth to come home. Even in his pool of afternoon sunlight he had a cold feeling.

The telephone rang, and he wondered how he would explain the manuscript to her. It felt old and important; it had a dusty weight that he couldn't describe. But there was nobody on the line. He said hello and then hung up, disconcerted but unsure why.

He returned to the floor and the manuscript and eased apart the folded edges. They crinkled and sighed, and he felt he was breaking something. The leaves wanted to close again, so he had to hold them down. The new pages were lighter than the covers. Two words centred on the right-hand side, a title in an embellished script. It was too complicated and faded to read.

He caught an edge with his fingernail and worked the leaves apart. The parchment complained as he turned it, brittle beneath his fingers. The next pages shimmered like light in water.

It was a controlled but frantic hand, a linear script wriggling between the creases. It had been written quickly but precisely. It was disrupted by two crude pictures: a superimposed man and woman on the top left of the page, arms and legs at various angles, and a squat tower in the opposite corner, crumbling to the margin, sprouting inkweeds.

He had seen illuminated manuscripts before: their giant decorated capitals, their gold leaf and diamond serifs – mostly reproductions, but a few originals in the dim light of famous libraries. The Lindisfarne Gospels and the Book of Kells, each a cathedral of parchment, the culmination of many lifetimes. All of their angles precise and identical, their proportions perfect, their pigments invaluable.

This was nothing like them. The crammed letters bunching at the bottom of the page, the tiny detail of the illustrations, the creases and folds and stains of the parchment. The other manuscripts looked like reason, ages of reason and illumination; this new manuscript looked like madness.

Jack had learned to read late, and could still remember his bafflement as parents and teachers had tried to explain how these curious marks could mean particular things. He'd taken their word for it, but for a long time he hadn't really believed in it. He'd caught up with his classmates in the end, but even now he suspected that his reading wasn't quite like everyone else's. He still saw the shapes and symmetries of words an instant before he recognised their meanings, and in that instant he wasn't sure they were words at all.

This was the same. The script was plain but graceful, the hand lean and confident. The letters were tiny sculptures, and he couldn't read any of them. He felt again like he had before he'd learned the trick, the secret that everyone else knew. This wasn't any alphabet he had seen: it had dots and loops and embellishments where none belonged. But he could swear it was some kind of writing.

He pulled at the page but couldn't read the next page either. He tried to flick further into the manuscript, but his fingers fumbled and the edge tore.

'Jack?'

Beth hovered above him, home at last. Her shadow passed over the manuscript and gave the writing another character. She leaned over and rested her hand on his shoulder.

'What's that?'

'In the crypt, under a stone. It's some sort of parchment, don't you think?'

She knelt to touch it. 'I think it's vellum.'

'What's the difference?'

'We've got some in the library. They make it from cows.'

'And parchment?'

'That's from sheep – they make it from sheep, or else goats.'

'I see.'

'It's all skin, though. It's all different skin.'

'Can you read it?'

She had looked away and didn't seem to hear him. He tugged at her shirt.

'Is it writing?' he said.

She squinted at the page. 'I don't know.'

It was bewildering. He'd seen nothing like it; he had no idea what it meant. He closed the manuscript. Beth picked it up and brushed it solemnly.

'This is it, this is what Dad was doing. Something to do with this.'

'You think he wrote it?'

She looked offended. 'Why would he write it?'

'I don't know,' Jack said.

'It's too old. He must have found it.'

'And this is what he was doing?'

She nodded. 'The Samaritan manuscripts, the Dead Sea Scrolls. He was always looking for more helpful originals. For ways out, I suppose.'

'You think it's like that?'

'Or some argument about – I don't know, God and physics. Or some extra gospel. Something that did something to his faith.'

Jack looked again at the battered vellum, the pile of pages. It didn't look like much, with its smudged cover and illegible title. But there was something dreadful about its opacity, its suggestion of dark meanings.

'Maybe,' he said.

'Can we find out what it is?'

He'd seen all kinds of alphabets: not only Cyrillic but the scrawl of Arabic, the landscapes of Chinese. He'd picked his way through them, learned a few of their meanings. This writing looked harder; it looked fused and ancient.

'I don't know,' he said.

'Maybe there's something like it in the library.'

There was something in Beth's expression. The unreadable writing made him nervous, but he had to help her if he could.

'We'll go tomorrow,' he said. 'first thing.'

ᴗ)

The wine was cool from the crypt and now the first chill of night, but it warmed at his touch. It hadn't aged well; it tasted dull and insidious. He resolved to drink it as quickly as possible.

Beth was asleep. She must have been exhausted, mourning Frank and trying to understand him, and Jack felt a sudden urge to protect her that he knew she would have smirked at. A patch of moonlight crept through the stained glass and over her face, and her brow creased.

He took another gulp of wine and held up the manuscript. The peaks and valleys of ink. The dots drifting into dashes, the personality emerging from the lines. The three dimensions of the calfskin's surface. There were pictures of plants and minerals, of the heavens, of strange machines and tiny squat people. He drained his glass and refilled it.

The wine reminded him of another old girlfriend, from long ago. He'd been driving through Italy with a high-school friend who went on without him. A golden and orange time, flooded with sunset. Rosa: she only spoke Italian, and he hadn't known a word. Her language, her unknowability terrified him – but her eyes, and her legs … Now he supposed it was probably just sex, but then he had thought it communication beyond words. They talked without needing to understand. They looked into each other's eyes and knew when they were thinking the same thing.

But he couldn't keep it up; he needed to know for certain. He bought books and language tapes and discovered he had an aptitude. He had basic Italian within six weeks. He could see the way the language and soon all languages fitted together; they made a spatial kind of sense to him. He only had to fill in their structures with verbs and idioms.

Of course he and Rosa had nothing to say to each other. She became self-conscious as his understanding grew. Her torrents dried up, and everything she said disappointed him. When he knew enough to translate the things he'd been telling her all along, she looked blankly at him, breaking his heart.

He threw out the books, but it was too late, the language was already growing inside him. Then French and Spanish, and a detour through German that led at last to magnificent Russian. A career in translation, despite everything. He'd left Rosa far behind by then. He'd never seen her again. Now she was just a taste and memory as he sat in the moonlight and touched the skin of a thing he could not understand.

6 Jack had met Beth three years ago at the library where she still worked, the state library in the middle of the city. He'd been subtitling a Colombian film and recognised a quotation from a book. He had to return to the book to get the line right, to get the movie right.

She wasn't at all like even beautiful librarians were supposed to look. She had long, dark hair and wonderful skin and wore a singlet; she looked like she had wandered there by accident. He cleared his throat and was nervous.

'I'm looking for *Love in the Time of Cholera*,' he said.

She said, 'I think I'm coming down with something.'

And he stared, and smiled, and that was it. A courtship of repartee: he translated poetry for her, she found poems about translation for him. At foreign movies he told her the dirty jokes the subtitlers had ignored. She took him to readings and let him thumb the rare books. They felt like the most romantic nerds, the luckiest nerds.

'Are translators like translations?'

In bed together, having slept together for the first time, after hours of undressing.

'How's that?'

'What is it – the more beautiful, the less faithful?'

He'd smiled and traced something unreadable into her skin. '*Traduttore, traditore*, they say.'

'Italian?'

'Translator, traitor.'

'Well. Something that rhymes in two languages just has to be true.'

'That's right. You've got to watch us.'

It wasn't true. But there weren't any jokes or diversions to express how he really felt – how he'd already felt, even then.

He remembered their beginnings as he carried the manuscript through the rare books collection. It was an airtight and temperature-controlled room in the library's depths. He felt a quiet awe as he searched the painstaking folios copied by monks, the first printed works. Different kinds of parchment, paper in all weights, rags and softwood and bleach. It muffled his footsteps and warmed the air.

There were books in many alphabets about many other alphabets. He copied them down until he ran out of pages. Reproductions of cuneiform and hieroglyphics, mathematical Greek. The letters of Hebrew were meant to represent the shape of lips and teeth and tongue – you could pronounce them by looking. Ogham was good for carving on sticks, Oriya perfect for palm leaves. He read Proto-Canaanite and Early Phoenician copied from tablets. Eastern European scripts derived from Glagolithic and Cyrillic showed many ways to write a little rain on Thursday.

Beth was returning books to their shelves and helping people through the decimal system. She kept stopping to check on his progress. He was startled every time, lost in the alphabets. A few looked promising, but it was just the handwriting. He matched some of the manuscript's letters to the examples in the old books, holding them awkwardly in the aisles. Gothic *othal*, Greek *phi*, Hebrew *kaf* and *chet*. He saw echoes of Arabic and Samaritan, Berber and Phoenician. The alphabets diverged wildly, but there was something that united them. And this new alphabet was related to them, though not closely. Beth saw him puzzling at his discoveries.

'Did you find anything?'

He shook his head. 'I'll show it to Thorn tonight, on the boat. He knows more about this kind of thing.'

Beth gave him an uncertain look. 'Just keep it away from Mum, maybe.'

'You're bringing Judy?'

'I thought it might be nice for her. Peter said there'd be room.'

'Oh, of course. It'll be fine.'

She nodded and wheeled her books away. He'd forgotten for a moment whose manuscript it was. And he couldn't help wondering how Frank could have made anything of a language nobody else seemed to know. He'd been a fiercely educated man, but as far as Jack knew his interest in linguistics was limited to the Bible's Hebrew and Greek, perhaps Aramaic, and the manuscript wasn't any of those.

But even untranslated it could have shaken the minister's faith. The mysterious illustrations, the worming script – you could go crazy just looking at it. Had Frank prayed for guidance, like the translators of the Bible? If he hadn't been answered, if he'd been left alone with this intractable thing – that alone might have used him up. As he brushed the vellum with his fingers and felt tiny shocks from the letters, Jack thought that he might easily have reacted the same way.

ʊ)

It had rained and then stopped, and the harbour seemed fuller than usual. A mild Saturday night: the autumn was holding on. Low clouds travelled between the two shores, and the city lights grew haloes of red and white and blue. Dozens of charters and cruises wandered among the bays and bridges: farewells and stag nights, office parties. They all looked slightly lost behind their salty windows, their old carpets.

Peter had met them at the ferry wharf and helped them aboard the patrol boat. It was sleek and new, spiky with radio equipment. It left a foamy spiral as it rose through the water. He was forty years old, tanned and crinkled, a diver with the water police. He took them on joyrides whenever he could; they all loved the unearned privilege, the escape.

'Are you sure this is allowed?' Judy asked.

'It's fine.' Peter took her hand as she stepped down to the deck. 'This one isn't even in service yet. We're testing it, and what better way?'

Thorn was already sitting like a figurehead on the prow. His real name was hard to pronounce, but he signed it with the old rune they still used in Iceland, and everyone called him by it. He translated sagas and eddas; he collected foreign idioms for Jack. He was tall and lean and seemed to shimmer with silver, his hair, his pale eyes. He turned to raise a hand to them, then sat back and rode the pitch and roll of the boat.

Peter watched him with pride. 'He just won an award, but he won't say anything.'

Beth looked impressed. 'For what?'

'His society of Norsemen, they give an award for best – what's it called? You know, the sea is the whale-road, the sky is the moon's way. He tried to explain it to me.'

'What was his?' Beth said.

'*The soul's sail and sun*. Love, you know?'

'That's wonderful.'

'Not bad, is it?'

Sandy climbed down from the bridge deck. She was strikingly beautiful, half-Indian with surprising green eyes. It was Sandhya, really, but her name had been tamed like everyone else's. She was the only single member of their small circle, and accepted their envy and pity with equal grace. She rarely bothered introducing her dates to them, just returned with stories or silence. She'd studied librarianship with Beth, and now worked at a religious collection in the old part of the city: the Deposit of Faith.

Jack kissed her carefully. 'Where's Dev?'

'He's a year old, he thinks this kind of thing is beneath him. My parents are giving him the attention he deserves.'

She looked tired, but there was a glow to her. She wore

Peter's denim jacket over a gold dress. She held a glass of champagne and could have been on a billionaire's yacht, anywhere in the world.

'Your police friends are gorgeous,' she said to Peter. 'Are they straight?'

'All policemen are straight,' he said.

'I know – but what about these ones?'

'Even these ones,' Peter said. 'Straight as they come, Dave and Warren.'

'I'd better get back to them,' she said. 'Is there any music?'

'Thorn's got some, but you might not like it.'

Sandy raised her glass. 'Thorn!'

Thorn clambered down to the aft deck; they congratulated him on his award and he glared at Peter. Sandy returned to the bridge, and Judy followed her in search of drinks. She didn't look like a widow in her limpopo pantsuit and silk scarf. Peter watched her as she stooped into the cabin.

'How's she doing?'

Beth shrugged. 'She seems all right. She seems – well, not fine, but almost.'

'She looks good.'

'I know. She always does. It's hard to tell what she's thinking.'

Thorn reached for her forearm. 'You should remember what the Germans say. Everything has an end – only sausages have two.'

Beth gave him a sad smile. 'The Germans say that?'

Thorn's eyes brightened. 'You know what else they say?'

'No, but that's all right. I'd better go and help her.'

She climbed the steps to the bridge deck. After a moment the boat made a series of showy turns and all the women in the cabin laughed; Peter's police friends were enjoying themselves. Thorn shook his head and turned to Jack.

'How's *she* doing?'

'She's getting through it. We found something in the church, we think it belonged to Frank. What do you make of this?'

He took the manuscript from his jacket and unfolded it. Thorn and Peter huddled over it, both attracted to the strange text. Jack felt their hands on his back, thought they might have touched fingers, just for a second. There were more pictures further in: an atlas of illustrations, a travel guide to earth. Tiny wobbling pyramids and a passable sphinx, a reedy delta. Short men in conical hats by pagodas; dark women dancing on volcanoes, naked but for strung skulls. The people were all small and fat, like sacks. Thorn leaned in and traced the writing.

'What language is it?' he said.

'You don't know?'

'I've never seen anything like it.'

'You're sure?'

'A couple of these, are they letters? They could be runes, perhaps stylised runes. But nothing else. I don't know what it is.'

Jack took the manuscript back. 'Who do you think would know?'

'One of the other translators, maybe?'

They had worked with all kinds of dubbers and subtitlers, translators of poetry and instruction manuals. They had dozens of languages between them. But Jack didn't trust them; he looked at the manuscript and knew that he couldn't stand to see it passed around.

'I'd rather keep it a bit quieter than that.'

Peter was staring at the pages with as much interest as Thorn: he only spoke one language, but he knew about secrets, about buried things. 'Maybe it's some kind of code.'

'What kind?'

'I don't know. You'd want to find out where it came from, and when.'

'How would I do that?'

Peter paused. 'One of the forensics guys we use, he's into all these old books. He even did some stuff for Thorn, he might be able to help.'

'Would I have to hand it over?'

'Some of it; you might have to destroy a bit of it.'

'I'm not sure I'd want to.'

Peter shrugged. 'He could tell you if it was real, at least.'

'Real?'

'Or a hoax. I think a lot of these things turn out to be hoaxes.'

Jack chewed his lip. The manuscript's time in the crypt, under the chancel, and if Frank had spent his last thoughts on it – it couldn't be a hoax. He didn't like people doubting it. And he didn't like the idea of giving it up, let alone destroying it – any of it. He didn't know why he felt so protective.

'I could arrange something,' Peter said. 'If you didn't want to go in.'

'Like what?'

'Bring this guy round, maybe. Some excuse.'

'What about your place?' Jack said.

Peter looked guilty, and Thorn said, 'We don't do that.'

'Sorry.'

'You could have a housewarming – a churchwarming,' Peter said. 'Imagine it, all that stone and atmosphere. With ultraviolet light, everyone dark and glowing, even Thorn's music. Do you still have those lights?'

'I don't want to make it a big thing.'

'The music would go well,' Thorn said.

'It just seems a bit soon.'

'What about dinner?' Peter said.

'Maybe. We could have dinner next week.'

'Good,' Peter said. 'We'll have dinner. Sandy might like him too.'

Two of the sack-people sat together on a hill, four in what looked like a lake or an enormous flower. One stood in a library of tiny books while another searched for it. They might have been legends of a lost culture. They might have been sackish kings and queens and heroes sitting there in flowers. It couldn't be a hoax. It might have been a code, but he felt it was something more precious than that. It had to be an old language, a lost language – lost until now.

The harbour opened up and the swell lifted as they travelled towards the east. Thorn's fingers wandered to whatever Peter was touching: the railing, the life belt. The boat passed a tiny island. A canopy of well-dressed people turned to watch as the police boat approached them and banked away. Sandy and Judy appeared with their drinks. Sandy sat down and made a show of looking grumpy.

'They're trying to teach Beth to drive the boat,' she said. 'How can I compete with that?'

'She's very charming,' Jack said.

'I know, she can't help it.' She turned to Thorn. 'What happened to that music?'

'Are you sure?'

'Sure.'

Thorn unfolded himself and swung into the bridge. After a minute his music drifted over them. Peter was right: it was nothing like the music that carried from the thinning party boats. It was bleak and tectonic; it howled along the boundary between high winds and human voices. It sounded eerie over the boat's loudhailers. Thorn emerged from the cabin and returned to the prow without a word.

Peter tilted his head towards the cabin. 'You should get back down there. They're sailors, anyone can pick them up.'

'Thanks a lot.' Sandy turned away from him. 'I was being all ditzy, I can't quite get it right. Did I tell you, I got dumped by a text message last week.'

'I've had that,' Peter said. 'And twice by e-mail, and before that by telegram. They don't even have those any more.'

'You think you're more tragic than me?'

Peter grinned. 'I was in a disastrous love triangle with identical twins. The ugly one loved me, the beautiful one spurned me.'

Sandy raised an eyebrow. 'I was living with a guy for three

months when he walked out without a word and I never saw him again.'

'Me too. And it was his house.'

Sandy pulled his jacket close around her shoulders. 'I loved someone, and he loved me. But over time, I saw that he was loving me less and less. Just a little less every day, and nothing I could do about it.'

'It happened to me, too. But I was the one loving less and less, and I couldn't do anything about it either.'

A headland obscured the city, and houselights dotted the shores. The clouds ranged above them, the air thickened, and the music was almost drowned by the wind and the slap of the wake.

'It's lucky we've got Jack and Beth,' Sandy said.

Jack turned to her. 'What's that?'

'You're our last best hope. I don't know what we'd do without you.'

The boat yawed, and Thorn slid across the foredeck and into the railing. He thumped the prow and shouted something in Icelandic. The boat returned to its course and Thorn righted himself, scowling.

Peter turned to Sandy. 'We've always got each other, sweetheart.'

She looked at him gratefully. 'I know, Peter.'

'Shall we dance?'

'We can try.'

They climbed a ladder to the flybridge and approximated a slow waltz in the night air, stepping out of time as the boat moved beneath them. Judy stared out at the darkness or the coast, and Jack didn't know what to say.

'I'm – look, I'm sorry about those two.'

Judy smiled. 'Oh, no. They're gorgeous.'

'I just mean – well, you must think they're so trivial.'

She leaned on the rail and looked out to starboard, and Jack joined her cautiously. It was a good way of talking, it felt safe. You could say anything to starboard.

'I'm glad you're there for her, Jack. They were right about that. She and Frank were something, there was always something between them. I feel better knowing that she has you.'

'She's pretty resilient.'

'To a point.'

Thorn's music had run out, or the policemen had turned it off. The boat continued through the silence, the beat of the hull on the water. Judy finished her drink and held the glass in both hands as if it were warming her.

'I have to tell you, Jack. Losing the man you were married to for thirty years – it's worse than being dumped by a text message, though I'm not certain I know what that is. But perhaps it isn't as bad as some of the other things.'

Jack shook his head. 'I can't even imagine.'

'Frank was a good man, but it wasn't always easy between us. Especially in the last few years. I don't know why I'm telling you this.'

'It's all right.'

'No, I mean I really don't know the reason.'

There had always been an element of performance in Judy's manner. Now she seemed truer in the wind and the night, and Jack didn't know what to do.

'I know when my father died – especially – there was a lot of idealising,' he said. 'A lot of revision. But I wanted people to remember how he really was, kind of flaky but also cold, in a way that was only him. That seemed like the right way, it seemed important.'

Judy gave him an untranslatable smile. 'Perhaps that's it.'

The boat accelerated as the lights on the northern shore gave way to darkness, and steered a gentle curve to pass on the right side of a beacon. They were back in safe hands. Judy glanced towards the cabin.

'Don't say anything to Beth,' she said. 'She's always idealised him.'

In a moment Beth was between them. She took their arms and stared to starboard with them. Her skin glowed in the

39

night, cheeks reddening. Jack felt her warmth and the warmth of their windbreak.

'They won't let me drive any more,' she said. 'Did you show Thorn your manuscript?'

'He doesn't know what it is.'

Jack reached into his jacket and felt the manuscript against his heart. He wasn't discouraged. There were failed and failing languages everywhere, in romantic tragedies, in the memory of whoever Frank had been – it was a miracle that any survived.

'What manuscript?' Judy said.

'Nothing, Mum. Just something Jack's working on.'

Beth squeezed his arm and looked guiltily at him before her attention was drawn once again to starboard.

'Oh, look.'

The boat had cleared the last bay and was approaching South Head, where the lighthouse swung its beams out to the horizon, solid and yellow in the mist. Judy had turned and was looking up to the flybridge, where Peter and Sandy were dancing through the silence. But Beth stared out to the lighthouse with a kind of rapture, as if she'd been at sea for years.

'Jack, I have to show you something.'

'Here?'

'Soon.'

And there on the starboard rail all languages seemed precious, and he and the world couldn't afford to lose any of them – not the codes of touch he shared with Beth, not the heresies of Frank's and Judy's lives, and not the loops and whirls crumpled in his coat. He felt a sudden rush of resolution – he would save them all. He was their last best hope as the boat carved a pale arc of surf, turned from the lighthouse and heaved again towards the city.

The best thing about translation, about learning new languages, was the texture it gave to everyday things. It wasn't just a chair any more. It was the French for chair, the Russian for chair – and they all meant different things, their sounds and connotations. It gave objects new dimensions, emotions new subtleties: it wasn't just love, it was all the words for love.

If the word was forgotten, the thing was diminished. Any mountain or ocean or wind, any city would be less if any of its names were lost. As the world was lessened when it forgot how to read the old scripts, Indus or Meroitic or Rongorongo. As it was lessening with every lost language, even now – especially now.

The first time, the hours of undressing. He had named each piece of clothing in every language he knew. All the words for shirt and skirt, for singlet and sock. And all the words for the parts of themselves they uncovered, stomach and breast, nipple, nape. It had taken hours. He had stumbled at the last words, and they had invented their own words that sounded stupid at first but became plausible. She was better at it than he was, and had turned his attempts into surprising and exquisite words, words for cock, words for cunt he wished he could remember.

Jack felt the manuscript growing familiar as he sat at his desk and turned it in his hands. Seven thick quires, each packed with ten or twelve doubled sheets, roughly cut, covered on both sides – almost three hundred pages. A strip of leather bound the quires and the cover into a codex. The vellum had torn and been repaired, but the stitching had failed and only the tiny holes remained. He thought about what Peter had said the night before, about his forensic friend. He wondered whether he could give any of it up.

A series of giant letters followed the sack-people. Some were the same as the script's smaller letters; they were all drawn in outline and labelled with lines and circles. It looked like a calligrapher's handbook, tiny comments marking each loop or diagonal. Or like the Asian ideograms in which every brushstroke had its own meaning – each letter a blueprint of sound or meaning.

Was the manuscript a last attempt to preserve the scribe's dying language – a last best hope? And with the language, all of the truths packed into it by the generations who had lived through it. Jack imagined himself writing down all the words he knew, as the desert swept in, as the seas rose and the hail pelted. This is who we are or were, and this is how we spoke to each other: if those are different things.

His stomach tightened as he turned the page and found familiar writing at last: a line of Greek, a line of Sanskrit, perhaps a dozen other alphabets. He recognised them from his search in the library. He thought for a shining moment that this might be a key to the manuscript's language, its own Rosetta Stone – he felt it between his shoulder blades. But it was just the letters of each alphabet, in alphabetical order. There was no comparison to the manuscript's own script, no clue, and after all his poring these old alphabets seemed as unreadable as the rest of the manuscript.

Peter's friend would flay the pages for their pigments and grit, their carbon. He might uncover the key Jack needed: the name of a city, a river or king he could use to crib his way in. But Jack couldn't part with any of it. You never knew what might be critical, a smudge of pigment, a stroke of the pen, even the creases in the vellum. Sacrificing any of it could leave the whole thing meaningless.

Here, a section full of plants and minerals, outlandish roots and leaves, magnified crystal and cleavage. Then a cauldron over a slow flame, flasks of various shapes and sizes, light passing through prisms. The colours still vibrant after centuries. It looked like the physics of a new world, but of course it was this world, the world of pyramids and pagodas – so it must have been a new physics for the world, many explanations for a complicated world.

Beth opened the porch door and a gust of wind slipped through the church. The final quire showed a contraption of gears and levers and glass, then a series of bizarre images: gnomes evolving giant foreheads, blank faces; a range of weather conditions, sun, snow, hail, heavy rain, light rain; and a tower topped by fire. The last picture was of stained glass, a Bible or other heavy book in leadlight. Jack felt he was watching himself being watched as Beth crouched to look at the manuscript, hand on his shoulder. She smelled like a day's work. She loosened her top buttons.

'What do you think it's about?' she said.

'I don't know. It could be anything, or everything.'

'Some kind of encyclopaedia, do you think?'

'Perhaps.'

'Can you read it yet?'

He shook his head. 'These letters – there are about twenty-five, it's hard to tell. Which would make it an alphabet, probably, not syllables or ideograms.'

'So maybe it's English? Before I and J were different, or before W? Or Latin, or Greek or something.'

'But look at these people, the way it's all drawn, it's not like anything. I think it's a whole new language – I mean, whole old language. A lost language.'

Beth looked dubious. 'You don't think it's a code?'

'It might be a code; it might be something completely

ordinary, in code. But it looks – don't you think it feels like more than that?'

'Like what?'

'I don't know. Creation myths, miraculous old stories, the deepest stories. Things we can't imagine, we don't have the language.'

He ran up against her look, and stopped. He knew he was getting carried away. He couldn't explain it; he couldn't tell where his hope ended and conviction began. Beth turned back to the manuscript with the look of someone adding or multiplying things.

'Like parables,' she said. 'Or contemporary accounts.'

'Maybe,' he said. 'Depending on how old it is.'

She glanced at him. 'I think – I can see how Dad could get caught up in something like that. What that would do to him – I can see that.'

He nodded with vigour. 'Can you.'

'How do we find out what it says?'

'We need to know more about the church.'

'I know where we can go.'

ᕮ

The *Depositum Fidei* lay beneath one of the country's oldest buildings, on the eastern ridge of the city centre. Built by convicts to a convict's design, the barracks had slept prisoners, infirm and destitute women, orphans and law clerks. It had been altered time and again over two centuries. Now it was a museum of its past selves. And the religious collection, the Deposit of Faith, had been there from the beginning, gathering in the basement and the catacombs, growing old as the world above it changed.

It was lunchtime in the central business district; the office blocks were emptying and the streets full of purpose. But the Deposit belonged to another time, and the city's sounds hardly reached it. There were miles of books and only Sandy to look after them.

44

'One of the marines who came out with the First Fleet,' she said. 'He brought a crate of books with him, and then bought up whatever else he could find. He left all his money to keep the collection going, quite a pile in the end.'

She wore a tight green skirt and a loose white shirt, and Jack thought again how remarkable it was that he knew such attractive librarians. Dev sat at her hip, swinging his enormous head to stare wide-eyed at them. His skin was the colour of various spices. He didn't know much English, but was fluent in all the other languages.

'*Blizok lokotok*,' he said.

Beth stroked his head. 'Aren't you handsome.'

Dev gave her a fat-cheeked smile. '*Da nye ukusish.*'

Jack took the manuscript from his jacket and unfolded it on the counter. The baby craned its head to look at it.

'What have you got there?' Sandy said.

'We found it in the church,' Beth said. 'We think it's Dad's.'

'What is it?'

'We don't know,' Beth said. 'Something religious, maybe. Have you seen anything like it?'

'Weird old religious books? Only every day.'

'No, but anything really like it.'

'I don't know,' Sandy said. 'They all look the same after a while.'

Jack looked around at the visible layer of the collection. 'What exactly do you have here?'

'Oh, everything,' she said. 'Any religion, from anywhere in the world. They filled up all the space twenty years ago. Now they want to start selling it off. It goes down there for miles, there's more than anybody knows.'

'We're looking for anything about our church.'

'What is it, nineteenth century?'

'Just barely.'

'Try over by the stairs.'

Two wings had originally flanked the main barracks, enclosing a large courtyard. The southern wing was gone, but

45

the foundations of all three buildings still met beneath the courtyard's gravel, joined by the tunnels of the Deposit of Faith. Even here, near ground level, the religious array was bewildering. Old Bibles creaked on lecterns; illuminated pages peered from behind glass. The shelves were of various sizes, and sloped into drifts of paper. Concordances and catechisms, tracts and manifestos, meditations and devotions.

There were piles of the Church's history in the colonies. The arguments with land-holders, the whittling of glebes. The First Fleet's provisions included one Bible and one prayer book; they looked noble among the hammocks and nails, the firkins of butter and puncheons of rum. Convicts had become priests, and priests convicts. Jack and Beth searched all day, growing dusty and reverent. Divine services in paddocks and huts, woodland congregations battling the clearers, the first stone churches – and finally a picture of their eleventh stone church.

'Jack, look.'

In fact it was two pictures, a stereoscopic photograph taken in 1861. Each half was about two inches across, and the colours were faded grey and pinkish white, but it was clearly their church. Jack looked down on the page and crossed his eyes until the new middle image fused and the church leapt into remarkable perspective. There were no trees, the churchyard was huge, and the single headstone floated above the page – he could almost read what it said.

'Oh—'

Beth had found the trick, and was staring enraptured at the tiny illusion. The blurs across the foreground might have been people crossing the empty yard; exposures took seconds, and bodies in motion would have smeared the plates with ghosts. Beth looked up at him, and her eyes returned slowly to their focus.

'That's amazing.'

'Isn't it?'

She returned to the caption beneath the photograph. 'Built for monks in 1811,' she said. 'I had no idea it was that old.'

'It's incredible.'

'Are there Anglican monks?'

'I don't know. San?'

Sandy hoisted Dev over to them. Nobody else had ventured into the Deposit all day; you needed someone to keep you company, apart from all these old gods. The baby god muttered unintelligible proverbs as Sandy explained the Anglican monks.

'There weren't any for a few hundred years after the Reformation – they were afraid of looking Catholic. Your guys would have been pretty experimental. I guess they didn't take.'

Beth was still looking at the picture. 'I guess not.'

Jack continued through the collection, searching for the monks. He kept finding trails and losing them again. There were a few references to the church in the twentieth century, but little of its early history. His eyes glazed.

He had never met Dev's father, a stockbroker or perhaps a stockman who sent money but had no other contact, which suited Sandy. Jack had driven her to the hospital and seen Dev at his tiniest: the miniaturist fingers, the green-black slicks he produced. Jack and Dev and now Beth – Sandy still had her *pitaji*, but the rest of them were fatherless, they were all old too soon.

At last he fumbled over a bundle of documents dated in the first years after their church was built, littered with Brothers – the experimental monks at last. They had lived in the nave and the oratories. Brother Aloysius was having no luck with his vegetable garden. The heat had finally broken Brother Liam's vow of silence. Everyone kept mistaking them for Catholics.

A single line caught Jack's attention, a dash across the page. It looked violent, like the stripe of a flogging. He stopped and leaned in to read it.

In his youth, our unlucky Brother ——, whose very name my Brethren now refuse to utter, and implore that I no more record, enjoyed some reputation as a fine expositor and translator of the Word, – though also provoked an equal jealousy, and even suspicion, – but he has since undergone a most persistent decline. In the wake of his arrival from England there arose certain rumours: – that in Cornwall he had acquired a mysterious and perhaps a devilish document, and that he had ceased giving sermons, and instead conducted experiments of a most particular nature; – and, certainly, the strength of his desire to join our Antipodean Order was the source of much speculation and small ease.

Though Brother —— keeps to himself entirely, and rarely leaves his cell, except to visit the Library, – where I have seen him studying late into the night, remaining sometimes for days, and saying nothing: – Even his study seems dangerous and strange, for he pores over books of writing, which only he can read; – and wanders the most heretical and occult of the Library's chambers, where his Brethren dare not, for fear of their souls. He carries with him a single candle, that burns a black and smoaky flame, and never diminishes; – he sends and receives mysterious packages, – and often hears news that greatly saddens or alarms him. Even his eyes, by all appearances, are retreating into his face, some say the better to watch the workings of his own mind. – And forever, from his cell, sounds a soft scratching, an eternal scratching, like a man's fingernails on stone, – that many have thought to be writing, – but no writing has been found.

Jack felt a chill. A mysterious document – it had to be his manuscript. And the books only one monk could read, the days spent in libraries. The monk had lived in their church, and perhaps in their crypt. Had he searched the Deposit of Faith? Had any of his strange books ended up on these shelves? Jack felt for a moment like an echo, following the same paths.

Beth was reading over his shoulder, pulling her breath over her teeth.

'Did he write it? The manuscript?'

'It says here he found it. In Cornwall.'

Her palm pressed into the curve of his neck. 'He was a translator.'

He read the page again. 'So he was. A Bible translator.'

'Over here.'

The Deposit held all the Bibles. It was the world's most translated book. There were dozens of English attempts, and Beth moved between them with confidence. Charles Thomson's Translation, Noah Webster's Revision – none of them had been translated by an Anglican monk in the eighteenth century. She worked through the minutes of translators' meetings, copyright disputes, court documents. She seemed to be enjoying herself, leaving coloured notes as she followed her trails. He loved to watch her, the efficiency branching into pleasure.

Suddenly the expression fell from her face, and she looked up at him.

'Here. I think I've found him again.'

He leaned in to see. It was another book about Bible translation, the committees responsible for the King James Version. Three of the translators remained unidentified, leaving tantalising possibilities. But Jack couldn't see the connection. 'Who?'

She turned the page. 'Someone from an Order of Saul and St Paul, at Land's End. Is that Cornwall?'

'I think so.'

'It's from 1777.'

It was a modest tract, only a page in length. He couldn't find a name, but the place and the date were right. He peered at it in the Deposit's dim light.

What Man can pretend, but that we *English* are greatly Blessed; who but a Moment past had no Scripture in our own Tongue, but relyed on the Exposition of Priests; yet now have such a Choice of Translations as would leave never Man lacking. Yet who may refuse that, as we are

Blessed, so are we Cursed; for we have no Translation but may be named Flawed, if not False. For we all know of the *Bible* that laments there be no *Treacle* in *Gilead*; or reports the *Breeches* sewn of Fig Leaves by *Adam* and *Eve*; or gives us Comfort, *Thou shalt not need be afraid of any Bugs by Night*: Indeed, we hear of a *Bible* so much abused that it complains, *I am persecuted by Printers*. Though these Errors be comickal Accident, no less do they shew the many Perils of Translation.

Even our esteemed *King James Version*, though the most poetick of History's many Translations, is imperfect: For it is stiled upon the *Bishops' Bible*, and shares its motley Ancestry; and it is the work of four and fifty Scholars, who are too many: For though one of them were *Shakespear*, yet three and fifty were not; and even were they all *Shakespear*, we must ask, would fifty-four *Shakespears* improve one?; and we must surely answer that they would not: They would squabble, and make Compromise, and leave their *Bible* imperfect.

In HIS Wisdom has THE LORD granted HIS Servant the good Fortune and Faculty both to read, and to commit to Memory, each of the Translations formerly attempted; and, which is of more Import, both the *Old Testament* in the *Hebrew* and the *New Testament* in the *Greek*, as recorded in Scrolls and Fragments from the Ages; and this Servant would bring this Fortune and Faculty to a new and final Translation of the *Bible* into *English*: By HIS Grace would he Resolve the Conflicts of past Translations; insure Fidelity to the Word of GOD; and lift our earthbound Language to the worship of GOD, as far as it may be lifted: That is my Proposal.

Another translator. Jack felt he understood him completely: here was a man for whom treacle in Gilead was at least as important as rain on Thursday. And he longed for the Bible the monk had described: an epic poem, a religious meditation, the last translation.

There was something uncertain in Beth's face. 'It's him, isn't it. The same monk.'

'It all fits. A translator, of the Bible – you can see how people would be jealous, suspicious, how he'd get a reputation.'

'And how a guy like this – how if he found something like what we've got, how that might ... do something to him. Like, what did that other one say – the eyes sinking into his head, and the scratching and muttering.'

'I suppose so,' Jack said.

'And he gave up his translation – his life's work. After he found this manuscript.'

'It seems that way.'

'He sounds like Dad. That's what he was like.'

She had a soft desperate look, as if trying to disbelieve something. It did sound like a painful transformation, from the upstart young monk to the gnarled old bogey. Jack hoped it hadn't happened that way to Frank. He looked carefully at her, the film of her eyes.

'Was he?'

'He knew a lot of the Bible off by heart, all the different versions – the English versions, at least. And he was always controversial, with his science and everything. He was always having to explain himself.'

'Do you want to keep looking?'

She bit her lip and nodded. 'Find out his name, at least.'

But the monk seemed never to have been named. Land's End was in England's southwest corner – in Cornwall, as he'd thought. The nearest church was St Sennen's, which had stood for eight hundred years. Baptisms and funerals and weddings, a list of rectors – but no mention of a monastic order. There were thousands of items left in the Deposit, and he couldn't be sure that they had been filed with any integrity. He had Beth, an expert researcher, but she was tiring. He didn't think they'd find anything else.

He tucked the manuscript back inside his jacket as Sandy

caught up with them. 'There you are,' she said. 'I'm sorry, I'm going to have to kick you out.'

Beth frowned. 'It's only early.'

'It's almost midnight. The library's been closed for hours.'

'Really?'

'I thought we'd lost you down here. I'm meant to be meeting someone.'

'Now?' Beth said. 'Where?'

'Just at home. He's a singer. He'll sing Dev to sleep, and then me.'

Dev stirred in his baby basket, and gave them a sleepy smile. Jack patted his great head. 'I think we're finished, for now.'

'I think so,' Beth said. 'I want – there's something else I want to do, anyway.'

There was a dissatisfaction in her forehead and around her eyes, as if the story of the monk had left her with more questions. Or maybe it was nothing like that; but Jack knew it was a specific thing, an unarguable thing. 'Sure,' he said.

'Will you drive me?'

'Of course.'

Dev seemed to know too. '*Dozhdichka.*'

つ

Jack drove east along the empty road that connected the city with the harbour's last headland. The suburbs brought down by the hailstorm, the shimmering bays, the forests of tilting masts, as the land rose and narrowed. Jack's old Citroën laboured and slowed. They took wrong turns and felt their way until Beth told him to stop.

Beams of light swept above them as they left the car, crossed the street and climbed the verge to the lighthouse. It was old and imposing and stood in the middle of a park at the edge of the world. Beth led him towards the cliff and sat in the grass, which was already dampening with dew. He watched the beams chasing each other, tired but no longer able to imagine sleep.

'I used to bring my boyfriends here,' she said. 'When there was nowhere else to go. I wanted to fool around but I always ended up just sitting and staring out to sea.'

The sound of surf against rocks rose and tumbled with the wind. The things that had to be done, the particular things. He'd thought they were going to Frank's grave, a couple of beaches to the south, but Beth had directed him the other way.

'So I used to come by myself, more often,' she said. 'I'd sit here and feel lonely. You know what they say about lighthouses, keepers especially. I used to imagine I was sitting there with the lighthouse keeper, two lonely people staring out to sea.'

'Did you ever think about dropping in?'

'It's automated. Since 1976.'

'Sad.'

'In the early days, you know, there was still a keeper. My parents would have brought me here when I was four or five. So I may have stared out to sea with the keeper, once or twice, without knowing it. But I wasn't lonely then.'

'And it was probably daytime.'

'It was. It was always daytime then.'

The sky was growing lighter, the horizon fading into view. A tanker appeared in the distance beneath a sulky light. The sea was slate, and hadn't yet caught the sun. The waves had stopped pounding the cliffs, and washed like the wind.

'There are things I remember that can't be right. Dad used to tell us stories from the Bible, the ones he believed, and from *New Scientist*, but there are some things – I don't know where they came from, but I feel sure I heard them from him.'

'Like what?'

'There was one about a lighthouse in the desert. In the middle of the desert. I don't know how it got there, or what happened to it. Maybe it was a metaphor and I got confused.

There aren't any lighthouses in the desert, are there? But I remember it, as if I'd been there.'

The beams were fading against the coming dawn; he kept losing sight of them. The swell was rising, the sound expanding in the uninterrupted air. Beth hugged her knees and looked out to sea. Jack thought about the Russian film, the ships rusting in the sand. He felt the manuscript's warmth under his jacket.

'Maybe there was an enormous lake out there,' he said. 'So big it had waves and tides and treacherous rocks, but it dried up. Or maybe there was a surveying error, latitude and longitude reversed, something like that.'

She shifted and assessed what he'd said. 'Where, what desert?'

'Inland. I don't know. But people used to drive out there, a hundred miles from the nearest town. They parked a way off and sat by the lighthouse and stared out into the desert. And they watched as the beam swept across the sky, and it looked like the dunes were rising and crashing, and the wind in the sand sounded like water.'

She nodded, as if tasting something she'd just decided she liked. 'The lighthouse worked.'

'Automated since 1976. But something happened and the light started to slip, the whole lighthouse was tilting into the sand. So the light ran aground and swept across the desert, far away at first and then closer, and you could sit in the sand and the light would wash over you, a couple of times a minute.'

When Beth spoke it was with the same voice. 'And if you were with someone – and especially if you were fucking them when the light ran over you – then you'd love them forever. So people used to go fucking in the desert and wait for the light to find them.'

'They said the light was so bright it went straight through them.'

She looked at him. 'Where did you hear that?'

'I don't know. I just made it up.'

'No, it was something like that. That's what I remember.'

'Maybe it was true. After all.'

'Maybe.'

The clouds grew orange and pink as they walked back to the car. She leaned into him, a hand in his back pocket, and he held her and tried to warm her. The Citroën looked like an insect in the dawn, carapace glistening with dew. He drove, and she began to fall asleep in the passenger seat. She flopped on his shoulder and woke up when he had to change gears.

'Are we going home?'

'Yes.'

'Let's go to the desert.'

'Maybe tomorrow.'

'Tomorrow's too late.'

'It's already tomorrow.'

A memory overtook him, and he reached into his jacket and unfolded the manuscript against the steering wheel, darting between its pages and the slowly filling streets. The tilting tower on the first page – it wasn't a lighthouse, there wasn't a desert. But he couldn't shake the feeling that the story of the lighthouse had somehow come from the manuscript. He felt that almost for the first time he'd known what to say, he'd found the right words.

He realised he was speeding, hurrying back to the church. To spend time with the manuscript, to search it for more secrets. He felt abstractly guilty, as if he had been unfaithful. He drove faster.

ᑯᴑ ᶆ·ᴑ(ᴡᴑ

Languages were dying all over the world, faster than forests and fish. Some were spoken by only a hundred people, or fifty, or three. Some existed in the mind of one old man or woman: perhaps they weren't languages at all.

Each was a massive human undertaking, hundreds of thousands of words, countless subtleties and distinctions. But they were all doomed; the richest of them would die with its last or second-last speaker. To say nothing of the dialects and vernaculars and shifting languages of slang, the private idioms of families and friends. Most of them sank without ripple. Only the lucky ones were remembered in writing, in letters and books and tablets like tombs.

And even then that wasn't enough. By itself, all writing was opaque. You needed something outside it, a reference or crib, a Rosetta. And Jack had nothing like that. He knew nothing about the manuscript, except what it had done. It had brought a monk from Land's End to their church at the bottom of the world. It had sent a brilliant mind spinning into insanity, perhaps in the same dark hollow where Jack had found it. It had derailed a translation. And whatever marks it had made on Frank.

After the lighthouse they had slept until the afternoon. Beth went to work a late shift at the library and Jack paced the church with the manuscript. No more stories had risen in his mind, no more clues. He felt like Frank and the nameless monk, making the same tightening circles in the nave. Beth came home and he went to bed feeling defeated.

The next morning was windy. The tarpaulin flapped against the hole in the roof and woke Jack up. The television station had sent him a letter about the Russian film, reminding him of his small advance and his most recent deadline. A weary tone – as if they'd written this letter on the day of his commission, and had a drawer full of similar letters to be sent as his failure deepened. Jack sat at the desk and flicked on the television.

The picture shuddered slightly, but otherwise the system seemed to work. Night had fallen; there was only a soft glow at the horizon and the tiny points of a million stars. Zhenshchina looked up at the silhouettes of the ships, black shapes against the constellations. A satellite was making its way across the sky. She turned around, but Chelovek was gone.

Fishermen had tried to dig a channel to keep their village connected to the sea, but the sea had outpaced them. The channel was a hundred metres wide and a hundred kilometres long, but it had been filled by the desert. It was marked only by twin ridges of sand, the salt of the evaporated sea, and the fishing boats that hadn't made it back. Chelovek walked along the shining path; he walked all night past the moonlit ships. Soon it seemed that he was walking through other landscapes, across the Siberian steppes, through blizzards and rippling heat, beneath eclipses and the midnight sun.

Zhenshchina watched him go, and the sand and salt reflected different colours, blue and white and red. Chelovek was walking past whatever footage the Russians could get their hands on. The landscapes were bluescreened behind him or projected against him, his skin bent with streetlights and rain. Zhenshchina's face picked up the colours. Not only landscapes but riot scenes, breadlines and tractors. He leaned and stared at each of the scenes, then walked on: it wasn't what he was looking for.

The fishermen had abandoned the channel but the sea had kept retreating. The last miles were broad desert. The patterns in the sand might have been left by the tide or the wind. At last Chelovek came to the water, thick with salt and filmed with chemicals. He knelt and put his hand out towards it, but decided against touching it. He stood up and followed his footsteps the way he'd come.

Beth sat on a pew and stroked the manuscript with her thumb. She was in the third quire, the sagas of the sack-people in their flowers and seed-pods. They set out to sea, they tumbled down mountainsides, they sat watching the skies explode with astronomy. They spoke and thought in seabed ripples, in the motion of campfire sparks in the night. Jack watched her, and he could almost read their language in the muscles of her face.

He thought again about Peter's forensic friend. He still felt protective of the manuscript. Only their small circle knew about it, and he liked it that way. But he needed help. He stood up as Beth turned the pages.

She looked up at him. 'Do you think they – either of them, do you think they ever figured it out?'

'I'm not sure.'

'Because this guy, this monk guy – it sounds like he spent a lot of time on this. And Dad was smart, but I don't even think he knew much Latin.'

'He might have had other advantages.'

'Like what?'

'They both might have solved it.'

'One of them should have left a note, at least. In case you were wondering, kind of thing. Save everyone a lot of work.'

'One of them should have.'

'Unless they were so blown away by what they'd found – or so horrified.'

Jack nodded uncomfortably. 'I suppose.'

'You know how sometimes you'll just be walking along and the most terrible feeling comes over you. Sometimes it's the opposite, but usually it's as if you've just remembered something so awful you can't believe you forgot it even for a moment.'

'But it can be the opposite?'

'Sometimes. But it's like if you could ever say what it was, if you wrote it down, this is what it would be.'

He looked at her closely, but she didn't seem to be caught by any terrible feeling or awful memory – or its opposite. He nodded again.

'Maybe it would.'

'You ever get that feeling? Of not being able to explain what you're feeling?'

'All the time.'

She was amused by the force in his voice, but he'd finally been able to agree with her wholeheartedly. She turned back to the manuscript.

'So what do we do now?'

He took a deep breath. 'Peter's got this friend who works at a lab, he can do some analysis of it. We'll just have to cut some bits off it, is the only thing.'

She looked pained, and he loved her for it. 'Really?'

'Or scrape them, or something.'

'Well – if it's the only way.'

'I'm not sure about it either.'

She held the manuscript out to him, and he weighed it in his hand before folding it into a satchel. It suddenly looked ordinary, like a battered first novel lugged around town, something autobiographical.

There was a knock at the door.

Beth half-shrugged and stopped. She swung her feet onto the floor.

'It's Dad's friend, the Catholic one. I asked him to look at the roof.'

'Oh. Good.'

Frank's friend O'Rourke was a serious man, and crossed himself at the porch door. He looked a lot like Frank, hale and white-haired. Beth dragged him into the middle of the nave and they looked up at the roof. She watched nervously as he tipped a ladder and thumped around in the hole. Her shirt was buttoned wrong. O'Rourke looked down and wiped his forehead.

'Looks like everything's well stuck up here.'

Beth peered up at him. 'You're sure?'

'All kinds of redundancies in these old things, built for all manner of whatnot. Hell of a storm, though, never would have seen that coming. My word.'

'Can you fix it?'

He climbed down the ladder and slapped the dust from his hands. 'No materials, love, and no time either. Not the only troubled roof around, you may've heard.'

She looked at the floor, hands in her pockets. 'We thought since you'd worked on the church before …'

He took a step backwards. 'I don't think I can be held responsible for—'

'Oh, no. I just meant, since you were a friend of Dad's.'

O'Rourke scratched his white head. 'Yeah, I'm – I'm sorry about Frank. I only heard about it after the funeral. But I'm real sorry.'

She gave him a pleading look. 'Thanks.'

'Listen, I'll squeeze you in as soon as I can. I'm training up a new guy, should help. It'll be a week at least, though, best I can do.'

She beamed. 'Thank you so much. Is it all right, with the tarp like that?'

'Should be fine.'

'Thanks.'

He nodded and turned to leave, but Beth wasn't finished; she stood in the nave, she weighed him down. He raised his eyebrows at her, forehead like a musical staff.

'When you were fixing it,' she said. 'When was that?'

'Oh, while ago, love. Seven, eight years, off the top of my head.'

She glanced over to the satchel on the desk, and Jack knew she was calculating the days, the hours Frank had spent here by himself. She blinked at the result.

'That long?'

'Well, it looked a disaster, but structurally it wasn't in bad shape. So it didn't take forever. And Frank was a man possessed, he wouldn't stop until it was done.'

Beth's eyes were glistening, but Jack could see the steel in them. 'And the chancel, when was it you did that? Was it early on?'

'The—' O'Rourke struggled to match the word. 'Oh, that. No, love, we didn't touch that. That's all original.' He swept a proud hand towards the rear of the church, and stopped, then looked back at Beth. 'Well, it was right there.'

'You didn't put in a new chancel? New boards?'

'Didn't have to. We replaced most of the – what's it called, the porch? And all the tiles, couple of the windows, a few new stones, lot of repointing as I remember. But that's all. Termites round here must all be Catholic.'

Beth smiled weakly. 'Must be.'

O'Rourke leaned in to her, encouragingly. He knew something was wrong but thought himself too old to imagine what. 'Anything else I can help you with, love?'

'So you didn't find anything under the floorboards – anything under the church?'

'Only rocks, maybe a few old bob'd fallen through the floor. What do you mean?' He scratched his head and peered over to the chancel – over to the trapdoor. 'Strike me. That's what you mean.'

'You've never seen that before?'

He shook his head. 'Anything down there?'

'No, nothing.'

'Mind if I have a look?'

Jack narrowed his eyes at O'Rourke, but Beth held her arms out. O'Rourke hefted open the trapdoor and stepped down into the crypt. Jack heard the wine bottles clinking together, thought he even heard the rasp of the loose flag-stone, but O'Rourke had reappeared before he had a chance to follow him.

'Cold down there,' the mason said.

'You didn't know that was there?' Beth said, without much hope. 'You're sure.'

'Reckon I'd remember a thing like that. That's for dead people, isn't it?'

'That's what it was meant for.'

'Creepy.'

This time she let him leave. The stained glass had changed colour during his visit, the light was different. Beth's foot-steps echoed as she backed across the nave and sat on the bed. Jack hurried to her.

'Frank could still have found it.'

She gave him a bruised look. 'How?'

'He could have done it himself, later on – he wouldn't have needed a mason to do that. Maybe there were loose boards in the chancel, one or two would be enough. Seven or eight years, he could easily have found it.'

She was running through the arithmetic again. 'It was so long.'

'Maybe they *did* find it, the two of them.'

'You think that guy was pretending, just now? Why?'

'I don't know. But he might have been.'

Beth turned her head sideways. He saw how important the manuscript was. Without it she would spin into guesswork and freewheeling guilt. Frank needed something magnificent, some shock to his faith – he couldn't have spent his last years slowly retreating. Jack knew she couldn't bear the idea of that minute-by-minute despair.

'We'll find out what it is.'

She shook her head. 'It doesn't matter.'

'It matters, you'll see.'

'Jack?'

'I'll be right back.'

The forensics centre was a bright, modern building on the fringes of the city. It shone with a light that left no shadow, like the midday sun outside. Uniforms and lab coats filled its foyer. Jack dug the change from his pockets and stepped through the metal detectors while security guards X-rayed his satchel. He caught a glimpse of the manuscript on the monitor, the tangle of writing.

He squeaked along the disinfected halls until he found the office. Peter's friend was a tall man with efficient movements. His hair and eyebrows were dark and flecked with silver. He wore a white coat and complicated glasses.

'Call me Ash,' he said. 'I knew Peter was up to something. I thought he wanted to set me up with somebody.'

'He might, as well,' Jack said. 'But this couldn't wait.'

Ash glanced at the manuscript and gave him an approving look. 'Well, this is the place,' he said. 'You know everything carries its whole history around with it. We all do. Everything we brush against, everything we've been.'

He spoke with a quiet enthusiasm that warmed the sterilised air. Jack watched him as he took the manuscript and held it to the light, testing its lines and planes.

'Have you done much of this?'

'It's mostly criminal around here. Forged wills, ransom notes. But old documents are kind of a hobby. This one's a beauty.'

'What will you do to it?'

'We'll need a small part of the material for dating and the ink for chromatography, and we'll take scrapings of the dirt.'

'How long will it take?'

'A couple of weeks, I'm afraid. We're pretty busy at the moment.'

'What do you think it is?'

'Oh, it's probably nothing.' He saw Jack's disappointment.

'I mean, it's probably a fake, or a hoax. But those can be more interesting than actual things, if you think about it. Why someone would do it, how they did it.'

'I suppose,' Jack said.

'Think of the possibilities. The Vikings discovered America, Saint Paul preached in London. Everything about art and truth. Can I take this bit here?'

He had turned to one of the pages of plants; a green creeper trailed a tendril to the vellum's edge. Jack nodded mutely and Ash sliced a strip from the bottom.

'This is good, there's ink and pigment in one here. People call Paul's Epistle to the Laodiceans a forgery because it was pasted together from other letters, but almost all of Matthew comes from Mark, or vice versa. What does that tell you?'

Jack thought that Peter was right: Sandy probably would like this quietly passionate scientist. But he was beginning to doubt his own hopes for the manuscript. A fake wouldn't help Beth, it was worse than nothing.

'I don't know,' he said.

Ash turned back to the pages. 'And just a bit more for the carbon, and for dirt and pollen too. So a corner off the cover here, yes?'

'All right.'

Ash drew his scalpel across the edge of the front cover. A clean triangle came off on the benchtop. It wasn't as bad as Jack had thought. But Ash looked startled.

'What's this?'

A strip of white poked from between the sliced inner and outer covers, like an exposed bone. Ash shook the manuscript and a corner of paper showed through the hole.

'Look, there's something in here.'

He peeled the covers apart. The vellum sighed again, and the paper slipped out and fluttered to the floor. It was folded in half.

Jack picked it up and unfolded it. All he could think was, *Frank*. He'd left a note after all – or someone had.

A carefully ornate hand, a quill and black ink. It was topped and tailed like a letter. He knew it was English – but he couldn't read it. He stood blinking at it, but it was useless. He was back in his childhood, suspecting a great conspiracy.

He squinted at the shapes, but they wouldn't yield. He just wanted a name; he wanted to know who the letter was to or from. It was no good. But there was a date beneath it, and numbers seemed easier. The numbers said *1781*.

It couldn't have been Frank. It was older than the church, older than the colony.

'What is it?' Ash said.

Jack heard a deeper interest in his voice. Did he think the letter was part of a more complicated hoax? Or had his talk of forgeries been disingenuous, had he caught a glimpse of something authentic and urgent beneath it all?

'It looks like a letter,' Jack said.

'Well, let's see it.'

Ash could have read the letter to him right away. But Jack instinctively stuffed it into his pocket. He'd trusted Ash's cynicism more than his sudden earnestness. He wanted to read it himself.

'No, it's nothing,' he said.

'Do you want me to date that for you too?'

'No. I have to go.'

Ash gave him an odd look. 'All right. I'll still see you on the weekend?'

'Sure.'

Jack picked up the scarred manuscript and bundled it back into his satchel. He took Ash's business card, a logo with an eye and a magnifying glass, and hurried back through the check-points. The stainless light and clinical steel, the ruthless attitude to secrets – it had all been a mistake. He'd find out on his own.

Sweat ran into his eyes as he sat in the car and stared at the letter. Clearly an address at the top. The text blurred and he tried to calm himself. The same pattern of letters repeated:

that was the name. *Bro, Brot? Brother.* The letter was addressed to a brother, an experimental monk. And that was enough. The reading flowed again.

To Brother Constant,
of the Church of Saul and St Paul,
at Land's End,   February 28th, 1781.

Dear Brother Constant,—

Altho' I have not the good Fortune of your Acquaintance, your Reputation is wide-spread, as a most learned Man, who must far surpass your Servant in all respects, excepting Age. I write therefore, to present to you this Manuscript: Which I acquired at Mr. Baker's Auction some Fifteen Years ago for no small Amount; it being describ'd as an Alchemickal Text, as an Atlantick Journal, & as a Profane Codex.

This Manuscript has weav'd on me from the First an Enchantment, by its fine Vellum, & the devoted Hand that improves it; but my Enchantment is become sour, and continues sour: For I do not know, & must know, its true Meaning & Nature. It is like a beautiful Church or Palace, which one has watch'd & admir'd for Years, 'til one first wonders what Treasures lie Inside; and, having now wonder'd, I may never more enjoy the Manuscript, until it has been Translated.

In the attempt of its Translation have I spent many Years; imployed a great many Techniques, viz., Books of many Tongues, mathematickal Tables, Kabbalistick Letters, the Principles of Secret Writing, &c.; & shewn the Manuscript to several of my Colleagues, who indeed regretted Mysteriously & Exceedingly having receiv'd the same. I now enclose this most peculiar Document: That you might succeed, where all Others have fail'd; & that I may rid me of its Enchantment.

I remain, &c.,
Johann Johnson

It was wonderful – the spelling not quite settled, the breathless description of the manuscript, a text of alchemists, a treasure of Atlantis, and another man who'd spent years negotiating with it. Most of all, his monk had a name: Brother Constant, his brother in translation. Constant, in a world of flux. He had received the manuscript in 1781, four years after he had proposed his Bible translation, and it had diverted him entirely. He had brought it from Land's End to Sydney, studied it in his crypt, hidden it beneath a flagstone – and why? To seal it forever, to protect the world from its secret, its mysterious regret? Or to await his successor? If Frank hadn't solved it, then Jack would. He scoured the letter again for clues. He'd find out, for all of them. He knew where Brother Constant had got the manuscript – and where Johann Johnson had got it before him.

ᴝ)

Samuel Baker's company was still auctioning books after almost three centuries. It had grown from its modest rooms in Covent Garden to cover the world. Jack drove from the forensics centre to the local branch, a narrow bluestone building on a sharp corner of the city centre. It was perhaps a hundred years old, but it seemed much older: the creak in the oak floors, the pipe-smoke burnished into the banisters. Stern auctioneers stared from oil paintings as Jack flicked through the old catalogues, exploring the 1760s: fifteen years or so before Johann Johnson's letter.

The posters and handbills gave a fascinating glimpse of London's eighteenth-century sales by Auction or Who Bids Most. Curious books in divinity, history, physick, mathematics, voyages, travels &c. Poetry and miscellany, curiously bound and gilt on the back, many in turkey-leather. Creased originals and smooth facsimiles, folio and duodecimo: *On the Correct Wearing of Hats, Encounters with Divers Small People, The Diagnosis and Treatment of Hysteria in Women.*

What endless libraries were written and collected, even in those old days. Jack wondered how many of these books still existed. Even his own collection held hundreds long out of print, almost forgotten. Beth had still more, crates of them that would have to be auctioned by weight. Were there enormous landfills, book graveyards, or did they just crumble into dust? The catalogues took on a solemn light as he leafed through them, looking for Johnson's auction.

He read that the entire and valuable library of Mr Jan Reynolds, lately bankrupt, had been sold by Mr Samuel Baker at his Auction-room in York-street – in 1763. Most of the books were unremarkable and briefly described; a few demanded more attention for their rarity or the excellence of their binding. And then:

105. Anon., ——. Vellum Manuscript, 300 pp in Folio. Inscrib'd in a fine, but mysterious Hand, with a Character, by all Accompts unique, whether of the *First Language*, or of Alchemists; & in any case acquir'd from a Founding Fellow of the *Royal Society* of *London*.

Jack stared at the description. Was it the manuscript Johann Johnson had bought, the manuscript in his satchel? It was the same size, made of the same material, and surely the same unique character. Jack read it again. The manuscript was older than Johnson and Constant, much older than Frank. He didn't know what it meant: the first language, the alchemists. And he wasn't sure what the Royal Society was, exactly – but it was real, it existed, and that gave him another step.

ᴜ)

He arrived at the church to find Beth lying on her back on one of the pews, one knee raised, sole flat against the wood. It was overcast outside; the floorlamps peered into the dim

68

light of the church. Six bottles of wine stood on the floor next to her, all open and drunk to different levels. She held a glass on her stomach.

'Sorry I'm late,' he said.

She smiled up at him. 'I was down in the cellar, I felt like a bottle of something but I couldn't decide what. I shouldn't have opened so many.'

'I can always help.'

'And look—'

She leaned over and knocked her glass against a bottle. It chimed through the church. A woolly concentration pulled at her features as she chose another bottle and clinked a higher note from it. She nodded, pleased, and picked a glass tune.

'That's nice,' he said.

'It's "The Bottle's-Half-Empty Blues".'

Behind the bottles' ramparts lay a pile of the childhood photographs she'd found: she was riding a wooden scooter, sitting on a seesaw, making a mud-cake. Frank was teaching her how to hold a cricket bat; he had her surrounded. Tiles of childhood in the indifferent light, and she slid them around on the floor.

He hovered over her. 'Are you all right?'

'Oh, yeah, I'm fine. Thanks.'

'What were you down in the crypt for?'

'Oh, just—' She waved her hand. 'I don't know. Did the lab turn anything up?'

His blood shifted gears. 'It came from a founder of the Royal Society, I don't know which one. And the monk's name was Constant.'

'They found that out just by looking?'

He put the satchel down on his desk and handed her the letter. She brought a slightly fuzzy focus to it. He left her and searched their shelves and boxes. Between them they had books about everything: all kinds of histories and biographies, books of fable and science, mismatched encyclopaedias collected from garage sales. He tore through them until he found a description of the Royal Society of London for the Improvement of Natural Knowledge, founded in 1660 and the oldest learned society still going. Another book listed its famous members: Isaac Newton, Joseph Banks, Benjamin Franklin. It was interesting, but it wasn't enough.

'That's great,' Beth said.

She held the letter out to him, smiling encouragingly – like someone whose child had managed to scrawl a snowman. He took it back and returned to the search.

Frank's magazines still cluttered the oratories. Old issues of *Vetus Testamentum* and *The Expository Times* argued for months about the meaning of chapters and verses; eventually Frank left them to it. He strayed into *Scientific American* and was soon tackling *Evolutionary Biology* and *Geochronology Today*. He kept reading the *Journal of Science and Faith*, or at least subscribing to it. Jack's memory of the old man grew shade and texture as he worked through the pile.

One of the magazines had run an edition celebrating an anniversary of the Royal Society's foundation. Its early existence as the Invisible College, its first charter – and its handful of founding fellows, Hooke, Glanvill, Wren. Jack felt like a drowner touching sand as he took the list back to the nave and looked up the names.

They were all men of science and religion, just like Frank. Robert Hooke named the cells of the body after monks' cells. Joseph Glanvill was a cleric who studied ghosts and witchcraft. Christopher Wren rebuilt London after the Great fire, fifty churches and St Paul's: he might have come across relics in the rubble, manuscripts in crypts like theirs.

Jack licked his fingers and turned the pages. The books and magazines piled up beside him.

Beth bent to blow across the tops of the open bottles, propelling breathy tones over the floor. The church prolonged the notes among its broken roofbeams. The room filled with spirits as she built an approximate scale. Jack looked up as she refilled her glass with white wine, red tails lifting like smoke.

'You're sure you're all right?' he said.

'I'm fine. Have you found him yet?'

'I don't know.'

It might have been John Wallis, a mathematician and cryptographer who had invented the symbol for infinity. Perhaps the manuscript was a code after all. A cryptographer, a founding fellow, a secret alphabet. Jack drew tentative arrows in the margin.

'It's just – I've been trying to remember something that isn't in one of these pictures. Something about Dad, the old days. Everything I can remember, it's all in here.'

She was dealing through the photographs again: the beach, the backyard, the botanic gardens. There were only a few pictures of all three of them, taken by self-timers or friends: they were all out of focus or awkwardly framed. Most of the shots showed only fragments of the family.

'You think your memories are so vivid and detailed and go on forever,' she said. 'But then you realise they all fit into these little rectangles, and they're flat and the colours are fading, and that's all you've got.'

He put the book down and sat beside her. 'I'm sure you remember more than you know. Things'll remind you, it'll keep coming back.'

She lowered her eyes. 'There is something. Maybe one thing.'

'There you go.'

'Can you drive me? Again?'

He'd been following the manuscript all day, but he knew O'Rourke had thrown her, she was no longer sure it had anything to do with Frank – and maybe she was right. If Frank had gone off in his own direction, none of Jack's discoveries could explain him – but perhaps it didn't matter. Perhaps the manuscript could help in some other way, its lost language, its forgotten wonders. He couldn't see how, but he'd felt it at the lighthouse.

'Anywhere,' he said.

'It won't take long.'

She went to put her shoes on, and Jack corked the wine bottles and tidied the photos back into their wallets. There seemed to be a lot of them, hundreds, but they didn't stack up to much. Not when they kept hurtling past, twenty-four to a second, the long unwatched movie of your life.

He began to gather the books, and a sentence caught his eye. The founding secretary was John Wilkins, a mathematician and bishop, a planner of moon cities, a philosopher of machines. He wrote books about secret writing, crypt-analysis, a language of musical notes – and his last work was *An Essay towards a Real Character, and a Philosophical Language.*

Jack's heart stammered. He hardly knew what it meant, but he had to find out. He closed the book, added the letter to the manuscript and left the satchel on a pew. He picked up his keys.

ᴝ)

They drove the same long road towards South Head, but this time they stayed low and kept to the harbour's edge. Past the old fishing village of Watsons Bay, its priceless weatherboard shacks, to Camp Cove. It was the last shelter before the ocean. The First Fleet had rested here, and perhaps Constant had too. A long sea journey, rumours of monsters – and the signal fire where the lighthouse would be.

'The monk, Constant – he would have come this way,' Jack said.

It looked the same now as it must have then: the city was hidden around the harbour's corners, and the opposite shore was still wild. Beth looked out at the failing light and the steel of the harbour and didn't say anything. Jack sat in the sand as she stepped towards the waterline. He knew what it was like, the ripples of grief and nostalgia, the need to forget or remember. Her eyes the colour of weather as she walked back.

'I nearly drowned here, once. Or I thought I did, I've never been sure.'

Patchy late-autumn rain was falling, and the sand was cold between their toes. There might have been people up on the terrible cliffs of the Gap, but nobody else was sheltering in the cove. He watched her as she sat beside him, her raised knees, her pale legs.

'I'd just learned to swim, this flailing sort of freestyle I had. And I'm out of my depth, all adventurous. My parents are calling for me to come back in. I never understood that, did you? In being land, out being water. I thought it should be the other way around.'

Jack shifted in the sand. 'It must depend on how you feel about water.'

'I thought water should be in. Anyway, I didn't want to go, I wanted to swim out. But I turned and I saw that the storm was coming, an amazing bank of clouds just sweeping in from the Heads. You know how it is in summer.'

'With the summer storms.'

'And I just panicked, I forgot everything about how to swim. It was suddenly this weird twilight, like now, and everything was still and quiet, and I was sinking into this huge grey silence of the harbour. The taste of the salt, you know? How it burns your throat. I was terrified.'

'What happened?'

'Dad came in after me. I remember – being dragged on my back, still swallowing all this water. Then crying into the sand, I never felt anything so warm and dry, trying to catch my breath. And Dad holding my face and crying all over me, wiping my tears and his own tears off me.'

'You were all right?'

'I must have been, it's all I remember. The drowning, the sand. And this powerful resentment towards him whenever I thought about it.'

'Towards Frank?'

She nodded. 'I always thought it was some kind of pride,

like I resented him for rescuing me, like I was ashamed or maybe embarrassed – for needing to be rescued. But then I was thinking – I was just thinking.'

It was beginning to rain again, fat and lazy drops that made dark craters in the sand. The wind had broken into occasional gusts. There was a chatter behind them, people hurrying along the paths towards the car park. She looked around and back to him.

'I don't remember him being wet. Apart from the tears. He wasn't wet.'

'What do you mean?'

'He wasn't wet, it wasn't him. It must have been someone else who rescued me, it must have just been the lifeguard, and not him.'

She looked up at the clouds and recoiled as a raindrop hit her face. She wiped it off with her hand, and looked up and down the beach and frowned.

'Do you want to swim?' she said.

'It's too cold.'

She shrugged. 'I thought I was panicking, but maybe I knew what was going on. Maybe I knew, and resented him for that. Nobody but your father should rescue you, if you're a girl of six or seven. He should be able to rescue you himself.'

As she spoke, she unbuttoned her jeans and slid them from under her buttocks, over her feet. She seemed to have decided on something. She tossed her jeans to him.

'Do you think that's too harsh?'

'Maybe. What are you doing?'

'I'm going to swim.'

'It's almost winter.'

'No, it's mild, it's unseasonable.'

'It's raining. And late.'

'Come down to the water.'

She unzipped her jacket and pulled her shirt off. She wore black underwear, and her body goosepimpled with fine hairs.

74

He felt she was telling him many things, but he was missing most of them. She stepped into the water.

'And now I wonder whether he knew, whether he felt the same way. I mean I stopped going to church, I practically abandoned him, I left him there while his eyes sank into his head, while he scratched on things.'

'We don't know that.'

'But maybe that was part of it – maybe he got so strange because we weren't there for him. You know things can start with nothing and get so far out of control – slowly, but in a second.'

Her long and slender body sank into the water, vertebrae marking the tide, her shoulders hunching. Lines of rain stood like skewers. She pulled grey ripples as she plunged.

He had a glimpse of Judy on the starboard rail. She had been the one who had drifted from Frank, if anyone had – or she had let him drift. He thought about telling Beth, despite what Judy had said.

The rain was getting heavier, lifting ragged patterns from the surface. Birds hovered in the distance, lost in the clouds' undersides. Beth swam in to shore, or out. He watched her as she found her depth and rose from the water, hair plastered, body running with salty rivers. She sat in the rain-pocked sand and shivered, feeling her arms. When he tried to cover her with his coat, she waved him away.

'You'll catch your death.'

'Feel my skin. Is it tingling from the outside?'

'It's frozen.'

'I swam out until I could see the city. It looks amazing in the rain.'

'You looked amazing, too. In the rain.'

'The lights are coming on. The bridge, and the buildings.'

He tried to rub her goosepimples away. Loose sand stuck to her body, a second abrasive skin. She stroked the grains from her wrist as she looked up at the water, a darkening slate; she narrowed her eyes as if trying to read its ripples.

'I heard there was a city once, built on the edge of a harbour of quicksand. Dry quicksand, the kind that lets you drop into it and sends a great jet of sand up after you. You can't even swim in it, you just sink. Only these enormous flat skiffs could sail across the surface of it, from one side of the harbour to the other.'

She was shaking from the cold. She had her knees together and her feet splayed. Jack put his arm around her. He didn't know how she was managing to keep her teeth from chattering. He didn't know what she meant. He thought about John Wilkins's real character – his philosophical language. Was that what Constant had brought here? A kind of writing, a manner of speaking ... but what, exactly?

'Nobody knew how deep it was, the sand,' Beth said. 'But they pressed it into stone and built their city around it, and lived that way for hundreds of years. And they all knew that every so often a young girl would try to swim in it, and the sand would swallow her up. She'd sink straight to the bottom, where all the other girls still were, never decomposing, only drying out, as the water from their bodies floated up – in little – bubbles.'

Now her teeth started in. She felt like ice in his arms: he'd never warm her, she'd drain his heat and leave them both frozen on the beach. Judy had said Beth was resilient to a point, and he wondered where that point was. She'd said she was glad that Beth had him, and he wondered whether that was right.

'We'd better get you home.'

She looked at him as if realising where she was. 'All right,' she said.

C

It was Thursday again, just over a week since the hailstorm. Jack had been battling the manuscript for almost that long, inching and then stalling, now making progress at last. He wished he had found the letter earlier. He regretted taking the manuscript to Ash. He felt its possibilities as he carried it through the library, still in its satchel; he felt its suggestions taking shape. It wasn't forensic knowledge he needed. It was something deeper.

A column of microfilm viewers stood in a dim corner, away from the afternoon sun. Beth had found the roll for him, a strip of black plastic wound around its spindle and tied with string. Pamphlets and prayer books rushed through the light until he braked a few pages into John Wilkins's masterwork. *An Essay towards a Real Character, and a Philosophical Language* was first printed by order of the Royal Society in 1668. Jack took notes as he read, resting his pad against the screen, and the projected letters wrapped his hands.

> It cannot be denied, but that the *variety* of *Letters* is an appendix to the Curse of *Babel*, namely, the multitude and variety of *Languages*. But supposing such a thing as is here proposed, could be well established, it would be the surest remedy that could be against the Curse of the Confusion, by rendring all other *Languages* and *Characters* useless.
>
> For *Alphabets*, they are all of them, in many respects, liable to just exception. They are inartificial and confused, the *Vowels* and *Consonants* being promiscuously huddled

together. Their *Figures* have not that *correspondency* to their Natures and Powers which were desirable in an artificially-invented Alphabet.

As for the ambiguity of words by reason of *Metaphor* and *Phraseology*, this is in all instituted Languages so obvious and so various, that it is needless to give any instances of it; every Language having some peculiar phrases belonging to it, which, if they were to be translated verbatim into another tongue, would seem wild and insignificant.

All the phrases Jack had collected. *Eat the soup or jump out the window. You want a drunken wife and a full barrel. After it rains a little on Thursday.* They were pretty baubles, insignificant in the end. There had to be a better way.

Wilkins wrote that the first language was given by God, and it was perfect. It gave the people dizzying power and ambition. It led them to the plain of Shinar to build their tower to heaven – Jack recognised the Tower of Babel. The people came close enough to trouble their maker. He confused their tongues and scattered them over the earth, and their languages had grown apart ever since. *Uren fader thic arth in heofnas, thu ure fader the eart on heofenum, ure fadir that art in hevenes, O oure father which arte in heven.*

Jack mouthed the words as they grew smooth, like riverstones, as they retreated from the language of God. It all seemed hopeless, they were all lost – but Wilkins wasn't finished.

But now, if there were such an universall character, to expresse things and notions, as might be legible to all people and countries, so that men of severall Nations might with the same ease, both write and read it, this invention would mightily conduce to the spreading and promoting of all *Arts* and *Sciences*: Because that great part of our time, which is now required to the Learning of words, might then be employed in the study of things. The perfecting of such an invention were the only way to unite the seventy two Languages of the first confusion.

Jack read the paragraph again. A universal character, legible to all people and countries. The manuscript had come from a Founding Fellow of the Royal Society – and here was the Founding Secretary, promising a new kind of writing. Jack tried to imagine what a language written and read by everyone might look like – how a book written in that character might appear. He had a feeling he already knew.

Beth found him among the viewing cabinets. She wore the expression she'd woken up with, a slight worry around her eyes. Her fingers hooked into her collarbone.

'Jack, you've been to that beach before – haven't you?'

'All my life, I suppose.'

'Do you remember seeing any lifeguards there?'

He paused. 'Not specifically.'

'It's a harbour beach. There aren't any lifeguards, are there?'

'I guess not.'

'Never have been.'

'It must have been someone else,' Jack said.

'Yes, it must have been,' she said. 'Someone else.'

She was wearing her jacket and held her purse in one hand. Jack glanced up at the library clock; it was after five, the end of her shift. The old book glowed against his hands: a remedy against the confusion, a perfect invention.

'I'm going to have to tell her about the church,' Beth said. 'About it being finished, all these years.'

'Judy?'

She nodded. 'She must have some idea. Maybe there's a simple explanation, something completely ordinary.'

He thought again of what Judy had told him on the boat. Had Frank even tried to explain himself to her? He might

79

not have thought it worth the effort. And if he'd left the house each morning simply because he didn't like it there … Beth wouldn't want to know that, and Judy wouldn't want to tell her.

'You have to?' he said.

'I have to know.'

'Do you want me to come?'

'No, it's all right.'

He was relieved, though he couldn't show it. He felt he could be more useful where he was.

It was an immense undertaking, a list of all the things and notions that needed names. Wilkins devoted metres of microfilm to his branching division of heaven and earth. Transcendental things, magnitude and space, sensitive and vegetative species. Herbs according to their leaves, nervous or succulent: trubs, fuzball, scurvy-grass, spunge. Or described by seed-vessel: gold of pleasure, yellow loose strife, dwarf medler. Fish were oblong and roundish or flat or thick. Rain could be mizling, showr, spout, storm or sleet.

The bishop had invented his own alphabet to express these divisions. Jack copied the letters down, practising their angles and intersections, still thinking about Beth. How much of her might he describe in a paragraph of this language?

Wilkins's alphabet wasn't the alphabet of Jack's manuscript. Jack couldn't help feeling disappointed. He thought he'd found the answer: Wilkins had invented a perfect language and used it to write the manuscript. Now he saw that it wasn't that simple. And yet there was something about Wilkins's work that reminded Jack of the manuscript, its structure and shape. They were related in ways he couldn't quite see.

The library was closing; the lights on the lower floors flicked off as Jack reached the end of the microfilm. The essay concluded with a prayer in fifty languages, including its own: *haz coba oo za ril dad, oche nash Izghae yease nanaebaesaegh.*

Jack found himself praying along, for wisdom, for strength: *our father who art in heaven.*

ᘮ

The satellite speakers filled the church with Thorn's windswept largos. Beth would be with Judy for a few more hours. Jack wandered between the floorlamps with the manuscript, holding it open, angling it into the light.

He couldn't stop thinking about what he'd glimpsed in the library. Not Wilkins's alphabet, but his amibtion. He had thought the manuscript a kind of encyclopaedia: the man and woman, the world's nursery of plants, flasks of chemicals. He had assumed, perhaps romantically, that it was a lost language. But instead – what if instead it were a new language, a new expression? Organised by logic and philosophy, a perfect language. The unfinished tower, the sack people and the different kinds of rain: perhaps they were part of an attempt to categorise everything, to express everything.

Jack paced the church, turning off lights. To speak such a language, to be its inventor and only native. What clarity of understanding – and what loneliness, like a god or angel, all-hearing, unable to respond.

He settled into the sofa with the last light. He wanted to stay up for Beth, but he could feel sleep lapping at him. He worried about what she was doing with Judy. Were they drunk together on great thermoses of whisky? She had abandoned the manuscript to solve some other puzzle, and he didn't know where the winds and tides might take her. He missed their teamwork, though there was something thrilling about the manuscript and its mysteries being his alone. A complicated emotion, and he doubted there was a word for it in any language.

ᘮ

Through a dream of letters he heard Beth's key serrating through the tumblers, the click of the porch door. The manuscript was splayed over his chest. Beth crept across the floor with a quiet sliding step. She sat on the sofa and huddled into him. He folded around her as she looked out across the nave, trying not to wake him. He twisted the lamp away.

'How's Judy?'

'I didn't tell her anything.'

'No?'

'I was going to, but I didn't.'

Her voice was flat with decision, soft with the time of night. He didn't know what to say. He kissed her behind the ear and she shifted deeper into him, and he knew there were certain kinds of silence that no words could improve.

cᴗ cᴛ)cᴛ

It was Saturday, a short day at the library. Beth had gone to bed with a puzzled expression and went to work looking the same way. Jack spent the day pacing the church, the manuscript in one hand, the notes he had taken in the other. It had been ten days since the hailstorm and the roof collapse, more than a week since he'd found the manuscript in the crypt. Constant had studied it for thirty years before his arrival at the church, Johnson had circled it for fifteen before appealing to the monk, and almost a century had passed between Wilkins's death and Jan Reynolds's last auction. Jack had only had it a week, but he read over his notes and jotted new ideas, and by the end of the day he had glimpsed his direction.

Wilkins had promised a language perfect at every level. One letter for every sound, and one sound for every letter. The phrases and sentences would be perfect, and the grammar would be precise and flexible. But it would start with the letters.

Jack propped the manuscript open on the kitchen benchtop as he flayed and dipped the fillets of six fish. They were oblong and roundish fish, at least in Wilkins's classification, and he was marinating them with some nervous and succulent herbs. He also had dough for half a dozen bread rolls rising on the cool side of the kitchen: he'd prove it in the last rays of the afternoon. He dusted flour from the manuscript's pages and leaned in to squint at its alphabet.

He turned back to his notebook. He was copying the symbols, trying to work out how many there were and how they might be arranged. Some seemed ligatured together, like *fi* and *fl*; it was difficult to tell where they ended and began. He made corrections and refinements until he was sure he had them all:

The single stroke / seemed to appear only at the end of words, so it might have been a full stop or some more basic kind of punctuation. The rest were probably letters: twenty-four of them. He drew up a table noting how often they appeared together, and by the bottom of the first page he had settled on a handful of rules: ⊂, ⊃ and ∩ were everywhere; none of ⊌, ⋔ or ⋒ was ever found together. He felt the letters' personalities emerging.

Wilkins said that words should sound pleasant and graceful and be easy to pronounce. Jack decided to arrange the different sounds – the vowels, approximants, nasals, fricatives and plosives – according to principles of sonority. The language might have *cleft* but never *lcetf* and certainly not *lcbtf*. It would avoid the horror clusters of Russian and Georgian, the *vzglyad* and *mtsvrtneli* and *prtskvnis*. It would respect the voiced and the voiceless. Jack arranged and rearranged the letters into their likely types until he had a rough list.

Vowels
C ∩ Ɔ U ○ ‖

Approximants
⊥ ＋ ┼ɔ ·

Nasals
ɼ̇ ⋔ ʊɔ

Fricatives
ʋ̣ ⅏ ⋒ ○ ᕹ

Plosives
ṅ ⋔ ℼ ʋ̣ ⊔ ᕹ

There was already a pleasing symmetry to the lists. The consonants ɼ̇, ⋔ and ʊɔ were mirrored and inverted: perhaps each shape stood for a part of the mouth, and its variations for the kind of sound produced there. At the lips might be *p*, *b*, *f* and *m*; behind the teeth *t*, *d*, *s* and *n*; and back towards the soft palate *k* and *g*, the fricative *kh* from *Chekhov* and *Bach*, and the nasal *ng* from *singer*. Jack sounded them all, and felt his tongue searching for the other letters. The last fricatives ○ and ᕹ were nearby, perhaps *sh* and the *zh* from *pleasure* and *treasure*; the approximants were variations on *l* and *r* and *y* and *w*. He could only guess at the six vowels, but knew they would be evenly spaced around the mouth: perhaps *i*, *a*, *e*, *o*, *u* and some kind of schwa, *ə*.

The falling sun sent planks of light through the churchyard and into the kitchen. He kneaded the bread for a few minutes, looking through the window. Outside, the lone headstone glowed orange; it had always been too worn to read, but among the stretching shadows he thought for the first time he could make out letters. He thought it said *Constant*. The sun hit the manuscript and the notebook, different shades of gold. He continued down the page.

Wilkins had begun his essay with the Confusion of Tongues, when the first language was broken into seventy or seventy-two of them. The manuscript's half-built tower must be Babel, gathering weeds. And it would say so, somewhere on the page: names weren't part of the philosophical language. Jack searched for the pattern: a plosive, a vowel, the same plosive, a different vowel, an approximant. ᗩᑎᗯᑎᕼ was close, but its vowel was repeated instead of its consonant. It was the same with ᒍᗪᗯᑎᕼ, which also started with an approximant. Neither of them quite matched.

But he found the exact combination near the bottom of the page, in the word ᑎᑕᑎᗪᒧᑎᕼ. It was too long, but its first five letters must have meant *Babel*. Perhaps the final ᑎᕼ was a grammatical marker. It was the most common of the letter-pairs he had listed, especially at the end of words. It might have been used for nouns, or even place names: Jack scanned the page and found it again, in ⟨ᑲᑎᕗᒡ·ᑎᓂ⟩. He stopped at the last word, growing used to this new kind of reading. Fricative-vowel-nasal-vowel-approximant: it was the pattern of *Shinar*, the Mesopotamian plain where the tower was built. He had the key, and the rest of the letters slotted into their places.

Ter sholpal tikim pu nashi owal lekim us owal tokim. Shol məshom pu ekayi bekh epim us pu ashəki latim is Shinarim us pu esti ushim. Akim pu utoki as rapim tizh wim azh atəki ef wim as kəltim us as bergim takh kir kotim namti əkh ostikim us wim azh təki ef wim as nipim atif wim ozh sherte aləkh tikir faltim. Er barakim pu sherti as akim bekh ushim aləkh tikir faltim us akim pu khepi as atəka tar kəltim. Er kim pu nipe as Babelim tizh re barakim pu ushim babi as shol tikir lekim us barakim pu bekh ushim sherti as akim aləkh tikir faltim.

Jack had no idea what it said, but it was something; it was a language. He tried a sentence aloud. It sounded like an incantation, a spell you shouldn't say all of or repeat.

He shaped the rolls and put them in the oven to bake, then poured himself a glass of wine and started on the fish. He felt the sudden urge to hole up in the crypt and hang something heavy from the trapdoor's ring, to grow his hair and fingernails and let his eyes sink mercifully into his head. It felt like a dream he might never return to if he woke. The fish sizzled and he shook the pan to dislodge them, still writing with his free hand.

All of the manuscript's drawings would have their own words, he realised. Every kind of plant and mineral, every mixture and alloy. All the kinds of rain, all the kinds of water, a word for rain meeting the ocean, a word for tears blinked away. Nothing Ash's forensics might uncover could compare to this.

The pan burst into flame and he jumped back from the stove,

snatching the manuscript away. He rattled a lid onto the pan and the kitchen eddied with smoke. The porch door opened and slammed and he heard Beth's footsteps, and his mind still hummed with words. Heavy rain, light rain, a rainbow, a flood. And the kind of rain that falls on Thursdays, but only a little.

She always returned in a bright cloud of professionalism, with the crisp corners of her library shirt, open at the throat, and the practised angles of her low heels. There were small fairy-tale transformations when she twisted her hair into a ponytail. He loved the small softening marks her bra straps left against her shoulders; as her skin smoothed he felt she was returning to him. And she lifted him from whatever translation he was working on; she discovered him every night.

But her movements tonight were stiff beyond efficiency, and the manuscript held him more tightly than his subtitles ever had. He felt they were stretching for each other as they pressed together; the spell lingered beyond her wakening kiss. She stood back and waved the kitchen smoke from her face.

'What's happened?' she said.

'Nothing. Uh, it's Cajun. Come outside.'

The sky darkened and lights began to flicker on behind trees and curtains. Constant's name disappeared from the headstone. Beth seemed to gather herself. He touched her again and felt closer to her. She looked around at the outdoor setting.

'And you've done the table.'

'It's a good night for it. Balmy.'

'Isn't it. We need another place.'

'Who?'

'Mum.'

'I didn't make enough food.'

'We can stretch it out.'

'Like Jesus.'

She seemed happier, but he wasn't sure of her plans for Judy. There was an expression on her face that he couldn't quite read. The manuscript reached for him, its siren-song of new words. He shook it off and turned back towards the church.

'They're here.'

Sandy unbuckled Dev from the baby seat strapped into Thorn's old Saab while Peter took a portable cot and a padded case from the boot. Thorn stood back, looking bewildered. He saw Beth and held out his bottle of wine.

'You all made it,' she said.

'Yes, we're quite the modern family.'

Judy arrived in a taxi while Peter was hoisting the cot up the porch steps. She looked unsure of herself; she kept patting her hair and straightening her clothes, though they were perfect as always.

'I hope it's not an imposition,' she said.

'No, plenty of room,' Jack said. He turned to Peter. 'Is your friend coming? Ash?'

'I told him when and where,' Peter said. 'But I left him a few messages this week and he hasn't answered. I want to ask him something.'

Sandy gave Dev a bottle and put him to sleep in the oratories. The night stayed balmy, and they ate bread and drank wine in the churchyard. Peter told them that the water police had fished an old sedan out of the harbour and found a suitcase full of women's passports, all from countries that no longer existed. East Germany and Yugoslavia, Upper Volta and Zaire. Peter hoped they were forgeries and didn't belong to stranded women. The car was covered in barnacles and weeds; it had been down there for years.

'Anyway, he's late,' Peter said. 'Can we start?'

Jack left Ash's fish warming in the oven and divided up the rest. He watched the outdoor table from the kitchen. A candle burned beside each of their glasses, and their faces floated in the darkness.

They were all getting along; Peter sat between Thorn and Sandy and draped his arms across both of them. Thorn leaned into his touch, and Judy drank steadily. But there was something different about them all, unusual pauses and silences. Jack saw how fragile they were, how much they depended on each other, as he returned from the kitchen.

Peter turned to him. 'Dave and Warren want to teach Beth advanced boat-handling. I think they're going to deputise her.'

'That sounds right,' Sandy said. 'They wouldn't even teach me how to put a lifejacket on.'

'Really, Sandhya,' Judy said. 'You're far too beautiful for those two.'

Beth gave her an indignant look. 'What about me?'

'You know you're beautiful, darling. But Sandy's so exotic. Men like that wouldn't know what to do with her.'

'They liked you too, Judy,' Peter said. 'They thought you were magnificent.'

'You should go for it,' Sandy said. 'They weren't that bad.'

'Sandy,' Beth said.

'I'd like to think I could do a little better, even if I am an old widow.'

'Mum!'

Beth and Judy gave each other the same glance, equal parts blame and contrition. Beth looked away first. She turned to Sandy. 'What happened to your singer, San?'

Sandy lowered her eyes. 'Bit of a one-hit wonder, it turns out.'

Peter gave an exaggerated shrug. 'I tried, I don't know what else I can do.'

'Weren't you bringing me someone tonight?'

'I tried that too. I don't know what's happened to him.'

Jack refilled Peter's glass. 'He seemed all right the other day.'

'You went to see Ash?'

'I gave him the manuscript to look at.'

Judy put down her glass and glanced up at Jack. 'That manuscript you were talking about, on Peter's boat?'

'That's right,' Jack said cautiously. Beth had wanted him to keep the manuscript from Judy when she'd thought it had consumed Frank. She didn't think so any more. But perhaps she was wrong – was that recognition he saw in Judy's face, or just curiosity? It was too late now.

'What did he say?' Peter asked.

'He said it was probably nothing.'

'Sorry.'

'Well, but that it could be something.'

Thorn took the bottle and poured himself a glass. 'Like what?'

'There was a letter with it, from the eighteenth century, it gave me some leads. I think it's some kind of artificial language, perhaps. A philosophical language, a perfect language.'

'Oh.' Thorn sat back. 'Disappointing.'

'Well, unless this one actually works.'

'Works how?'

Jack tried to put what he'd seen into words. 'Well, you know about language and thought, language shaping thought. What if there really is a better way of expressing things, words for all the important ideas, and the relationships between things – a better way of thinking about things?'

Thorn gave him a tired look. 'You know all these philosophical languages are idiotic. Grand ideals, but all they do is list the hang-ups of whoever thought of them.'

'There haven't been any good ones, but that doesn't mean there can't be.'

Judy pointed her glass at Thorn. 'I think it sounds wonderful. It sounds very useful. Good for Jack, discovering a perfect language.'

Beth turned on her. 'Mum, he hasn't discovered a perfect language.'

Judy put her glass down. 'He says he has.'

Beth shook her head. 'It's like – San, remember at college, when we were learning the Dewey Decimal System? And that joke about the Chinese encyclopaedia that divided the animals in funny ways. They're all – one category is stray dogs, and one is mermaids, and ones who just broke the water pitcher, and those that from a long way off look like flies. It's Foucault or somebody, isn't it?'

'Yes, but he was quoting Borges.'

'Right, but isn't the point that all language is arbitrary, any time you divide up the world it's always in some way stupid.'

Thorn spread his palms. 'I think she has you, Jack. At least natural languages evolve, over centuries, everyone contributes – and look at the problems they've got. Imagine if you had to start over.'

Jack looked around the table, the faces in the candlelight. Only Judy's offered him any encouragement or hope, and she'd been drinking all night, great elegant gulps of wine. He felt a sudden doubt.

'But think of a language with all the best words,' he said. 'Everything we're always struggling over. *Schadenfreude* and *esprit d'escalier*, and *saudade* and *duende*.'

It wasn't an argument; it was an escape. He knew that it would divert the conversation away from his perfect language, suddenly tarnished. He felt a dull shame as Judy folded her arms in displeasure.

'I don't know what those last ones are,' she said.

'None of us do, or we can never be sure that we do. *Saudade* is a kind of yearning, *duende* is – I don't know – some sort of inspiration. But you have to know the whole language first. There are loads of others.'

Thorn put down his glass. He knew what Jack was doing, but he didn't mind. 'Now what Sandy has, that's *torschlusspanik*,' he said. 'Gate-shutting-panic, the fear of being left on the shelf.'

Sandy made a face. 'What about these bloody men who won't stick around, what have they got?'

'*Türschwellenangst*, of course: threshold-fear.'

Jack poured the last of the wine and thought about words for a surrender worse than defeat, for a cause that vanishes halfway through the battle.

'All the Russian words are about drinking,' he said. 'They've got different words for happy-drunk, maudlin-drunk, singing-drunk. There's a word for the last bottle you don't need but always have.'

Judy drained her glass. 'That sounds perfect.'

They'd drunk all the wine they had handy, so Jack tiptoed through the oratories, past Dev in his cot, then through the trapdoor and down the stone stairs. The bottles were already swaddled in dust.

He reached for a familiar label and felt he was back where he'd started. Perhaps he'd been fooling himself. There were patterns in the manuscript, but they weren't the strict patterns of a philosophical language, where every letter had to mean something. The patterns were in endings, in clusters, in particles – like the patterns of a natural language.

He took the wine back up to the nave and found his notebook. *Er kim pu nipe as Babelim. Wim azh doti af azh babi as akir lekim.* He mouthed the words. Dev was standing against the side of his cot, peering into the darkness of the oratories with his great deep eyes. Jack leaned in and whispered to him. *'Ter sholpal tikim pu nashi.'*

He didn't know why he'd said it. Dev blinked and took a step backwards. He sat heavily and looked up at Jack with an inquisitive expression.

Jack glanced at his notebook. *'Owal lekim us owal tokim?'*

The colour fell from Dev's face and he screamed, a ragged chord that reached for the reptile part of Jack's brain. His whole tiny body flared and crumpled, and Jack threw up his arms against the noise.

Sandy was first; she scooped him up and let him holler over her shoulder. The others followed a few steps behind her. She had to shout at Jack.

'What happened?'

'Nothing, I don't—'

But she was already trying to soothe him; she walked him

in circles, patted him into different positions. The others huddled into corners, trying to escape the noise. Peter was quite clucky, but Thorn looked professionally horrified. Beth and Judy held their hands to their collarbones in exactly the same way.

'I'd better get him home,' Sandy said. 'You don't mind, do you, Peter?'

'Not at all, darling. We'll roll down the windows, or turn up the music.'

'I'm sorry, Jack. Beth. It was wonderful.'

'Is he all right?'

'He'll be fine, it's probably just—' She shook her head. 'He'll be fine.'

Judy edged towards Peter. 'I don't suppose you've got room for me, as well?'

Peter looked surprised. 'Oh, plenty – if you're sure.'

'We can drive you, Mum. In a minute.'

There was a slight tone in Beth's voice. But Judy was her mother: she knew all her tones. 'Don't be silly, Peter's going the same way.'

They all kissed each other and hurried through the porch and into the night. Dev's voice rang through the streets for more than a block. Jack wondered what he'd said.

$\cup$)

Judy had slipped away before Beth could tell or ask her anything. Jack felt it between them as they worked through the dishes. Beth took a long time drying. She looked out into the churchyard and not at him. The hot water was running out; the sink was full of fish-oil and tannins. He took Ash's dinner from the oven and put it into the refrigerator.

Beth put down the dishrag and leaned into him, cheek at his shoulder, surprising him. 'I'm sorry about before. About Borges.'

He watched her in the window's reflection. She was an

94

inch shorter than he was. He stroked the fall of her neck. 'Borges isn't your fault.'

'No, I mean – I'm sure you have a perfect language.'

'I'm not so sure I do.'

He caught her eye in the reflection in the window; there was something evaluative about her look. She looked away.

'It's just – I found something today, about Dad. It kind of threw me.'

She was always surprising him, always two or three steps beyond him. 'What did you find?' he said.

'Here.'

She led him back through the oratories and into the nave. The stone still rang with Dev's howling. Her handbag sat on one of the pews; she opened it and pulled out a thick wallet of photographs.

'I thought Dad must have left these for a reason, here in the church. To let me know, if I wanted to know.'

Jack wasn't sure. The simplest reason was often no reason: things happened, people had heart attacks, they left boxes behind. 'You think it's something?'

'Do you notice anything about these?'

She handed him the photographs and he shuffled through them. The black-and-white miniatures, the faded colours. All the pictures were of her. She was a beautiful child, blonde at four, brunette by six, and had an ease with the camera that he didn't recognise.

He didn't understand. 'You're very cute,' he said.

'That's not it. Look at these two.'

In the first photo she was sunbaking at a suburban swimming pool, wearing a blue one-piece and oversized sunglasses that must have been Judy's, posing like a film star. She was more tanned than children were allowed to get these days. In the next photo she was sitting on a picnic rug, wrinkling her nose as she peeled a broad strip of skin from her arm. He looked closer, at the faces and figures.

'This guy here?'

'You see him?'

'Maybe.'

A man stood in a pale blue turtleneck and what looked like a brown corduroy jacket, hands in his pockets. First outside the cyclone fence surrounding the pool, looking towards Beth, then in the shade of a tree behind the picnickers. He was about an inch tall in the first picture, smaller in the second. It might have been different men wearing the same clothes, but it looked like the same man.

'Who is he?' Jack said.

'I don't know. He seems familiar, but I don't know why. Maybe just because I've been looking at him all day.'

'Maybe.'

'But something made me look at him, there was something about him. It's a bit weird, isn't it? Having the same person in two pictures?'

There were dozens of people in the backgrounds of both photos, filling the pool, dotting the park. But now the man Beth had identified looked like the only figure in the landscape, alone in all the metropolis. It had to be a trick, it was all suggestion.

'I don't know, Beth. There are lots of pictures here, the same guy turns up in a couple of them ... And this was twenty years ago, there weren't nearly as many people then.'

She gave him an uncommitted look. 'I suppose.'

'And the inner suburbs, it's like a little world. You're bound to keep seeing the same people, and unless they've got some physical deformity you'll probably never remember them.'

'Or if they're remarkably attractive.'

'But even then. I mean, we've lived thirty years within five miles of each other; it's impossible that I'd never seen you before. And I certainly would have gone all—'

He blew through his rounded lips, as at a painfully desirable passer-by. She smiled on one side of her face.

'Not for the whole thirty years, you wouldn't. I mean in

the eighties, with the hair and the braces, you would have gone all—'

She held her palms out in front of her and gave a voiceless *wargh*. She had great timing; Jack had to laugh.

'But it's frightening how little we remember,' he said. 'How much we forget. A moment and it's gone; people lose their features, they blend in.'

She nodded. 'It's scary.'

'I'm sure it's nothing bad.'

'I'm sure you're right.'

He felt his perfect language fading as he ran his fingers along the bookshelves. Words writhing and curling on the church floor, brittle as insects. He found a book of essays and short stories by Borges, in Spanish. He turned to the index and the *Emporio celestial de conocimientos benévelos*, the Chinese emperor's encyclopaedia. The outlandish categories were all there. Tame, fabulous, shaking like crazy, innumerables, *perros sueltos* – it mocked classification, the whole endeavour. He turned back to the beginning of the essay, a short piece, entitled – of course – *El idioma Analítico de John Wilkins*.

Not a general objection: a precise assault. Borges praised Wilkins for the diversity of his interests, his moon cities, but wasted no time in dismantling his universal language with its ambiguities, its redundancies and deficiencies. It was a reasoned and reasonable assessment, and held a current of regret. There was no arguing with it.

As the shadows thickened and Beth's breathing slowed he knew he had made a mistake. He had no idea what the manuscript was. He had exposed it to daylight, and now nobody had heard from Ash. Jack had glimpsed his quiet fascination, the secret wonders he saw in the world, and hated to think anything had happened to him. But if the manuscript wasn't a perfect language, perhaps it was the opposite.

The next morning was sunny and mild. It seemed treasonous to worry about anything under the cloudless weekend sky, the harbour full of yachts, the snap of sails and clink of rigging on the breeze. But the sunlight never reached far into the oratories, and the crypt stayed cold and dark all day.

Ash's business card listed only his office numbers. Jack called all day but there was no answer. It was Sunday, after all. A recorded message at the switchboard recited the office hours; he would have to wait until tomorrow. He called Peter for Ash's home number, but he didn't have it. Jack paced the church, as Frank had, clutching the manuscript as Frank might have – but that seemed less likely, now, and even less as the day wore on.

It wasn't a perfect language; there was no such thing. It was probably a hoax or forgery, as Ash had said. But Ash was missing, and Jack couldn't help thinking that his disappearance had something to do with the manuscript. Some occult power of the kind that had terrified the experimental monks, the mysterious regret.

Beth was sorting through the photographs, arranging them in piles. She attached sticky notes and drew arrows. There were more pictures now than before; she must have found more wallets and envelopes full of them. She held them up to her face, angled them into the sunlight. It never seemed quite bright enough.

On Monday he called Ash again, and the phone rang out. He tried the switchboard, and nobody had seen him. He hadn't applied for any leave. Jack told himself that it could have been anything. He couldn't think of any plausible harm the manuscript might have caused. He tried to put it out of his mind.

Beth was hurrying through her morning preparations. He still hadn't grown used to her body: every time he saw her it seemed to be from a slightly different aspect. She caught him looking as she shrugged into her shirt, and gave him a small flattered smile. She turned her back on him as she threaded her earrings, but he could imagine the concentration on her face. She stepped into her pants, and straightened up as a rap sounded at the porch door. She turned back to him.

'Are you expecting anyone?'

He shook his head and went to the door. The last couple of days had made him nervous: Ash's silence, his failures. The suburb's cheerful sounds rose through the porch, but he still felt wary.

Frank's man O'Rourke stood on the doorstep with a ladder and a silent companion. The promised apprentice had dark hair, grey eyes and skin that looked tanned for the first time. There was something about his eyes, even at a glance: pale and unblinking eyes. O'Rourke put his fingers to the peak of his cap.

'Ah, hello there. We've just come to fix your roof. This here's Max.'

O'Rourke had denied finding anything under the chancel, but Jack wasn't sure. He'd poked around the crypt as if looking for the manuscript, or making sure it hadn't been disturbed. Jack knew it was paranoid, but he couldn't help it.

'You couldn't come back, tomorrow maybe?' he said.

'Can't lose a day,' O'Rourke said. 'We can come back in six weeks, though.'

'No, no. Come in.'

Beth was working at her shirt's buttons. The hollow of her throat, the curve of her breasts. The apprentice's stare shifted to her. She turned away.

'Can I get you a cup of anything?' Jack said.

'Maybe later, thanks.'

Beth stepped into her shoes as Max and O'Rourke disappeared outside and clattered against the wall. He heard them dancing across the roof, the cat-like footsteps Max's, the cautious tread O'Rourke's. The tarpaulin was whisked off and a beam of sunlight fell to the floor. Beth kissed him and left for the library.

Halfway through the morning a shadow passed the porch door and the day's mail slid into the church. There was another letter about the Russian film, signed with the same pen as the first one. He hadn't thought about it for a week, but he was glad to be reminded. He sat at his desk and set the tape rolling again.

Dark clouds sailed over the desert sea, hiding the stars and the moon. Zhenshchina huddled by the keel of a listing ship; its bulwarks and funnels faded into view as the clouds thinned. Chelovek had returned from his travels. He leaned in and told her the wonders of his long walk. He'd seen geologists drilling miles below Siberia and covering their ears as the screams of the damned escaped. A cathedral full of stained glass that had flowed slowly out of shape. A country at war built airfields of wood to fool its enemy; the enemy carpeted the airfields with wooden bombs. He saw libraries sinking because their architects forgot about the weight of the books.

Chelovek was speaking softly but quickly; there wouldn't be time to subtitle half of what he said. You were only allowed to have two lines on-screen at once, fifty or sixty characters. Jack kept up as well as he could, but he had the feeling that everything meant something, everything was critical. He had to keep going back and starting again; it took all day. Max and O'Rourke rapped on the door and told him they'd be back in the morning. He tried Ash again, no answer. The world outside seemed dull and treacherous.

Beth came home and sorted through her photographs while Jack battled the Russians, and their sleep was brittle and tiring. The next day she had a late start. She spent the morning back on the floor, arranging the photos against the dark boards. Jack watched her as he ate a bowl of cereal and tried to call Ash.

She had separated all of the pictures in which any strangers appeared – anyone apart from herself and Frank and Judy. It looked as if she'd spent her life surrounded. In all of the scenes at least one person was watching her from the background, a blurry observer.

'What have you found?' he said.

She slid a photo across the floorboards to join the two she had chosen before. She was reflected in a funhouse mirror, perhaps at Luna Park, with gaping eyes and a pumpkin grin. And just at the mirror's inflection, where the concave smeared into convex, the blur of a man's figure. Making no vertical sense, reduced to strokes of colour: a camel brown and a pale blue.

'You think this is him?'

'Don't you?'

'Well. It doesn't really look like much.'

'Not on its own, but with the others. There are more, too, but he's wearing different clothes, so it's harder to tell.'

Jack looked through the rest of the photos. They seemed to be arranged in some pattern of likelihood, but he couldn't tell which of the background figures she had chosen. They were all out of focus, obscured by trees and each other.

'I'm not sure what I'm looking at,' he said.

'They're a bit small, I want to get them blown up.'

'What do you think it means?'

'I don't know.'

She returned to the pictures, exchanging a pair in her unknowable hierarchy. What was she looking for? Frank's science and heresy, his talk of lighthouses and the universe, then the drowning and the rescue, the years in the church – what connections could she see? The stories, the photos – they were signs and symbols, but he didn't know what they meant.

The telephone rang and he answered it, expecting more silence or the blather of a telemarketer, a cheery bill reminder, all betrayals of language.

'Jack? It's Ash.'

Relief washed over him. 'Ash. I thought something terrible had happened to you.'

'Like what?'

He didn't know. He struggled for an explanation that didn't sound ridiculous. He shook his head.

'Nothing. I don't know.'

'You're going to want to come down here,' Ash said.

A pulse of interest. 'Really?'

'Right away.'

ᴜ)

It was another clear day, the sky a dazzling blue; it seemed impossible that there were secrets in the world. But the air was cold in the bright corridors of the forensics centre, and Jack remembered the note in Ash's voice as he knocked on the door.

Ash looked exhausted. His eyes were rimmed with red, his coat stained with dull colours. His laboratory was piled with pizza boxes and soft-drink cans. The strips of the manuscript lay among them, burnt, scraped, discoloured with solvents. He trembled as he picked his way through the rubbish, and his old vigour sounded like delirium.

'You see what happens is, things that are alive absorb carbon-14 at the same rate as it decays out of them. If you want to know what happens. But when they die, they stop absorbing, and the isotope breaks down over time. So you can measure how much carbon-14 there is in the dead thing compared to how much in the atmosphere now, and work out from that how long ago the thing died.'

Jack tried to keep up. 'You mean, the cow.'

'Yes, or the cows. We assume that atmospheric C-14 is

always constant, which it isn't. It's affected by nuclear tests and the industrial revolution and so on. But we calibrate using old tree rings and so on.'

'And?'

'I would say that these cows died some time between 1090 and 1120.'

Jack was astonished. 'Old cows,' he said.

'Yes, old cows. The vellum could have been written on much later. But I can tell you that the inks used here were available then. They're iron gall inks, which you make from wood galls and iron sulphate, also called vitriol.'

'So it's real?'

'It depends what you mean. But it's old. It was written a long time ago.'

Jack's head spun. Nine hundred years – how many books that old still existed? And they were all in fragments, kept behind glass in darkened rooms.

'Where's it from?' he asked.

'I'm not sure. They're Aleppo galls from Turkey and also gum Arabic, probably from Egypt, but they were available all over Europe and the trade routes. And the dust, the pollen – it looks like it's been everywhere, it's hard to pin down.'

'Is it.'

Ash nodded, but there was a kind of hesitation in his eyes. Jack looked down at the strips of the manuscript, then at the scientist.

'What is it?' he said.

'The thing is, iron gall inks are meant to stick by biting into the parchment, there's a reaction that binds them. Eventually the ink eats all the way through. But here it's like the ink is floating on the surface; it's made no impression.'

'What do you mean, the writing's too new?'

'It's way too new. There'd be more reaction if it had been written this morning.'

'What does that mean?'

Ash evaluated Jack with a long stare. 'You know, when we

– when science – proved that the Shroud of Turin was medieval at best, they tried to argue that the Resurrection must have skewed the results. Can you imagine, radioactive Jesus, bombarding his shroud with isotopes.'

'What are you saying?'

'I'm saying I don't know. But take a look at this.'

Ash turned off the overhead light and took the corner he'd clipped from the cover to a lamp on the worktop. The lamp had a dark tube that reminded Jack of Constant's eternal candle, its black flame. A click, and the room was filled with an intense ultraviolet light. Ash looked like a spectre in his lab coat, and its smears looked like blood as he held the corner to the lamplight. Jack felt his breath escaping.

'What's that?'

'I don't know, there's not enough of it.'

It was almost nothing, a series of loops and tails against the new purple of the vellum, veins beneath its skin. A clipped corner of writing: the scratching, the invisible scratching that all strange old books attracted.

'It's probably an inscription of some kind, a name or date,' Ash said. 'A signature, you know, inside the cover. If you bring the rest back we can see what it says.'

He was being careful, but Jack recognised his stare. Like Johann Johnson and his friends, like Brother Constant: Ash had to know. Intellectual curiosity was darkening into passion and need. And the mysterious regret was gathering. He was on Jack's side for now, but he'd want this discovery for himself.

'I'd also like to have a look at that letter, if you've still got it.'

'Yes, I see.'

'So, you'll bring it all back?'

'I'll call you in a couple of days.'

Jack didn't know what to do. The manuscript had disappointed him – unforgivably, he'd thought. But if it was centuries older than Wilkins, nothing to do with him – nine hundred years old, it could be anything. Europe had been lost in its Dark Ages, searching for candles. The world was thrashing with conquests. Pierre Abélard was writing in Paris, Thomas à Becket in Canterbury, Omar Khayyám in Nishapur, the skalds of the sagas and eddas in Norway and Iceland. Great advances in theology and mythology, in astronomy and romantic love.

He'd been wrong about the forensics. The lab whispered its promises as he passed back through security and walked across the grass towards the car park. Ash and his colleagues would map and specify the manuscript, model its history, expose it to every kind of light. Jack could give up his obsession and return to the world, its blue sky, its trees in the wind. It would be so easy, he couldn't really think of any—

But gravity had gone wrong, and somehow he was falling headfirst. The ground flew beneath him and he plummeted towards the line of trees by the car park. He tried to flail his way upright but he couldn't work out directions, dimensions, and now there was nothing but a giant fist crashing through a glass table, and the sound itself seemed to bear him up into the trees, and he knew he would, he couldn't help, it was too late to—

He tried to open his eyes, but everything was red and black and seemed to be meltign as he wáchted adn hx—

And he tried again, he struggled with the drak and tried his best to saty where he wqs but great fogners wr pull he jnto the eartk søft xentel stoft—

Af gim zh mendi takh gim ozh shesti ukhotal as azim—

He raised his head to see a plume of black smoke pouring from the forensics centre, its broken windows. Lights flashed and sirens dopplered towards him as the emergency services converged. Time seemed to be running strangely. He was lying on a stretcher. His ears pounded with echoes, and his vision flickered as he stared at the ruin before him, and befroe he knəw it once agaín—

At last he got two fistfuls of consciousness and held it. Something soft and absorbent had been taped to his forehead, but his face was still warm and wet with blood. His neck clicked as he looked around. The grass was covered in glass and broadcast vans, and everyone seemed to be rushing over to the other side of the building – Ash's side.

He sat up dizzily and was restrained by an ambulance officer.

'Whoa, you don't want to do that.'

They weren't the official ambulance service; they wore the black and white uniforms of the St John volunteer brigade. Jack had seen them patrolling outdoor concerts and cricket matches and never quite knew what their story was. The Maltese cross epaulets, the four white arrowheads meeting on a black field. The real ambulance used the same cross, but it was red. He tried to get up again.

'Where are you taking me?'

St John holstered his two-way radio. 'We're just first aid, we can't take you anywhere. We're waiting for an ambulance.'

'I think I'm all right.'

'Mate, a minute ago you were speaking in tongues. I'd wait right there.'

'What did I say?'

'Beats me. Sounded like the last days.'

Jack peered at him. 'The last – you're involved in all that?'

'What?' St John followed Jack's gaze to his shoulder. 'Oh, this? No, mate, you're thinking of John the Evangelist. We're John the Baptist, we're just here to help.'

'But you're still – you're still religious, right?'

St John gave him a steady look. 'Officially we're *pro fide* – for faith – but we're also *pro utilitate hominum*, we don't discriminate.'

'I really think I'm all right.'

'You just relax.'

'But you can't stop me, can you?'

St John raised his eyebrows but stood back from the stretcher. Jack tried to stand up. It was harder than he'd thought. Half of his vision was obscured by a dark fog. All the world's birds swarmed in the sky above the lab, stretching into great accordion clouds, swooping to pick the flesh from the bones of kings and captains and mighty men. No – that wasn't right. He shook his head and the last days lifted, apart from the smoke and the flashing emergency lights. He staggered around the building.

The leeward side of the lab had crumpled into a blackened hole, and a slick of debris spread across the lawn. Splintered wood, more glass, and a group of scientists streaked with carbon. They were pointing and muttering; some were taking notes. Jack breathed again as he saw Ash picking his way between them, his coat burnt, his hands and head marbled black and a disturbing dark red. He righted a charred office chair and sat in it as Jack approached him.

'What happened, what is this?'

Ash was trying to separate a wad of crumbling paper. 'Look at it – now we'll never know who stole what, where the treasure was buried. All the secrets. I suppose that was the idea.'

'What do you mean?'

'Usually they just bribe somebody; they've tried this before, but never …'

'Are you all right?'

'I'm fine, it's just …'

'Don't tell anyone I was here, all right?'

'What?'

'The police. Anyone.'

But Ash had turned back to his paper, scarring himself with more charcoal and soot. All the footprints and dental impressions, all the unsolved mysteries. Someone patted Jack on the shoulder. Camera flashes burst around him. At least the manuscript was safe. He hadn't been paranoid; he'd been right, they'd all been right. Mysterious regrets, exceeding regrets. He didn't know who was responsible, but it felt like the end of the world.

5

He avoided the ambulances and made his way to the car. He had to get home to the manuscript and the sanctuary of the church. He fumbled the key into the door and the ignition; he stalled in reverse and in first gear. He limped out of the car park and drove along the back streets as slowly as he could. Even his good eye was smearing and flickering. Cars hurtled shockingly into his field of view. He didn't know these streets. He couldn't find his way home.

A winding road took him to the edge of the harbour, and he realised with a shock that it was empty. The oceans had boiled, and dry sand stretched to the opposite shore. It was littered with shipwrecks: ferries and steamers covered in oysters, old barques and cutters slumping into the sand, staves like skeleton bones. Hundreds of shopping trolleys and a midget submarine. The sky was the colour of rust.

The next thing he knew he was stuttering past a park full of men in pale blue shirts and brown jackets. They were all different men, but dressed the same. They stood in clumps and followed him with their eyes as he stalled and bunny-hopped away. His head was too small; he could feel the faultlines of his skull.

He only wanted to go home, but the roads or the wind eased him north and east, towards South Head and the lighthouse. The ink wriggled over his vision, making a tunnel to the grass of the verge. He was afraid of what he'd find there, what apocalyptic outlook. But the sea had returned, it swelled and crashed against the cliffs, and he felt better. He sat and listened to the endless argument of the waves until he could open his eyes. He must have been driving all afternoon. He ran out of petrol halfway down the hill and had to coast in neutral, the wheels eerie against the road.

Beth met him at the porch door. He had left the car and walked for half an hour, and now she was flooding the nave with light.

'It *was* you,' she said. 'I saw you on the news, I called Peter but nobody had heard of you.'

'I hit my head. I'm all right.'

'God, you're concussed.' She looked into his eyes, or at them: her expression made him think she couldn't see through them. 'They said it was criminals.'

He remembered something about bank records and title deeds, ordinary regrets. But it must have been more than that. 'There were four of them,' he said. 'On horses. And a woman on a – on a kind of beast.'

She soothed his forehead and pressed her body against his. Over her shoulder, the pews were covered with photographs.

'Was Peter's friend there, did you find him?'

'He got burnt, a bit.' Jack held his hands out as Ash had, staggering through the ruins. 'I don't think it was too bad.'

She'd blown up sections of the pictures, then blown up the enlargements, to the limits of the film's resolution. The random grain, the overlay of colours. Smudges and shapes, illusions. They looked like the things he'd been seeing all day through his ruptured sight.

She traced his bruise softly. 'What are you getting into?'

The dusk was draping his eyes. He felt the strength draining from his body, felt her feel his collapse and prop him up and help him to the bed. He didn't know what he was getting into. She turned out the lights and the night was welcome. He caught her scanning the blurred pictures, all funhouse pictures now, and as the last veils of darkness fell he thought he could ask her the same thing.

ꡀꡁꡂꡃ

6 Jack slept for the whole of the next day. He was half-aware of the builders climbing on the roof, of Beth moving quietly around him, sometimes laying her body against his. He kept telling her he was fine and didn't want to go to hospital, but he might have been asleep. The day seemed to unfold in the wrong order; the sun was always somewhere unexpected. He tried not to remember his dreams.

In the deepest part of the night he woke, or thought he woke, and saw a splinter of moonlight between the church-stones. He tried to look closer, but his eyes were still shut. He was looking at a notion, a memory ... and the splinter lengthened into a thread, it flexed and shimmered. He knew what it was: the trace of handwriting Ash had cut from the manuscript, glowing with his forensic light.

However Beth fell asleep she always ended up facing away from him. He left the bed and crept to her dark side, a rare view of her unguarded face. He'd only seen it a few times: her lips slightly parted, features soft and unshaped, ten years younger or fifty years older. But tonight her face was harder: she was holding on to something, working at mysteries in her sleep.

He followed her blind stare into the space of the church, where her photos ranged across the pews and the floor-boards. The faces looked like bruises as he wandered among them. She'd been sorting through them when he'd come home, bandaged and reeling. She'd left them behind, but not far. He was touched by her concern for him and wished he could be sure he'd react in the same way. But here he was, leaving her in bed, following his silver thread beneath the shadow of the tarpaulin and into the oratories, with only the excuse that it was somehow also for her.

The lab had exploded, but he'd got off lightly. He'd lost the slivers Ash had cut from the manuscript. But if he'd left the whole thing there, if it had gone up in flames … He could never take it back there. He couldn't take it anywhere. But maybe he didn't have to. Peter had reminded him of the parties he'd lit with strobes and gels, with all the kinds of light. He'd had Halloweens full of startling bright teeth and underwear glowing through dresses – and he still had it, his ultraviolet tube, his black candle, in a box of cellophane and wire. He slotted it into a desklamp, took the lamp and the manuscript down into the crypt and closed the trapdoor behind him.

He sat on the stone steps and turned on the lamp.

The light beyond light. He glowed, and the manuscript glowed, and veins or imperfections in the rock dotted the walls with tiny stars. Some trick of perspective made it look as if there were no walls, only flecks of light diminishing into the distance. He was suddenly a long way from the crypt and the church; he was floating in the first few seconds of the universe. He felt dizzy and had to touch the rock to locate himself.

He opened the manuscript, and the cover shone with signatures, silvery-black in the purple light – as Ash had suggested, but dozens of them. Johann Johnson had signed his name, twin giant Js cut off at the bottom corner. Jan Reynolds had added his name in 1723, and even John Wilkins – in 1638 he had signed himself Jo. He'd been there after all, not the manuscript's author but its student, its slave. The earliest date Jack could read was 1554, but there were names without dates. Rossignol, Argenti, Giovanni Porto or Porta – they all overlapped, as if the older ones had sunk and been written over. He traced them with his fingers, hardly believing what had appeared before him like a miracle, a vision. At last he found Constant, as he'd known he would.

He angled the page under the blacklight, searching for Frank's name – for any hint that the old man had found the crypt and the manuscript after all. If only he had, if only he'd sat here and stared at these pages, if only he'd discovered what Jack just had. Then Beth could give up the static and grain of her childhood, and she could avoid the conclusion that Jack was circling – that in the end her parents didn't love each other as much as she loved them, and Frank couldn't stand it or do anything about it. But he couldn't find the minister's name, or anything like it.

He turned the page, and the manuscript was full of glowing notations – it always had been. Like the notes he'd made on his own books and journals. Straight and rippling and doubled underlines, bars that traced the sides of paragraphs, tiny abbreviations in different handwritings. The notes might disappear for pages, particularly towards the end of the manuscript – but they always came back.

Most of the comments were as cryptic as the text. Some of the plants were identified with the distinctive symbols of Wilkins's real character: he had thought they were fuzball or scurvy-grass. Other notes could have been English or German or Italian or Russian, mostly illegible. But they were all clues, flashes of understanding. Someone had written *Babel?* by the half-built tower, and another hand had written *Pharos* over the top of that. Was it a conversation over the years, or just two men, each alone, asking questions of the darkness?

Some of the notes were confined to certain sections, the history or calligraphy, the plants or metals. But the most persistent attempt continued almost to the end, thinning only after the machines and potions. The marks floated beneath the vellum's surface; they said things like *1 Cr 14 2, Dan 5 8, Rev 5 4*. Jack remembered Constant's scratching, his knowledge of the scripture – these references must have been his shorthand. It might have been Frank, but it was probably Constant. The vellum had grown old and brittle, and his pen had battled with the long chains of its cells. And even he had been lost to madness and death in the colonies, and even his scratchings had been silenced.

Jack sat and ran his fingers over the page, watching the inscriptions fade and reappear. He had no idea what time it was, but he could hear the first sounds of the suburb grinding against the day. He felt like a prisoner in a dungeon, listening to the bright superterranean world. The dawn chorus couldn't agree on a key, or a tempo – and now Beth was padding over the churchboards. The desklamp suddenly jerked to one side, and he knew she'd found the extension cord.

'Are you down there?'

The trapdoor opened and daylight fell into the crypt; the silvery notes blinked from the manuscript. He brushed the page with his fingers but could feel nothing of the old scratchings. He squinted up at Beth.

'I woke up early,' he said. 'I wanted to check something.'

'Are you all right?'

He felt at his forehead, remembering the bruise. 'I'm all right. I'm much better.'

She bent into the crypt. 'Maybe we should get you checked up.'

'No, I'm fine.'

'Because you look kind of insane down there.'

'I'm not insane.'

'Come up.'

She climbed backwards up the steps and he followed her into the nave. The morning's sounds were all amplified: blenders and coffee machines, leafblowers and traffic. He steadied himself on the cool wall of the church.

He'd brought the manuscript up with him. She looked at it, and he saw an expression almost like jealousy cross her face.

'Did they say anything at the lab? Before it, you know.'

'It's from the eleventh or twelfth century. It's almost a thousand years old. And a lot of people have tried to crack it.'

'Is it worth a lot of money?'

'Probably, I'd imagine – I didn't ask.'

She narrowed her eyes. 'So what is it – do you think it's something amazing, do you think it's full of important secrets. Or what?'

He couldn't help looking at it, and it looked more ordinary in the morning light. But he still felt the traces of what he'd seen, pulsing between his fingers. It wasn't about Frank, or not directly. He wanted to tell Beth he was doing it for her, even if he couldn't explain how, but maybe that wasn't it either. He held it out to her.

'I don't know. It feels like it is. But even if it's not – even if I knew it was trivial, I'd still want to know what it was.'

She didn't take the manuscript from him; she folded her arms low across her stomach, making a hollow of her chest. The sheets had left creases at her cheek and temple.

'Why?'

She didn't sound resentful, only bleary and confused, but she needed an answer.

'I just – I feel like otherwise there's something wrong with me.'

'You need to work it out.'

He felt a cautious relief. 'I'd like to.'

'If you can't work that out, nothing makes sense.'

'Almost, yes.'

She gave him a look that was half sceptical and half pointed. Obsessions were like dreams, he thought, actual rapid-eye dreams – your own were always more interesting than anyone else's. But you tried, when you loved someone. You woke up and listened, you tried to understand.

Her photographs still littered the pews and the floor-boards, and in the daylight he could see how far she'd pushed the film; she'd brought it into sandstorms. She gave him a sad expression and he thought she might have been talking about her own search. He felt like a professional fraud: he'd been calling himself a translator for years, and he didn't understand anything.

She picked up one of the pictures and moved it forward and back. 'I guess I lost him. I thought I had him, but look. Can you see anything?'

The colours were scarlet and gold. They were halide crystals, chemically sensitised to the primary colours of light, spread in clumps and islands across the film. He couldn't see anything in it.

'Not really.'

She took the picture back. 'It's just static, isn't it? But everything is, when you look close enough.'

He supposed she was right. Pictures in newspapers, frames of film – they were all illusions, they all divided into their parts. And even the thing itself gave way to its atoms, the spaces between its electrons.

'Dad used to say that this is where God was,' she said.

He watched her, thinking how he'd studied the pores of her skin, the shards of light in her irises, the lines of her tattoo – but every avenue of knowledge teetered over a wasteland of ignorance. He knew she missed Frank, but he couldn't see the shape of her need: he didn't have the resolution, didn't have the grain.

'In pictures?'

She showed him the dappled photo. 'In chaos, in the place beyond measurement. Dad had to believe in physics; he knew God wouldn't bend the rules. But there's a limit to the laws, there's a place where there's nothing but probability – and he thought that's the only place left for God to be, where he can pull strings and you'd never know.'

'That's not bad.'

'He brought home a picture of that Mandelbrot fractal, and he said it was a map of heaven. The coastlines, the inland seas. He loved it.'

'That's a bit different, though – that's detail no matter how far you zoom in.'

'Yes, but eventually you stop; you have to. You stop before you get to God.'

She had arranged the photos in order of their fidelity: first the two pictures of the man in the pale blue and brown, the faces blotched and shadowed but still faces; then a slow deterioration as the grain took over. The final pictures were nothing like the first ones. They had lost their colour, resolved into inkblots. They looked like nothing.

'And this guy, is he God?' he said.

'Maybe he is. The closer you look, the less you see.'

She gathered up the pictures again, the most blurred on the top of the pile. She put them back in the cardboard box, on top of the originals. 'He's not God. He's a dead end.'

Jack looked into the box. Some of the black-and-white prints were the size of business cards; he could see how they had collapsed into grain so quickly.

'Who took these?'

'Dad did. He had this tiny camera, one of his little devices that he loved.'

She dug into the box again and held out a dull silver case, slightly bigger than a cigarette lighter. Jack took it from her and felt its compact weight. It had a slender light meter, dials for shutter speed and focus. He pulled its ends apart to reveal a viewfinder and lens, each less than a centimetre across.

'It's a spy camera,' he said.

'Originally. It's from the fifties, I think, or sixties.'

He pressed the most obvious button and the shutter blinked; a hundredth of a second later Beth was smiling at him through the viewfinder. He took it from his eye and turned it over appreciatively.

'It still works, it's completely mechanical.'

The camera gave a precise whirr as he closed it, and one of the dials shifted from one notch to the next – the last notch. He frowned and pulled the camera open again, revealing a groove. When he pressed it the camera slid apart and a cartridge popped out. It was about an inch across and looked almost exactly like a coil of microfilm.

'Look,' he said.

He wasn't sure it was the right thing to do. She had put away the pictures and their imagined trespassers. Perhaps she might settle for missing Frank and not understanding him. But he held out the film, and she turned it over in her fingers.

'Can we get it developed?' she said.

'I don't know if they still have this kind of film.'

'Can you find out for me?'

'Sure. Of course.'

She touched his arm, and they were back in the hunt together. It was the wrong one – but it was better than nothing. Her face had shaken off its morning mist: her eyes were clear, her skin smooth. The sun poured through the squints. She kissed Jack on the cheek and pressed the cartridge into his hand.

'If you've got time.'

She closed the door behind her, and Jack stood alone in the sudden space of the nave. He spun the film in his fingers, a tiny miracle. But it was still early; the camera shops wouldn't be open. He put the film down on the pew by the porch door, looked cautiously up at the roof, and turned towards the crypt.

ひ)

The notes revealed in the black light had seemed impenetrable, but now Jack saw hints and traces in them. A history of handwriting followed the margins and found its way between the lines. He had seen the various hands in the library, searching for his lost alphabet: the angular minuscule of southern Italy, the thick Gothic scripts used in Germany, the light Secretary hand of medieval England, and the Humanist cursives of the sixteenth century. It was a clamour of old voices, an argument in which nobody was listening.

A Gothic hand commented on the first section; Jack managed to untangle the word *Engel*. The scribe had thought the sack-people were angels, high above the world in their flowers and creepers. Jack was warming to the idea of these misshapen angels when the script disappeared. On the next page, notes in a French hand argued that the sack-people were fairies and knights; they were labelled *Oberon* and *Huon* and *Amir*. By the time he had reached the section on calligraphy, several Italians were debating codes and ciphers in their cursive hands. They underlined certain letters in every word and spelled out plots against the Pope.

Jack marked with his fingers the places where one commentary finished and the next began. When he turned the manuscript over he saw that he was clutching apart its seven quires. The quires didn't seem to correspond to the manuscript's sections; there was no reason why his commentators should start and stop at those precise boundaries. Unless – unless. The manuscript must at one time have been divided.

That had to be it. At some time, for some reason, the book had been split into its seven parts and scattered across Europe. Each part had been studied by the local scholars, and its interpretation had been flavoured by the local concerns. Its meaning had fragmented into dozens of possibilities. And then it must have been reassembled, perhaps centuries later.

A very faint gloss ran from the beginning of the manuscript to its end, hardly discernible even in the ultraviolet. It looked like a form of Carolingian minuscule, a tiny script that retained the daggers and hooks of the hands used for *Beowulf*. The manuscript must have been separated shortly after that: the next complete commentary seemed to be in the more recent English Secretary hand and was adorned with alchemical symbols. Then the glyphs of Wilkins's real character, and finally Constant's references.

Constant was always with him, and he tried to imagine what the monk had made of his long journey between the manuscript's towers. Frank would have known the history and variations of all these Bible verses without looking them up. How much trouble would have been saved if only Frank and O'Rourke had pulled up the chancel and found the crypt, and how much comfort might have been given to Beth?

He realised the church was silent above him, no footsteps or clatters from the roof. He stood up, feeling in his knees and back the hours that must have passed. But he was unprepared for the dusk that hung in the church when he opened the trapdoor. The tarpaulin stretched back over the roof. Max and O'Rourke had let themselves out.

Beth's film cartridge was still sitting by the door. He saw it in the lamplight, knew it was too late. He'd missed a whole day. He thought about hiding it, making something up; but in the end he left it where it was.

꒦

The translators' preface was Jack's favourite part of the King James Version, the only part he really believed. *Translation it is that openeth the window, to let in the light; that putteth aside the curtain, that we may looke into the most Holy place.* He sat in the nave with his facsimile edition, checking it against the manuscript and Constant's references.

It was a magnificent translation, and he wondered what Constant would have done to improve it as he looked up the first of the monk's reflections. *Dan 5 8* and *Rev 5 4* came from the great apocalypses of the Old and New Testaments. *Then came in all the kings wise men, but they could not read the writing.* Jack felt the shadow of the laboratory explosion, the last days. He touched his bandaged forehead. *And I wept much, because no man was found worthy to open, and to reade the book.*

Genesis and the confusion of tongues decorated the tower on the first page, where he had found Babel and Shinar before his perfect language had crumbled. *Goe to, let vs go downe, and there confound their language, that they may not vnderstand one anothers speech.* Constant had agreed with him. Then the series of alphabets, surrounded by miracles from Acts and Corinthians: *And how heare we euery man in our own tongue, wherein we were born?* And the section of flasks and potions, a generous distribution of gifts: *To another discerning of spirits; to another diuers kinds of tongues; to another the interpretation of tongues.* He saw their outlines illuminated as he followed the tiny poetic clues.

Beth paused at the door, and her eyes settled for a moment on the pew where the film cartridge still sat. She loosened her top buttons as she leaned over to look at his Bible. She gave him a puzzled expression and ruffled his hair.

'You're not looking for God too, are you?'

'Maybe, I'm not sure.'

'Because if this church is going to end up like *The Shining*, if I'm going to come home and see you typing Hail Marys over and over ...'

He grinned. 'I thought it was an Anglican church.'

'Yes, but it's being fixed up by a Catholic, so who knows.'

She looked up to the ceiling. Nothing seemed to have changed from that angle. She shrugged and straightened up, and in the moment before her face was eclipsed he thought he saw a frown notch her forehead. He was about to apologise for the undeveloped film, but then decided it was probably something else.

He kept reading, past the apparatus of flasks and levers. *Yea, a sword shall pearce thorow thy owne soule also, that the thoughts of many hearts may be reuealed. Behold, thou desireth truth in the inward parts: and in the hidden part shalt make me know wisedome.* And Daniel again, that great translator: *I came neere vnto one of them that stood by, and asked him the truth of all this: so he told mee, and made me know the interpretation of the things.*

If only, he thought.

Beth returned with a glass of wine and sat next to him on the sofa. The lamplight striped her skin with shadows. She took a long draught and all the muscles of her face relaxed. She watched her hand as it moved through bands of light and dark.

'Do I look the same to you?' she asked.

He put down the Bible. 'The same as what?'

'As before. I saw myself in the mirror today, at work, and I thought that can't be right. That isn't how I look.'

'Sometimes those mirrors aren't very flattering.'

'I don't need flattery, I just need consistency. I mean if a mirror shows someone who isn't you, it's not doing a very good job, is it?'

Her library shirt was open to the sternum. She bit her lower lip, slightly off-centre. Her hair was gathered into a loose ponytail, and a few bangs crossed her face. She looked tired, but she looked the same as she had before.

'You still look like you.'

'Really?'

'You look beautiful.'

She gave him a crooked smile, not entirely satisfied. The thoughts of many hearts, truth in the inward parts, and the interpretation of the things. Frank hadn't believed in miracles, and neither did Jack – but if there were some way of lifting Constant's references from metaphor and into fact, he would move all the possible heavens to get to it. Some lost science, some sleight of mind … He didn't know what it could be, but he knew that he needed it right away.

The last entry was from the Song of Solomon. It was one of the two books in the Bible that never mentioned God. Jack remembered Frank's odd funeral and its secular references. The scratched abbreviation decorated the fiery tower on the final page. Jack couldn't make any sense of it, but there it was, in the Bride's voice.

By night on my bed I sought him whome my soule loueth: I sought him, but I found him not. I will rise now, and goe about the citie in the streets, and in the broad wayes I will seeke him whom my soule loueth: I sought him, but I found him not.

cn out

6 Jack hadn't left the church since he'd stumbled home from the laboratory; he had spent two days in the darkness. He took the manuscript down to the crypt and hid it under the flagstone where he had first found it. He unwrapped the bandage from his head and had to will himself to step into the dawn light. He wasn't sure what was going to explode next: this house, that letterbox. He was still flinching with every footstep when he reached his car.

The Citroën was parked at a getaway-car angle half a metre from the kerb. Three tickets wrapped its wipers. He found a petrol station that would sell him a jerry can and poured five litres into the tank. He sat for a minute with his eyes closed before turning the key in the ignition, then blinked and drove into the city.

The teenager at the photo lab was playing with a compact digital camera when Jack walked in. He took the cartridge with a sceptical expression and said he'd have to check with the manager. The older man's eyes sparkled as he held up the film.

'Eight by eleven,' he said to Jack. 'I haven't seen one of these for years.'

'Can you do it?'

The manager nodded. 'End of the day. How big do you want them?'

Jack thought of Beth's enlargements. He knew how quickly the film would lose its definition, how its edges would mist. But she didn't want the illusion; she needed to see what was really there.

He made an expansive gesture with his hands. 'Big.'

The manuscript had passed among spies and poets, clerics and occultists; it might have overcome them in the end, but it had convinced them of its secrets. It had something to do with translation, with truth.

Beth wasn't working, so Jack had to make his own way through the library. He collected a pile of books and took them to a quiet corner. Books from each of the places where he thought the manuscript had been, books about everything the notes were about. A pale beam of sunlight moved across the desk.

He started with the Italians, whose minuscule had surrounded the giant letters and the densest text. Leone Battista Alberti, perhaps: an architect of cathedrals and aqueducts, a father of Western cryptography. Or Giambattista della Porta, who recommended writing invisibly on hardboiled eggs, who listed words likely to be found in coded messages. *Dear* and *yours truly* in letters; and in love letters *heart*, *fire*, *flame*, *death*, *pity*, *cruelty*.

In the next book he read about Johannes Trithemius, abbot of Sponheim in the Rhineland. His *Steganographia* was written in the late fifteenth century but not published until his death: it told of networks of angels who carried his messages across the planet, and was quickly banned. Later his works were thought to be metaphors, elaborate examples of cryptography – but perhaps the censors had been right after all. The angled Gothic handwriting in the manuscript must have been his.

The same stories kept rising from the pages as the light in the library changed. All of the early scientists were accused of sorcery and witchcraft. Their guilds were disbanded, their treatises burnt. There were no clear lines between physics and magic, and it seemed to Jack that everyone was an alchemist. He read along as they searched for the true nature of things, as they invented alphabets for their secrets and used code phrases that would have baffled even Thorn – the green lion, the toad that eats his fill. Roger Bacon and Thomas Charnock, with their alchemical symbols. And George Ripley, who was mentioned only in fragments and hearsay but kept drawing Jack's attention. Ripley was a monk from Yorkshire who travelled to France, Germany and Italy and returned in 1478 claiming to know the secret of transmutation – who said he could turn lead into gold.

The pattern was faint, but it was there. All of the men he read about, all the works of science and wonder reminded him in different ways of the manuscript. He knew that its several parts had found their way across Europe, and now it seemed that each had provoked a remarkable reaction. Alberti and della Porta had set their codebreaking skills against their section, and soon led the world in the industry of secrets. Another quire had lifted Trithemius and his students from secret writing to the talk of angels. They had seen in it the blueprint for their heavenly network. Other parts had fed into the tradition of the trouvères and troubadors of France, who had given magical powers to their knights and kings. They had all read something different in the manuscript, and perhaps all of them had been partly right.

But the alchemists had taken the most from the manuscript's page. Jack felt its influence most distinctly as he read about their trials, their errors. They had been its most careful students, and they weren't content with their slender seventh. They needed all of it. So George Ripley had travelled to Europe and had gathered and reassembled the manuscript – it must have been him. Later the restored pages had inspired John Wilkins to attempt his philosophical language, had perhaps bankrupted Jan Reynolds, had puzzled Johann Johnson and then deranged Constant – but first they had to be collected by George Ripley.

Jack felt his respect deepening as he continued through the books. Alchemy wasn't only about metals, he realised; it was every kind of transformation. Not only lead into gold but sickness into health, and death into immortality. Its great work was the perfection of souls. The gold didn't hurt, of course. And Ripley had grown rich – staggeringly rich. Every year after his return to England he had donated £100,000 to the Knights of Rhodes. It would be worth a thousand times that now, not bad for a cleric and scholar. Jack wondered who these knights were, and what they'd done to deserve their billions. He already had a reasonable idea.

The librarian took his request slip with an expression of mistrust. Jack supposed that his books on cryptography and alchemy might make him look like a crackpot or worse. Maybe these were books that got you flagged on government lists, like *Mein Kampf* and *The Catcher in the Rye*. He should be covering his tracks more carefully. He wished Beth were working. He checked the library clock, determined to make it back to the photo lab before it closed.

He returned to his table and opened the first book. It told him that the Knights of Rhodes had once been the Knights of the Hospital of St John of Jerusalem, first a monastic and soon a chivalric military order established after the capture of the Holy City by the first Crusade in 1099. They were older than their chief rivals, the Knights Templar, and later acquired most of the Templars' property. By that time Jerusalem had fallen and the Hospitallers had conquered the island of Rhodes, which they made their headquarters for two centuries. They repelled several Saracen attacks with the help of George Ripley's donations, but were ousted by Suleiman the Magnificent in 1522 and relocated to Malta, where they lingered until Napoleon.

Jack had heard about the Templars, who in their brief existence had inspired a still-burgeoning mythology. They were said to have found the Holy Grail and the Ark of the Covenant, to have brought the Shroud of Turin from Jerusalem. They were arrested for heresy on the first Black Friday, in October 1307; they were accused of worshipping false gods and denying true ones, kissing each other on the lips and buttocks, and amassing obscene wealth with sophisticated financial instruments. Since their dissolution they had been associated with a series of deranged conspiracies, some playful, some earnest, some fraudulent, all indistinguishable in the end.

But Jack didn't know anything about the Hospitallers, who had watched the Templars come and go, happily accepted their treasures and gone on for another five centuries, maybe longer. Since the loss of Malta in 1798 there had been continuations or revivals of the Order all over the world, most influentially in Russia, in Rome, in England. But the Hospitallers had always operated an extensive international network, formalised after their assimilation of the Templars into seven *langues*, seven tongues: Provence, Auvergne, France, Italy, Aragon, Germany and England.

He felt that a complicated shape had found its space and slotted in. Seven tongues, seven quires to the manuscript. He had already traced its hands to England, Germany, Italy and France. He hadn't identified writing styles for Provence and Auvergne, or the old kingdom of Aragon – but it couldn't be coincidence. The Hospitallers had divided the manuscript into its seven parts and delivered it to their seven regions, where its ripples had spread until George Ripley had paid huge sums to heal it again. Why they had split it up? To increase their chances of interpreting it, or to protect its secret? And where had it come from in the first place?

The Hospitallers had crusaded under a number of flags and standards but had finally settled on an eight-pointed cross, four arrowheads meeting. It was the Maltese cross, named after them. Jack thought he'd seen it somewhere before, but he couldn't place it. The memory seemed to be shrouded in smoke: the burning of infidels, the crumbling of ancient walls, the end of the world.

The church was full when he returned from the photo lab: Beth was already home, and Max and O'Rourke were ending another day. He heard them through the oratories as he passed the television, a murmur over the Friday evening news. They were drinking coffee in the kitchen. The back door opened to the churchyard. A bank of clouds changed colour as different angles of sunset caught it. Beth turned to him.

'Jack, look at the clouds.'

'They're stunning.'

O'Rourke raised his cup. 'I was just saying, we've found some stone to work with. Just lovely sandstone, sheer pleasure.'

'Good. That's very good.'

The clouds were losing their colour; the merest traces lingered for the longest time. Max looked at Jack, a slight sharpening of his eyes. His mouth was set in a forgotten smile, fading like the sky's colours.

'Max was telling us about Vladivostok,' Beth said.

'Really?'

'Look.'

Max moved away so that Jack could see the block of sandstone on the kitchen worktop. It had been carved: a relief deepened its surface a half inch. A harbour, a peninsula, a spray of wharves. A cargo ship in the foreground, ripples in the water. A pile of new sand spilled from the worktop onto the floor. O'Rourke rested his cup.

'Amazing story, I was just saying. His wife met some bloke here on the Internet, got the bloke to buy her a ticket, all the way from Russia. All her friends were doing it, Max reckons. So he comes looking for her, no luck, decides to stay instead. He's got this letter on him, takes it everywhere, my name's Max, and here's what happened. I've been teaching him a bit of English, just the names of things.'

'Jack speaks Russian.'

Why not, Jack thought. '*Ya govoryu po-Russki.*'

Max stared blankly at him. His pronunciation, or did Max have another dialect, near enough to a different language? Strange place, Vladivostok, an outpost surrounded by Asia, Cyrillic in a sea of ideograms. He tried to imagine Max storming from the seaport to persuade his wife back there, but he couldn't imagine him persuading anyone of anything – even trying, with those sphinx eyes.

'I told you, all he speaks is stone,' O'Rourke said.

'He did this just then,' Beth said. 'Right in front of us.'

'Don't worry, this one's spare.'

'Or they can put it in the roof for us.'

Jack reached out to touch the sandstone. It was rough beneath his fingers, catching the ridges of his fingerprints; a few particles came away. He traced the lines of the harbour, the parabolic cables, the wash of the ship. Max took hammer and chisel and carved a crescent moon in the sky, almost before Jack could move his hand.

'Let's have it in the roof,' Jack said.

O'Rourke nodded at Max, and the apprentice picked up the block and hefted it outside. Jack and Beth stared after him as he lowered it to the ground beside a pile of blank stones, beside Constant's blank headstone.

'Hell of a postcard,' O'Rourke said.

They nodded. The sky was darkening to blue and indigo, the clouds to charcoal. The carved block caught the kitchen's light on its edges, smearing the scene. It reminded Jack of the prints stashed in his jacket. Max and O'Rourke packed up, and he and Beth followed them to the porch and closed the door after them. He turned to Beth and handed her the new wallet of photos.

'Have a look at these,' he said.

'Oh, hey.' She took the pictures with a surprised smile and ruffled his hair. 'Maybe I won't sign up as an Internet bride after all.'

He leaned in to look. The grain had opened up, leaving the edges ragged. Many of the pictures didn't seem to be of anything in particular. Intersecting beams, bright wedges of sunlight, the texture of stone. But then he saw a pattern he recognised: a circle, the outline of a book. He looked up at the stained-glass window in the roof, still the same.

'This was here?'

'They all are.' Beth was looking too, at the leadlight, around the church. 'I took these. See?'

The pictures began to make more sense as young Beth got the hang of the camera. The congregation was heartbreakingly small. The walls were stained and crumbling: it might have been the film, or the film might have been doing the church a favour. There was Judy, looking like a good minister's wife, hands in her lap, lips pressed together. And Frank at the pulpit, listing slightly with the frame, leading his flock through the world's strict miracles. He looked inspired and inspiring. He pressed at the air with an emphatic forearm and splayed fingers. And with the picture taken from below Jack thought he could see Frank as Beth had seen him: as a prophet, as an adept, as every kind of father.

'You took these?'

She nodded. 'I'd forgotten. He wanted me to try it. I must have been eight or nine. I suppose—' She laughed. 'I suppose this was all I could think of, to take pictures of.'

'It's great.'

'God, it's like being there again. You know when you're a kid and everything's a bit indistinct, people are always standing in the way, you don't have the vantage point. But suddenly the clouds part and you see things, you understand them.'

She was still looking at Frank through the ancient congregators, and he wondered what she'd seen. The grain seemed to give up more meaning as he watched. In the weather of Frank's features he thought he could make out a gleam of curiosity and insight. He looked like a great leader, and Jack felt a small collapse as he imagined the slow decline that had left him to pace the church for the last years of his life.

But he was heartened to see Frank as he had been, and through the eye of the one who loved him best. Even if you wound up alone, it was what you'd been that counted, and what you'd done and tried to do. Beth's eyes glistened.

'I thought he must have been like Jesus's best friend. When I still believed in Jesus, but before I knew about blasphemy – I loved Jesus, but I thought how lucky he was to have a friend like Frank.'

'You were probably right.'

'When I was older, when I stopped believing, I was mortified that I'd wasted all that time in church. But in the end I didn't mind so much, I thought maybe it was worth it. Because I got to feel like that about him.'

'See, you do remember.'

She held the pictures out to him. 'But it's photos again, it's like I was saying.'

'That stuff isn't in the photos.'

She looked at him gratefully. 'And I've never seen these pictures before.'

'No.'

She nodded with a modest kind of satisfaction and continued through the photos. He hoped it would help. She might be comforted by the man Frank had been; her grief might settle at last. She seemed closer to peace as she tilted the prints to match the angles of the spy camera. He turned back to the television news.

'Oh my God,' she said. 'It's him.'

He wanted to turn and see who she meant, but he was watching himself on the television. The news was wrapping up the week's events. It showed the charred laboratory, the screen washed a rhythmic red and blue. Jack was staggering across the grass, shirt untucked, putting his hand to his forehead, until for a moment he stared straight into the camera. It only lasted for a moment. But it sent a jolt through him, drew him back to the great fist, the slippery daylight, the St John Ambulance.

There they were again. Their black-and-white uniforms, their Maltese crosses. The penitent's black robe and the white mark of the redeemer: the first colours of the Knights of the Hospital of St John of Jerusalem, nine hundred years later, less wealthy, less warlike, but wearing the same cross and using the same name.

He glanced at Beth to see if she had spotted him on the news. She looked the same as he felt, a bewildering system of realisation and confusion pressing at her features. But she wasn't watching the television; she was staring at one of the photos. It was a random shot of the congregation, blurred by the grain and the shutter speed but picking up a shiny pate, a head tilted at a familiar angle, a pale fabric gathered around the neck ... Jack wanted to turn back to the news, to see what they had found, but she was facing him with an expression drained of all hope and happiness.

'I didn't want it to be him. I didn't want him to be there.'

∽)

She wouldn't say anything more about it. She returned the photos to their envelope and didn't answer any of his questions. Her movements slowed as the evening stretched. She ate a few cold leftovers, undressed and left her clothes in a pile on the floor, and Jack held her as she sank into a defeated sleep. Her body twitched but her eyes were steady behind their sheets of skin, as though her distress had sunk to her sinew and bone. She kept him awake with her jitters and shifts, but he wouldn't have slept anyway.

The laboratory had been bombed, and the Hospitallers had been there first. Was it some secret continuation of the Crusades? The letters had always looked slightly Arabic; was this part of the great clash of histories? The Knights were now practising first aid, the Saracens cooking up explosives, either or both of them sworn to discover the manuscript or prevent its discovery.

His heart wouldn't slow down. He eased Beth from his arms and sat on the edge of the bed. He tried to stop the floorboards from creaking as he crept to the trapdoor. A square of moonlight fell across the manuscript as he carried it into the nave. The porch door was locked, but anyone could see through the squints. The manuscript might have been safer in the crypt, but he didn't want to let it out of his sight. He returned to the bed, lay on his back and folded the vellum to his chest.

Or perhaps the Hospitallers were on the side of the bombers, searching the rubble they'd made for the secret they shared. *Pro fide* and *pro utilitate hominum*, faith and the good of humanity – but what monstrosities had been committed to those ends, long before the quest for Jerusalem and ever since? The very words sounded sinister these days, when everything meant its opposite.

He told himself they were coincidences. Beth's breathing changed, and her eyes flickered and darted; she was dreaming at last. He should have been helping her, but he had called a terrible danger to their church. His chest clenched as he watched her in the blue light. He told himself he was imagining things. But as the night heaved past he couldn't stop thinking of everything he knew about the manuscript, its age, the great minds that had dashed themselves against it – and compared to all that, in the first hint of daylight, as Beth finally rolled away from him, like she always did, nothing seemed very difficult to believe.

6 Jack slid into a dream of insomnia, of terrible books and unspeakable writing. The dream was colder and emptier than the true night, but it was hardly stranger. Crusaders and alchemists, spies and clerics, all kinds of lunatics: even without the credulity of sleep he wouldn't have been able to tell the difference – until he woke suddenly into the grey light of the church as if someone had whispered something terrifying.

Beth sat on a pew, wearing one of his T-shirts. She had drawn a knee up to her chin and was staring at the front of the church where the chancel and altar had been. He thought he saw faint outlines drifting before her gaze: Frank wearing out the floor-boards, the congregation a mist behind her – and a kind of shadow on the gospel side. It was the dream, or the bruise on his temple. She pressed her mouth to her raised knee. He stood and creaked over to her; he put his hand on her shoulder.

'Are you all right?'

'I woke up early,' she said.

'What's the matter?'

She looked surprised. 'Nothing. What time is it?'

'Almost eight.'

'I'd better get ready for work.'

But she didn't move from the pew. The photo of the blurred bald man lay next to her on the floor. It was the clearest picture since the first two she'd found, and even in its shades of grey it looked like the same man. A twist in the lower half of his face, a self-assured smile that made Jack uneasy.

'Who is that?' he said.

'I don't know.'

She kept her head angled so that her peripheral vision wouldn't catch the photo. A truck thumped past.

'But you think it's someone, right?' he said.

She let out a long breath. 'I don't want to think about it. If it's the same guy, and it's someone from the church – from right here – if he was following us around, following *me* around, and suddenly Dad shut up shop and never came back – I mean, what could this guy have wanted, what could he have done?'

'You don't think—'

He couldn't say what she didn't think. A cold line traced his scalp as he remembered all the pictures he'd seen of her as a girl, in swimsuits, naked – she'd been a beautiful child.

Beth shrugged. 'It's a church, they can't turn anyone away. Lonely people, crazy people. Sometimes it's the only place they can go.'

'You don't remember anything?'

'No, but I *don't* remember anything. There's so much I don't remember.'

'Surely you'd remember something like that. If anything had happened.'

'I don't even know.'

Her voice was measured and absent, as if it were an old movie she wasn't sure she'd seen, but he thought he could hear in it the sound of great hollows. She gave him a weak smile that suggested that nothing much could be done for anyone.

'I'd better get to work,' she said. She crossed her arms and pulled his T-shirt up over her head, and without meaning to, without thinking about it, he looked away.

उ)

He wanted to keep her safe in the church, but he couldn't stop her leaving. He knew how it would sound. An ancient Order of Knights had absorbed the heretic Templars and acquired their relics and spoils. Besieged on a fortified island, they had sold to an alchemist their most precious possession, a manuscript so alarming it had to be dispersed across their secret empire, where even divided it could be felt in the obsessions of an age. The alchemist had found its secret, but it had been lost with him; the Order had evolved into a volunteer brigade and still wanted the manuscript back. She'd think he was mocking her, he didn't take her own worries seriously. A prowler in the congregation with an interest in beautiful girls – it did sound more plausible than the story of the manuscript. But Jack had evidence: from his books, his crypt, the mark on his forehead.

'I'll drive you,' he said.

'Are you going to the library?'

'No, but I've got some things to do.'

She gave him a curious look. 'What things?'

'Some more research.'

'It's all right, I can catch the bus.'

'It's no trouble.'

She shrugged and didn't look pleased. He made sure he started the car before she got too close. He had looked up the St John Ambulance in the phone book and was disturbed to learn that its head office lay on a side street off the main road into the city. He had walked and driven past it hundreds of times. Now he took the long way, and got tangled in one-way streets.

'I'm going to be late,' she said, more an observation than a complaint.

'Sorry.'

He found his way into the city and dropped her at the library. He watched until she was safely inside, then sat for a minute at the side of the road. He wanted to hurry back to the church and lock himself in. But he couldn't just huddle there and wait for them to find him – to find Beth. He had to go out to meet them.

The St John headquarters was an austere sandstone building hidden behind fig trees. It was no wonder he'd never known it was there. But the Maltese cross was etched into the stone, like the battlements of Valetta, and as he gathered his courage and swung open the heavy doors he knew he was walking into an enemy stronghold. Even the least paranoid observer might have been unsettled by the sight of so many uniforms in the same place. Two or three strolling the parks were innocuous, but a whole building full of them, and the same thing in cities across the world, their ranks, their chains of command – it suddenly seemed much more like a fighting force. And to know that its members had worn these arms in battle for centuries, at Jerusalem, at Acre and Antioch – and then to know everything else Jack knew. He stopped in the middle of the lobby as the knights brushed past him with their slouch hats and walkie-talkies. It was too dangerous; he should never have come. He turned back, shielding his face, hoping to make it to the street before they realised who he was.

A young volunteer with short black hair held the door for his partner and followed her inside. Jack's vision bruised as he realised it was the man who had helped him after the laboratory explosion. He felt again the trembling ground, saw the scrawls of smoke across the sky – and St John had been there right away. That was it: Jack would never escape.

But the volunteer looked straight past him and waved at the receptionist behind him, a tall woman with olive skin and a bright smile, and Jack breathed again. Perhaps St John had treated a dozen people at the forensics centre, a hundred in the last week. The Hospitallers might not know about Jack after all; they might only have learned that the manuscript had surfaced, and not who had found it. He could still slip away.

Jack took a step and paused. St John had known a lot about his organisation, its Latin mottos, its namesake saint; he might know more. And he had helped Jack, whatever his motives. If Jack left now, he might never be certain – or not before it was too late.

'St John! Hey – St John!'

He said it without thinking; he didn't know what else to call him. He was surprised when the volunteer stopped and turned around.

'I'm sorry – yes?'

He knew he didn't have long. 'I need some information.'

St John pointed to the reception desk. 'You should ask Carol. She'll give you a fact sheet, or the annual report.'

'This won't be in the annual report.'

St John narrowed his eyes at Jack, trying to place him. 'How did you know my name?'

'I just called you St John – you know, it's on your badge.'

'Oh, yes. Right.' He looked at the Maltese cross on his shoulder. 'The thing is, my name actually is St John. Although it's pronounced Sinjin.'

'Really?'

'My old man was a Knight of Justice.'

'You still have knights here?'

St John gave him a cautious look. 'Knights of Justice, Knights of Grace, and Dames of both.'

Jack lowered his voice. 'Can we talk somewhere?'

St John stared more closely at Jack, the mark on his forehead. His face fell into an expression of recognition. 'You were in the bombing. At the forensics centre.'

The blood pounded through Jack's head. He thought about denying it, but he couldn't see where that would lead. 'That's right,' he said. 'You gave me some first aid.'

'You had a concussion. Are you all right?'

Jack touched his temple. 'I think so.'

'We can talk in here.'

Jack teetered, thinking as quickly as he could. St John knew he had been at the forensics centre, but he couldn't be sure about Jack's connection with the manuscript. He would try to draw Jack out, baiting him with information; Jack would have to try the same thing. It was too risky, he wasn't up to it – but he found himself following St John through the corridors.

The building was a cross between a hospital and an office block. Jack tried to imagine subterranean levels beneath them, mossy and damp and lit by torches, but it was difficult. St John swung open an unmarked door and Jack paused for a moment. Perhaps he'd overthought St John's intentions, there wouldn't be a contest but an ambush. But he thought of Beth and stepped into the darkness. St John closed the door behind them and flicked a switch. The ceiling stuttered alight to reveal a room full of bodies.

There were at least a hundred, stacked on the floor and packed together like prisoners on a grim freight train. None of them had arms or legs, and their identical faces were graceful and tranquil. St John saw him looking.

'Do you know the story?' he said. 'It's the death mask of a young girl pulled from the Seine in the nineteenth century. Nobody knew who she was, but she was so beautiful they made copies of the mask and hung them on walls around Europe, and people wrote poems and made sculptures of her – and eventually these training dummies.'

They gave the room an atmosphere of tragedy. All these poor French girls, mouth-to-mouthed every day but never rescued. Was it meant as a warning – one of those baroque gangland threats, a kiss on the mouth, a fish in the bed? Jack gathered his attention and directed it at St John.

'Your father was a Knight, and near the top?'

'He wasn't ever an office-holder or anything. Though he was shortlisted for Hospitaller. He should have got that. But it's all politics, of course.'

Jack's heart stumbled. 'What do the Hospitallers do?'

'They administer the Eye Hospital in Jerusalem. Corneal grafts and so on.' He looked at Jack's expression and smiled. 'What did you think they did?'

'Nothing, nothing in particular. I don't know.'

St John looked around. 'Look, I'll save you some time. A lot of people come here looking for big secrets of whatever kind. But my father got as high as almost anyone, and he was a perfectly normal guy. He went to conferences and talked about developments in medicine. He never told me anything miraculous.'

'So there's no connection with the original Order?'

'There's a connection; there are loads of organisations that have revived the old Order, or were inspired by it or even established by a few genuine Knights. But there's no real continuity. Once they lost Malta, that was really the end of it.'

He spoke like someone who had signed up in search of mysteries himself: a flash in his eyes, a crack in his voice. Perhaps he had been driven by the riddle of his father, as Beth had – but more likely he was looking for the Hospitallers' great prize, he was after the manuscript. They were both stepping around it, its unsayable name.

'But their treasures, their secrets,' Jack said. 'They didn't just leave them to Napoleon, they must have taken them off the island.'

'There's no evidence there ever were any. They were wealthy, they practically invented banking, but they'd lost most of their European holdings, they were reduced to piracy and slave-trading. We're closer here to the original vision than they ever were on Rhodes or Malta. But even at their worst, they were businessmen.'

He was stonewalling; they had trained him too well. Jack would have to reveal himself, at least partly. He swallowed.

'They weren't funded by the proceeds of alchemy?'

St John stopped and looked at him. Suddenly it seemed that all of the faces in the room were turned in his direction. They wore slight smiles.

'The Ripley gift,' St John said.

'Lot of money.'

'But George Ripley had a lot of money, he always did. His family owned half of Yorkshire. He used to throw it around so people would think his alchemy worked. But in his old age he admitted that he'd never transmuted anything, and he told people to burn his books wherever they found them.'

'He told people to burn them?'

'This was after he'd retired to the Carmelites in Lincolnshire. They were to burn them, or afford them no credit, because they were false and vain. Something about having found all the gates, but no key.'

'What kind of key?'

'I don't know. None of it matters, anyway.'

They were knowing smiles, all twisting slightly. Jack felt a sudden deflation. St John had spoken of Ripley's retraction with regret, as if his own hopes had been as ambitious and his disappointment as complete, and Jack could almost believe that the volunteer was trying to save him from the same frustration. His story was touching, if it was true. But there were other explanations for St John's knowledge of the Hospitallers and their unsaintly patron. Jack couldn't trust him.

'So what was all the money for?'

'I don't know,' St John said. 'It bought the Hospitallers forty extra years on Rhodes and probably helped them on Malta. But for Ripley it was a waste.'

Jack looked around at all the bodies. He remembered Beth's near-drowning and her story about the harbour of quicksand and the paper-skinned girls who lay at its floor – and he wondered what that had meant. He hadn't been wrong about the manuscript and its dangers, but he felt confused, he couldn't see quite so clearly how everything fitted together. And perhaps in his fear for Beth he had overlooked her own fears. He hadn't believed them, or he hadn't wanted to. He had left them far too long. He knew where he had to go next.

ʊ)

When Frank had decided to stay at the seminary his brothers had bought him out of the family farm, twelve hundred acres at the bottom of the grain belt. They had struggled with drought and blackleg, and Frank's share hadn't been worth much. But it had bought a small house two suburbs away from the church that would take the rest of his money and his time. Jack drove slowly, as nervous as he had been on his way to the Hospitallers.

It was a simple double-brick cottage in a street that in recent years had been renovated to the limit of the local regulations. It had always been immaculate, though it had grown dark and old-fashioned. Jack had been here for dinner parties, for barbecues. A precise garden, a shed, a parlour: it had been a nice place, and he'd always enjoyed coming with Beth, watching the family show they put on for him.

Frank had been dead six weeks, and the place already looked worn down – even though it was Judy who had taken care of the garden. Weeds were pushing between the flowerbeds, and leaves had blown over the driveway.

Judy wore her usual satin housecoat and baseload make-up, but a few wisps of hair had wandered in the wrong direction. She stepped out onto the doorstep with her arms crossed and looked nervously up and down the street.

'Jack? Is everything all right?'

'Can I come in?'

She considered him for a moment, looking for the first time as old as she really was. She held open the screen door and scanned the horizon before closing them both in. She grasped his shoulder, and it sent fingers of ice into his chest.

The hint of decline he had seen outside thickened into the house. The dirty plates spilling from the kitchen sink, wine glasses and whisky tumblers scattered across the counters and tabletops – even an ashtray packed with cigarette butts, all smoked to the filter. He felt a faint dread. He was counting on Judy's matter-of-factness: she knew what her marriage had been, and her clarity had explained everything. In anyone else these new lapses might have been signs of mourning, but in Judy they seemed more ominous.

At the dinner party she had asked about the manuscript, and for a moment he'd thought she'd recognised it. If Frank had found it after all, and Judy knew what it had done to him – was that it? Did she know the Hospitallers were after Jack now? He wasn't sure it made sense. He tried to remember why he'd come.

Judy's eyes darted over the mess and returned to meet his defiantly. He felt emboldened by her imperfections, but wrong-footed by everything they might mean. She moved to the half-bottle of whisky on the cabinet.

'Would you like a drink, perhaps?'

'It's only eleven o'clock.'

'I know what time it is.' She glared at him. 'It's my first one.'

'All right, then.'

He felt disappointed that she hadn't bothered with the thermos and the teacups. The whisky thickened his tongue and knotted his stomach; it was much too early. But he felt the warmth spread through him, the complicity build between them.

'How's my daughter?' Judy said.

'Yes – actually, that's why I came.'

She looked at her glass almost petulantly, as if offended that he hadn't just come for a couple of short ones. But after a moment she looked up at him.

'What can I do for you, Jack?'

'I'm sorry to ask you this. But what you said on the boat, about how things were difficult between you and Frank. I was wondering—'

'I shouldn't have said that.'

There was a ragged edge to her voice: it could have been the whisky, but it sounded more like her mood. He took a slow breath and looked carefully at her, the cracks in the old varnish.

'I'm sorry,' he said. 'Things weren't difficult, then?'

'Of course they were.' She glared at him. 'Of course there were difficult things. We were married for thirty years. I've no idea what sort of relationship you have with Beth, but if you plan to be around for a proper length of time you ought to be prepared for a few difficulties yourself.'

He felt his face grow hot. He was surprised at the vein of contempt in her voice, but he realised he didn't know her at all. They'd met many times, but they were strangers.

'I know it's none of my business. It's just that Beth, she just wants to understand Frank, to feel like she can make sense of him, all the way to the end. But for some reason she thinks something terrible must have happened.'

'You didn't tell her anything, did you?'

He saw the fear in her eyes. What had broken her detachment? It wasn't the manuscript. The unwashed dishes, the drifts of unopened mail – there were secrets after all, about Frank, about Beth. Had Judy found her way to the same conclusion Beth had? Sorting through Frank's things, happening on a diary – or had she always known?

'I didn't tell her,' he said. 'I think you should talk to her, though.'

But suddenly he wasn't sure. He didn't know Judy, and now she seemed more dangerous than he'd guessed. If Beth was right after all, if Judy could confirm everything and give her phantoms breath and life – he'd been wrong to come here. He'd made a terrible mistake.

'I can tell her that we had our problems,' Judy said. 'We didn't see eye to eye on everything. It wasn't particularly serious and we didn't want to worry her, so perhaps we kept some parts of our relationship from her.'

'Is that true?'

Her eyes ran back over the unwashed glasses, and this time he realised it wasn't house-shame – it was something more like panic, and again his reassessment left him unsure of everything. He stared at the plates.

'We always loved each other,' she said. 'That is true, it's the truest thing. You're right, it's no business of yours, but I don't want Beth ever to doubt it.'

Was it a dinner party she hadn't cleaned up, was she ashamed to have held a dinner party six weeks after Frank's death? No – there were different traces of food, none of it dinner-party food. There were four plates, six saucers, eight wine glasses. He looked at the ashtray and couldn't count the butts, but everything else was even numbers, everything divisible by two. The shadows seemed to clear from the room. It was an outrageous inference, but he counted again and knew he was right.

'Judy – I'm sorry, can I use your bathroom?'

She looked surprised and then suspicious, but waved him along the corridor. He knew he'd find something. A recent razor, a toothbrush. He searched the cupboards and cabinets, the basins and bath recesses. If a man had been here for long enough to smoke all those cigarettes, he'd have left something behind.

But there was nothing but a fresh bar of soap, a bone-dry handcloth and a spare toilet roll hidden under a crocheted cover. It was as pristine as the rest of the house was grubby. She'd outsmarted him: she'd sent him to the guest bathroom.

He held his breath and listened. The man might be in the house right now, in the bedroom, in Frank's den, sweating as Judy tried to steer Jack away. The silence resolved into small noises: the clink of ice in Judy's glass, the creak of her chair as she wondered what was keeping him. He had the sensation that someone was in the next room, sitting like a sculpture, waiting for Jack to leave so he could breathe again.

And then he heard it. A soft affricate, and immediately another. Each a kind of *ch*: the flint of a cigarette lighter, tried twice. It hadn't come from the kitchen. The man was sitting nervously and hadn't been able to resist lighting up; perhaps he was smoking out of the window, trying to stop his hands from shaking. Jack took a deep breath and smelled a trace of smoke – he was almost sure of it.

He ran the tap and returned to Judy in the kitchen. He thought for a moment that he'd been wrong, that she'd be the one smoking, but she wasn't. She'd poured herself a fresh glass and was beginning to slump in her chair. She pointed the tumbler towards him and gave him a look that repelled him and broke his heart at once.

'But nobody understands anybody, Jack. Not really, not in the end. Nobody makes sense to anyone else.'

He drained his glass and put it back down on the table. It suddenly seemed like the only thing they had in common.

As Jack drove through the back streets he felt the world was brighter and shallower than he'd thought: it had fewer shadows, its failings were plain to see. There was a man in Judy's house, and Frank not two months dead. She'd hinted at their problems, but Jack couldn't have imagined they'd be as bad as they now seemed.

He parked the car at the water's edge and sat on the sea wall. He'd been here days ago, he realised: after the laboratory explosion, when the harbour had been drained and the sand or quicksand had reached to the far shore. It had been an illusion, he'd been concussed. Now the sparkling water had returned, and everything was clearer.

If she'd been seeing him before Frank had died – or even if their marriage had worn so thin that she could fall for a man so quickly – then of course Frank would have retreated to his church. And how could he have preached again? His faith was abraded into ghostly shapes by his intellectual curiosity, his scientific journals; his hope was like the nave where he found himself, empty apart from the dust; and hard to expect charity of any man in his place.

It might still have been the manuscript – it had drawn Frank or frightened Judy away, it had started everything or made it all worse. But there were a thousand simpler reasons, thirty years of reasons.

So the mystery was solved again, and the answer was unbearable but better than it might have been. He felt terrible for Frank and even felt bad for Judy, for the choices she had and didn't have – but beyond all that he could only feel relieved for Beth, that the man in the pictures was an invention, a creature of looking too hard. Jack had saved them after all.

He left the car a street away and cut through a park, looking over his shoulder. The light was failing by the time he reached the church, and the shadows slowed his footsteps. He thought of the water corpses and Beth's story at the beach. Could he really tell her about the man in Judy's house? Perhaps she was better off wondering. Perhaps that was better than knowing that Frank had been betrayed, his church in ruins for all its rebuilding.

Beth sat on the porch steps, looking out as the neighbourhood's colours and shapes ran together. She wore her library clothes and a strange expression as she scanned the churchyard and the street. Her hands were pressed between her knees. Jack crunched over the gravel.

'Forget your key?'

'No.'

She tilted her head slightly so he could kiss her on the cheek, then nodded towards the porch door.

'I can't seem to go in there.'

He sat down beside her on the step, his back to the old wood. The skin over her collarbone was raised into tiny points, like the wind over the ocean. He looked out across the churchyard, the driveway, the low shrubs. He thought he saw movement. Perhaps they had followed him after all.

'It's no good out here,' he said.

'No, I always hated this time of night. Of day.'

'Dusk.'

'No, twilight. Dusk is all right, it's practically night. But this twilight.'

'I don't like it either.'

'It's not one thing or the other. When I was little, it was always robbers and monsters, unpleasantness. All of my nightmares were twilit.'

'Mine too.'

He tried to put his arm around her but she twisted from his touch; there was suddenly a layer of air between them. She gave no sign of shifting from the step, so he sat with his arm a centimetre from her back and felt the heat ebb from the day. Beth huddled closer into herself and shivered.

'It was about this time, this light. I think. It's been coming back to me all day, but I can't remember it properly, it's all in this not-colour. It must have been about now.'

'What was?'

'It was about now and I was here by myself. I don't know where Mum and Dad were, I don't know why they weren't here. Nobody was here. I must have been twelve or thirteen, I had to go to the toilet, out the back, and I was walking through those – you know, the oratories, towards the kitchen. They were dark, they were very dark, and there seemed to be a lot of them.'

There was less uncertainty in her voice now. Jack tried to catch a glimpse ahead, but the light was wrong, there were only shadows.

'And he was there, he was suddenly there. Sitting on one of those stone ledges, with his knees all gangly and sharp, and the most appalling expression on his face, this bottomless – kind of – *hunger* that would make you weep and run away.'

He tried to remember the pictures she'd shown him, the smears that had obscured the stranger's face. Where had the appalling expression come from? He felt a prickle seize his scalp.

'And it was almost like I *did* know him. As if I'd seen him all those times when he was hanging around, in the park, at the church, and there was something between us. And then he – I don't know how it happened, but he was – I just remember him—'

'Beth.'

'I don't know. I don't know. And Dad finally came but the man was gone, and Dad was asking me what had happened, where'd I got to and I said nothing, I was fine, but I couldn't stop crying and he knew. He wouldn't say anything, he just set his face, but he must have known.'

Her eyes were bright and her forehead folded along complicated planes, but she kept her mouth and her voice firm. She had taken her praying hands from between her knees and now sat as if she didn't want any two parts of her body to touch. Her elbows held out from her sides, her fingers splayed – most of her cells had been replaced time and again since then, she'd had hundreds of new skins, but her body still repelled her. It wasn't that, it couldn't be that.

'Beth, it didn't happen.'

A look flashed across her eyes, but it was unconnected to her lips. 'That was the last time I went to the church. I never went again. And then he closed it down and couldn't bear to open it, not after that had happened, after what he'd seen.'

He took her hand. She winced at his touch but he held on. 'You left the church because you were a teenager. That's all. And the church didn't close until years later, until ten years ago. Why would he even buy it, if all that had happened?'

She gave him a betrayed look. 'What are you saying?'

'It didn't happen.'

'Young girls get molested. In churches.'

'I know, and it's terrible. But you didn't. They do, but you didn't.'

'But I remember it.'

'What do you remember?'

'I remember something.'

He heard the edges of her voice and moved back from her. 'You've never thought anything like that happened before. You're a beautiful, well-adjusted woman; you never even had an eating disorder.'

'I have a clear memory of this guy, this man, there in the church, in the dark, and the cold air, the draughts—'

'You're looking for a reason why all these things, these bewildering things have happened.'

'Well, why did they happen?'

All the drowned girls, all the water corpses. A woman had fallen into the Seine, a hundred years ago, and they'd hung her face on parlour walls, teased out her smile in poems, while deep in the dry quicksand the young girls papered away and their fluids rose and burst back into the sky, and all because one day a father wasn't there to rescue his daughter. Now she was looking for freak waves and sandstorms, reasons for her drowning.

'He bought it so he could close it down,' she said. 'He worked for as long as he could so he wouldn't have to open it up again. Something awful happened here, and he blamed himself. And when he'd finished building he pretended he hadn't, so it would never open.'

'But then why would he give it to you?'

'I don't know, to – I don't know.'

A sandy tear left a streak down her cheek. She slumped backwards but recoiled when the arc of her spine touched the porch door. He couldn't bear it.

'It wasn't that.'

She looked up at him. 'Something happened.'

'Something might have happened, but it wasn't that.'

'Then what?'

He closed his eyes and thought he saw pale beams of light sweeping over unidentifiable shapes. He opened them again and everything was shadow and treacherous twilight. He took a deep breath.

'What if your mother had met someone else?'

She laughed, but there was a fleck of panic in her eyes. 'She'd never do anything like that. Judy?'

'What if she did? Or even just came close?'

'Did she tell you something?'

He felt the old wind between the grains, the thin skyward jet as he sank. 'That night on the boat, she said there'd been problems. Particularly towards the end, she said. And then today I went to her house, and there was somebody there.'

'You went to the house?'

'She had someone living there. A man.'

It was getting hard to read her expression. Her features blended into each other; her skin smudged into the air around her. Her voice was flat and edgeless, like the light.

'Are you sure?'

'There was all this stuff lying around, cigarette butts, and the way she was acting, the things she said. And then I heard him, and it all made sense.'

'You didn't see him?'

'No.'

'What did you hear?'

'A cigarette lighter. Twice.'

She leaned back from him. 'A cigarette lighter?'

'Twice.'

She looked at him in disbelief. 'That could have been anything!'

'And I smelled smoke, and there was an ashtray full of cigarette butts. And Judy doesn't smoke.'

'She *says* she doesn't smoke. She says she's not an alcoholic, but you've seen her. I think she'd be more likely to start smoking than to take up with another man.'

He had stopped sinking, but he couldn't feel the bottom. He was suspended in the sand, no way up or down. 'It was a feeling I had,' he said.

She stood up. 'You're telling me my mother had an affair. I need more than a feeling and two sounds that might have been a cigarette lighter.'

The night arrived, and a certain contrast emerged in the world. Jack didn't know what had happened. He'd wanted to help Beth. He was afraid his discovery might have upset her, but never thought she wouldn't believe him. He should have confronted Judy, he should have found out for sure. Beth took her key and slotted it into the lock, pushed open the door and stepped into the empty church.

'Sorry,' he said.

6 Jack had never had an affair himself. He didn't entirely understand them. He noticed other women only when Beth pointed them out. Isn't she pretty? Or isn't that a pretty dress? Then he would say sure or yes, pretty, because that was all Beth wanted him to say.

He was aware that some men had more than one lover and took all the necessary steps. Some women had affairs and were able to dedicate themselves at different times to different people. But he didn't understand them, and had assumed he didn't know any of them. He was confident, or arrogant, or trusting: he was unjealous. He would never ask a woman where she'd been.

Beth understood, he thought. She wouldn't suspect him of any affair, and knew he wouldn't suspect her. But he had accused her mother, and though he was right he could have done it better. She hadn't said much to him after that, and had left in the morning without much more.

And yet she had stood and unlocked the porch door, despite everything she thought had happened inside, and now he saw that she had tidied all the photographs back into the box and returned the box to the oratories. He didn't know what it meant.

Max and O'Rourke were back on the roof, earning double time. A patch of light and shadow played over the floorboards. The suburb's sounds had fallen to a late-morning quiet. The Russian film's sound-track lifted through the church with its abrasive consonants, and up on the roof Max laughed, and Jack couldn't imagine why.

The sun was rising over the abandoned fishing village. The salt blushed, and the shadows that had reached for the sea crept back towards the stranded ships. Chelovek and Zhenshchina stood apart from each other and watched the light spread across the desert. They began to pray aloud: the Lord's prayer, spoken together.

At least it was easy to subtitle. He only had to choose a Bible version; it had to be the King James. But he noticed after a minute that their unison was dissolving. One or the other kept saying a wrong word. *Hallowed be thy rain. Give us Thursday our daily bread.* The script didn't help, it just repeated the standard prayer. But the actors, or filmed lunatics, weren't paying attention. He'd have to fill the screen with subtitles, or a series of surrenders. *Beats me. No idea. Damned if I know!*

They must have set out to create an untranslatable film: some inscrutable Russian pride, some Cold War torment. He wanted to drag Max down from the roof and make him explain what it meant, but he'd still had no luck talking with him. Perhaps his story hadn't even been true.

He thought back to St John and his ambulance. He hoped he hadn't given too much away. The Hospitallers were after the manuscript: St John had been lying, or he didn't know the truth. A secret detachment within the order, ignored by the charter and the articles of association, searching for gates and keys. Jack was disappointed that Ripley's alchemy had failed, that he'd recanted his claims. What had happened? Was part of the manuscript still missing? But he didn't think so. Seven quires, seven *langues* – that had to be all of it. The key must be something else, perhaps another document. Ripley had retired to the Carmelites in Lincolnshire, to study the manuscript, to write his last books – or to look for his key? *I sought him, but I found him not: I found him not.*

Jack turned back to Chelovek and Zhenshchina, who had stopped praying and were sitting in a drift of sand against a rusting hull. They spoke to each other in tones of despair, or so Jack thought. He couldn't understand a syllable of what they were saying. It had started subtly, a few words he didn't recognise; he'd thought they were regional variants. But the dialect continued to broaden and soon lost all meaning. He was beginning to doubt what he'd known. He had thought them an old couple, but perhaps they were unmarried siblings, or perhaps they had just met.

The sand darkened as clouds slid across the sun, but Jack had seen enough. He stopped the tape, turned off the screen and left for the Deposit of Faith.

ひ)

It looked like it had been ransacked: half of its shelves were empty, half the collection piled into towers. The air was dusty, and the books caught crisp edges of sunset. Sandy sat in a carpet of yellowed catalogue cards, studying handfuls of them. Brown dust had settled over her face. He crouched to her.

'What's going on?'

She looked up at him. 'The auction's on the weekend, but the whole thing's a nightmare, we've no idea what's even here. There's much more than anyone thought. They've got whole teams in to try and catalogue it.'

He stared at the religious ruins around him. The battle between chaos and order, as always. She was right: there was too much of it, it wasn't reasonable. There were too many wrong turns, too many inventions. There was altogether too much faith.

Sandy surveyed the piles. 'Worse things than being left on the shelf, aren't there? That's what I tell myself.'

'Nobody's going to leave you on the shelf.'

'They'll take me off, browse a little, and put me back again. I'm a library book, or worse. A newspaper or periodical.'

'You're overdue.'

'I think so. How's our last best hope?'

'All right.'

'Beth's all right?'

She'd been trying to joke with him, but he saw in her eyes that she hadn't come close. She was almost always confident and strong, but she sometimes wandered bleak plains in which she and her baby loved each other but nobody else would. He didn't know why: she was attractive and kind and eager. Maybe there was something important that she couldn't bring herself to believe. She needed something from him, or from them. But he didn't have anything.

'I need to find some Carmelites,' he said.

'I don't know where anything is, exactly. They might not have gone far, they might be anywhere.'

'Where were they?'

She waved at him. 'Bottom of the stairs.'

'Thanks.'

There seemed to be no order to it. Whole shelves had been emptied while others had been passed over. Or every third book was missing, or books in patterns he could sense but not see. All of the world's religions were there, its gospels and sutras, its jealous and generous gods. There were too many of them, and none of them could do any good.

He found an old picture of Mount Carmel, rising high above the Jezreel Valley and the Mediterranean Sea. He read that it had sheltered hermits and seers since Elijah beat the prophets of Baal there, but the modern Order of Carmelites had emerged during the Crusades. They fled the Holy Land before it fell for the last time to the Saracens, and established themselves most successfully in England. But they were dwindling by the late fifteenth century, when George Ripley joined them, and soon after his death the Order in England was dissolved by Henry VIII along with all the others, all the monasteries destroyed or converted.

The shelves piled higher and squeezed closer as he burrowed deeper into the Deposit. Voices rose from the depths and footsteps passed behind and below him. He kept finding dead ends and having to retrace his path. The lights became dimmer and less frequent and he had to bend and peer at the titles, feeling the dust in his throat.

He almost wept as he read about the dissolution. In 1534, Henry sent Thomas Cromwell and a battery of commissioners to visit the monasteries, the abbeys and convents, to inventory their holdings and soon to seize or destroy everything they had. The worst destruction was visited on the cloistered libraries: books torn apart for their bindings and inlays, manuscripts used to wrap candlesticks and shine boots. Henry selected a handful from each library for his own collection, and the rest were desecrated, hundreds of thousands lost. Jack listened to the cataloguers and felt a sinister echo. He was glad Ripley hadn't lived to see his scrolls used to pack fish and fire ovens.

But some of the works had survived. The Book of Kells and other treasures were smuggled out by monks, and even Cromwell's visitors had taken a few for themselves. Jack felt a cautious relief. Perhaps a tenth had been preserved, and most of those ended up in the other great repositories, the universities. The manuscript must have been spirited to one of those safer libraries, in Oxford or Cambridge, hidden beneath a robe or jerkin – along with the key, if Ripley had ever found it.

Jack heard a soft noise and looked up to see Dev staring at him. He had used a bookshelf to hoist himself to his feet, and now stood swaying with one hand on a volume of *Strong's Concordance*. His jumpsuit was dusty with crumbled pages.

'What are you doing here?' Jack said.

Dev tilted his fat chin towards him. '*Ter sholpal tikim punashi.*'

Babies made all the world's phonemes, all its clicks and whistles. But this sounded different from Dev's usual babblings, and something about it chilled Jack's blood. He felt a dark shape somewhere in his mind, but he couldn't bring it into focus. He looked at Dev in astonishment.

'*Owal lekim sowal tokim,*' Dev said.

A long chord echoed in Jack's ears. It sounded like a huge assembly singing together, a single word he didn't know. It froze him to the library floor. He wondered what was happening, and why Dev's chatter sounded so familiar.

The baby was getting impatient. '*Owal lekim* oos *owal tokim.*'

Then it dawned. He'd spoken the same words to Dev in the oratories; they had set the baby screaming. Jack had thought the phrase a fragment of perfection, then. Now he had no idea. How could Dev have remembered it? And why did it sound so different in the baby's mouth, old and serious and full of suggestion? Jack shivered and realised the library had fallen silent: the cataloguers had left. He scooped Dev up in one hand.

'We'd better get you back to Mum.'

Peter was leaning on the front desk, serious in his navy pants and heavy boots. He held his police cap in his hands. Sandy took Dev and brushed the bookdust off him.

'There you are,' she said. 'I thought you might have been catalogued.'

'Beth told me you were here,' Peter said. 'We pulled this off the cameras at the centre, we think these two planted the explosives.'

He handed Jack a sheaf of folded pages, consecutive frames of security video. Two men in overalls were digging in the bark-chip garden that surrounded the forensics centre. The camera caught them from an angle, obscuring their faces. One of them might have been dark-skinned or else just tanned; the other one had a beard but no moustache.

'Have you caught them?' Jack said.

'No, we don't know who they are.' He gave Sandy a sly look. 'We thought San might have been out with at least one of them.'

Sandy leaned over the photos. 'Are they single?'

They both looked like ordinary gardeners. Their faces didn't suggest any reason for blowing anything up. But Jack looked closer and saw that each of them had a tattoo on his wrist – a simple winding figure. It was difficult to see through the blur of the video, but he recognised both of them.

'There's a guy asleep on a bench outside you might like,' Peter was saying. 'Laid-back type. Outdoorsy.'

'Bloody ha.'

The headless snake, the dotted curl, ℧ and ∩̇. He'd thought them both plosives, when he'd thought the manuscript was a perfect language: voiced plosives, *b* and *d*. Now he didn't know what they were, but there they were, on the bombers' wrists.

He'd doubted himself, he'd let his attention slip. Were they connected with the Hospitallers, a militant wing? Or were they another group entirely, named only in an unknown language, with an even older claim on the manuscript? Did the cataloguers fit in somehow as well, was O'Rourke feeding them all information about him? He had no idea who they were or what they wanted. But they were out there, and they were after him.

℧

Beth lay on the floorboards in the middle of the nave. The church was dark beyond the lamplight pooling around her. She looked like a stage death, a fall from the rigging. She wore her library pants and a black bra. Jack closed the door behind him and locked it; he struggled to control his breathing and his pulse. Beth didn't move.

'Aren't you cold?' he said.

'It isn't cold.'

She was drawing. Cartridge paper in the ellipse of light, crumpled attempts across the floor. She shifted and knelt before the paper, face an inch from the pencil. He felt calmer in the church.

'What's that?'

'You're in the light.'

'Sorry.'

He crept past the lamp and floated above her. She had drawn herself, very simply: an oval face, long curves of her body. Her eyes and mouth were slants of anguish. She had trouble with objects and landscapes, couldn't get the shapes right, but her figures were always simple and heartbreaking. The tilt of her head.

He crouched in front of her and saw that she was crying. She was still in her library make-up, mascara bleeding black tears down her cheeks.

'What's wrong?'

'Nothing. I'm just – I'm method drawing.'

'This is you?'

'What do you think. It's quite a likeness, don't you think?'

He sat on the floor beside her. The muscles in her shoulder stood out with the effort of drawing. The figure was off-centre, leaning into the corner of the page.

'What's it called?'

'I don't know. Something desperate. *Sunshine and Flowers*, something like that.'

'*A Day at the Beach*.'

She looked up at him and he realised what he'd said and not meant. He climbed awkwardly to his feet, disturbed by the picture and her tears, the wells of distress that they kept stumbling over.

'You'll get cold,' he said.

'It's not cold.'

But it was cold; he felt the church's age and emptiness, and her skin was goosepimpled. He leaned over to rub some warmth into her shoulder. The picture looked like her, huddled into itself against the cold.

'Did you see Judy today?' he said.

'No.'

'Did you ask her?'

'Ask her what?'

'If it's true.'

'It's not true.'

He looked down and saw that she had run her thumb along the picture's edges, smudging herself. She was emerging from fog, or dissolving; she looked even sadder. She rolled the paper into a cylinder and held it in both hands. He tried to look into her eyes.

'Are you going to ask her?'

She put the picture down and cradled the back of his neck. 'That's enough. That's enough questions.'

But her lips at his throat were a question, her fingers at his buttons a series of questions. There was a tentative quality to her touch that he hadn't felt since the first time. The arch of her back, the tilt of her hips – she was asking him something as they folded together on the floorboards. Something about Judy, about Frank, about him or her. And he responded as well as he could. He pressed at her body, echoed her rhythm – but he knew he wasn't answering, any more than repeating a question was an answer. He stared into her eyes and watched the small expressions tug at her face. He wanted to answer her, but he didn't have any answers.

lang ucruc.

The rising sun sent columns of pink and orange into the church. Jack watched as they slid over the bed and clipped Beth's bare foot. How strange it was that you could wake with someone in the dawn light and know so little about her. The blue veins tracing her breastbone, the charcoal-rubbings at her armpits, but nothing beyond that. You could wake with her a thousand mornings and still not know what her first thoughts would be.

She had a way of stretching that looked as if she were trying to press her body into a tiny space. Her gaze settled on him and then flicked away, and there was a reproach in the angle of her neck that made him think he'd hurt her in the night. He'd worked his way into her too roughly or too soon, or he'd called her by the wrong name – but it wasn't that. It had to do with the questions, but he didn't know what those meant.

'Is anything the matter?' he said.

'Nothing's the matter.'

She sometimes slept in a slip or T-shirt, but she was never as unreachable as when she was naked. She would let herself be touched, but would huddle inside her skin and feel nothing. He was relieved when she sat up and shrugged into her dressing-gown. She smiled at him but he wasn't convinced. She said she was fine but he resolved to follow her to the library.

υ)

Beth had done an Arts degree and then a Masters in Information Management, where she and Sandy had learned about Dewey and the Chinese encyclopaedia. Jack had read a lot of books in and about various languages, books in and on translation, but he'd never been to university. He wished he had, sometimes. He liked the earnestness and impracticality of it – at the highest levels the determined uselessness of it. He particularly would have liked to have been at one of the ancient universities when they were still young, their colleges brand new, their limestone pale and unworn.

Each of the rivals had a College of St John, which seemed like the best place to start. Oxford's hadn't been built until 1555, more than a decade after the dissolution of the monasteries had ended, but Cambridge's had been founded in 1511 on the site of the ancient Hospital of St John. Light and sacred draughts – Jack felt the creak of the stacks as he read about the old students and fellows, searching for hints of the manuscript or its key. The ghosts of books filled the gaps in the shelves, and the library was washed with the rustle of pages and whispered arguments; it sounded like the wind or the sea.

Beth had been appearing and disappearing all day. She wore a searching expression as she wandered the shelves. Several times she opened her mouth but then turned away, as if she'd remembered he couldn't help her. Or perhaps it was just the library that had silenced her, its endless *shh*.

In the rare books collection, beneath the old maps with their unfamiliar coastlines and blank spaces, he came across a thin man who seemed to be made of triangles, his nose a hypotenuse, his beard a long isosceles. The man's portrait prefaced a treatise about a complicated symbol of crosses and circles, meant to express the unity of everything: the sun, the moon, the elements, and the use of fire. Its lines could be rearranged into all the world's alphabets. Jack had seen the glyph scratched into his manuscript; now he read that this was John Dee, who had attended St John's Cambridge from

1543, just after the dissolution, who had travelled to Europe and gathered the most extensive library of books and manuscripts in England. Books about mathematics, about astronomy and astrology, cartography and navigation, and especially about magic.

Jack could almost see the old conjurer there in the library beside him, though his view was obscured by the missing pages of his diaries and notebooks, by the allusive language he used, and by the intervention of publishers who had meant to discredit him. Dee flickered in his corner, as if lost in a storm of library dust. He lit the walkways and wheeled ladders with a pale fire as he worried over his books and papers, as he laboured with his prisms and globes.

As his flesh withered and his bones and beard sharpened he withdrew from his measurements and raised his face to call to angels. He looked searchingly in Jack's direction but his eyes wouldn't focus. He built his crystals and lenses into windows to other worlds, and wept when he realised he had no gift of sight.

Jack couldn't make out the arrangement of stones and lenses that made up Dee's apparatus. But he saw glimpses, there in the library, and they matched the diagrams of his manuscript. It all fitted. Dee had been happy drawing coastlines and conic sections until something had turned him to the world of angels. He had found the manuscript in the library at St John's, and had seen in it much more than a perfect language, something of another order. Jack wasn't sure what it meant, but it was something mystical, communication with angels, a new kind of alchemy.

Dee searched England for anyone who might see into his crystal, but a parade of mediums failed to convince him. A prophet told him he would find a chest of precious books buried near a ruined castle, but there was nothing there. *Many years, in many places, far & nere, in many bokes, & sundry languages, I have sowght, & studyed; and with sundry men conferred, whereby to fynde or get some ynck-*

ling, glyms, or beame. Jack knew how he felt. But there was nothing.

Then came Edward Kelley, an apothecary's apprentice and forger from Worcester with heavy eyes and a pitchfork beard. He said he'd found a red powder that could turn lead into gold, and a strange bundle of papers – not in a castle but in the ruins of Glastonbury Abbey. He had heard of Dee's attempts and was certain that the papers he had discovered held the key to his world of angels.

Jack read the paragraph again. It had to be the key that George Ripley had pursued: the document that would unlock the manuscript at last. Ripley hadn't found it. It wasn't with the Carmelites in Boston: it was with the Benedictines, at Glastonbury. It seemed to be the part of England most over-grown with legend. Jack passed between books of history and myth in equal numbers as he read about the Abbey. It was said to be England's first church, visited by Joseph of Arimathea with the infant Jesus and later with the Holy Grail, the tomb of Arthur and Guinevere. Before the draining of the fens it had stood high on the island of Avalon. It was the richest abbey after Westminster, and one of the last victims of the dissolution; its ruins must have been fresh when Kelley uncovered its true secret.

Jack hurried back to Dee's story. Kelley stared into the mounted stone and described the spirits in the room: one with very long arms, one with a pot of water, one with a trumpet. Forty children in white silk robes, a pretty girl of seven or nine wandering among the books of Dee's library – and all of them carrying letters or numbers, on rings or amulets or tablets, written into their hearts or the veins of their chests, all spelling out the language of angels. Galas, Gethog, Thaoth, Horlwn, Innon, Aaoth, Galethog ... Dee wrote it down over seven years, as they travelled together to Amsterdam, to Krakow and Prague, dazzling princes and emperors, promising lead into gold.

If Kelley was a fraud he was a clever one, weaving long

arguments among the angels, repeating languages he claimed not to know. Dee was slowly but deeply persuaded. Even when Kelley told him the angels wanted them to share their wives, he went along with their instructions: he never again asked Kelley to look into the stone, but he sent his young Jane to the charlatan's bed. Kelley left to work lucrative deceptions on Emperor Rudolf, and Dee and his family limped back to England. Kelley had taken the shewstone, the frames and altars they had used, and most of the books they had consulted together – but Dee had kept his red powder, and the Glastonbury papers.

Jack looked up from the old copy of *A True and Faithful Relation of What Passed for Many Yeers between Dr John Dee and Some Spirits* and saw the outlines fading from the library air: Dee with his stone and his compass, Kelley with his promises, the parade of souls. Jack wasn't sure what he'd seen between the stacks. The angels had promised the Philosopher's Stone but hadn't delivered. They had made predictions that never happened. But the language they had taught the alchemists stayed with him. *Od saga toltorg camliax l astel od l chamascheth* – something about it sent colours through him. It sounded like the sort of language angels would speak, if there were angels. Could Dee or Kelley really have invented it?

It wasn't a philosophical language; it was a language of untidy splendour. Single words stood for whole clauses: *bams* meant *let them forget*, *moooah* meant *it repenteth me* and *apachana* meant *slimy things made of dust*. It didn't have the perfection Wilkins had sought, but perhaps it had another kind of perfection. And as he turned back through the pages he saw how this heavenly language might also have embraced the other theories of the manuscript: it was a transformation, a secret messenger, a cycle of song. The scholars of the whole and divided manuscript had all been right, in their way. And Dee hadn't seen or understood everything with any clarity, but perhaps he had been closest. The language of angels: Jack felt a sudden warmth spread from his chest to his shoulders.

Beth looked tired, as if she'd walked further through the library than he had. She glanced up at the skylights.

'I'm supposed to have a drink with Sandy,' she said.

'Where are you going?'

'I don't know, some bar she's found.'

'Sounds like fun.'

'You know about Thorn's thing tomorrow?'

He rubbed his eyes. 'What thing?'

'The award. The ceremony.'

'Oh,' Jack said. 'Of course.'

She paused, and her fingers brushed the leather spines. 'Do you want to come to the bar with us?'

He thought he should go; the dim light was hemming his vision.

But he couldn't stop thinking about Kelley's papers, his key made of vellum or rags.

'I'd better keep at it.'

After she'd turned her head he thought he'd caught a shade of relief in her expression. But he hadn't been looking closely enough, and then she was gone.

Almost nothing had been written by or about John Dee after his return to England. Jack searched through piles of books before he found a footnote remarking that he had died in the last days of 1608. The few mourners who visited his house at Mortlake were surprised at how little remained of his great library. Dee's own writings were nowhere to be found, except in rumours: they had crumbled at the moment of his death, or their words had caught fire. The last Jack read of Dee was in a biography of antiquarian Robert Cotton, who had heard the rumours but thought it more likely that Dee had hidden his books. He spent the next ten years buying up the nearby fields and ploughing them for the magician's secret estate.

The shelves shifted around Jack as he read about this new collector, finding his way through the library as swiftly as Beth had. Cotton had a gift for locating manuscripts that were already rare and would prove priceless. Many of the treasures of the monasteries had already surfaced in his library, beneath his busts of Caligula and Nero: the Lindisfarne Gospels, the only copies of *Beowulf* and *Sir Gawain and the Green Knight* – and after a long search he quietly added the exhumed papers of John Dee. Cotton's library was soon the largest private collection ever established, surpassing Dee's and never itself surpassed.

But secular libraries were no safer from the kings of England than religious ones. Cotton was also a politician, and the old papers in his collection were among the best evidence of the grants and reservations of Charles's power. The king and his advisers feared the information he had gathered; they charged him with treason and seized every shelf and bookpress from Julius to Domitian. It was like taking a living organ, and the antiquarian died the next year. Most of the books were returned to Cotton's heirs, but many were sentenced to be burnt by the hand of the common hangman.

Jack had to check the line again, but there it was: books condemned for heresy or treason were taken to the public squares of Westminster and Cheapside and set alight by the hangman. A heavy feeling gathered in Jack's stomach. The courts and houses of parliament had consigned thousands of pages over hundreds of years: arguments about life after death, calls for sport on Sundays. And as Charles searched Cotton's library, he burned as seditious a series of legal decisions about the power of the crown, as blasphemous several books pondering the nature of the Trinity – and as forgery a long and strange letter to the Abbey at Glastonbury.

As Jack climbed from the reading room he had the impression that all of these books were empty, the pages yellowing at the edges but otherwise blank, the leather bindings unembossed. Back at the church, the movie posters had been stripped of their words and letters. And the manuscript, hidden again in the crypt, was more dreadful than it had ever been; he would never know its language or its secret. He sat alone on the floor and watched as the light faded, as the shadows filled the nave. He was too tired to stand up and turn on the lamps, and as the darkness claimed the walls and the roof he realised he was glad of it. He couldn't read anything, he didn't want to see anything.

ʊ⟩

He thought he was asleep when Beth arrived home. He heard her at the door, footsteps on the floorboards, but he was dreaming. He was dreaming the whole thing and she was still out, or her return had insinuated itself into his dream.

'Jack?'

He had been thinking in the language of angels, the few words Dee had written down before his key had been burnt and the language lost forever. It was a wonderful language, a language that revealed the soul, that would flow in and out of them and teach them everything, up in flames.

'You're asleep.'

Perhaps he was, though his eyes felt open; he could see across the floorboards. The rise and fall of his chest, his breath almost catching his palate. He didn't want to leave this language and break back into the world.

'See Jack sleep.'

She was drunk. She spelled it in the footsteps circling behind him. She was leaving her clothes around the church floor, and he felt naked shadows caressing him, teasing him awake. Perhaps it was *iudra*, the shadow of someone naked. It needed a word of its own.

'Sleep, Jack, sleep.'

He slept or pretended, staring asleep at the church door. She crawled into bed behind him, pubic hair against his buttocks, fingers tracing his hips. The scents of her evening flowed over him: smoke, alcohol, perfume. He thought she'd had a pleasant night.

'I was thinking about our lighthouse, Jack.'

She was whispering.

'The lighthouse in the desert that shone through people? I was thinking – that's all very well. But what if the light isn't strong enough? It can't get all the way through, it's barely to the edge of you. Then you can't see anything, not properly.'

He tried to keep up with her, but her argument spiralled away from him, the private logic of drunk.

'A light that shone through you – but there aren't lights like that, Jack. Everything happens in the shadows, every-thing's in the corner of your eye. So that when you go to look ... when you try to look behind you ...'

She was fading now, joining him in sleep. If he woke he would startle and embarrass her. He let her catch up with him. It would be all right in the morning; he would solve it in the morning.

'It's the twilight, Jack. It's the only light there is.'

Car headlights swept past the stained glass and sent inverted colours against the ceiling, ellipses shrinking to circles and stretching again. A *semoroh* light: he hadn't noticed it before.

6 Jack woke late and exhausted, and Beth was gone. The floor was covered with lilies of crumpled paper, scattered while he slept. He bent to uncrumple them, feeling the age in his back. It was the figure she had drawn before: three lines of expression, the long sweep of her body. But this time it was doubled. Each line had a ghost or was the other's ghost, a cross-eyed or drunken vision.

A day at the beach. On the next page she had drawn three of herself, red and green and blue. The lines were less sure now, as if affected by static. There was a pleasing asymmetry to the drawing, the green Beth further from the red and blue Beths than they were from each other. It was a good picture, and he almost thought he understood it.

Another picture showed four of her: black and yellow, a kind of pink and a light blue. Something about the colours. He didn't know where Beth was. They were supposed to be at Thorn's award ceremony. The rest of the pictures were the same, or unfinished drafts. He let them fall again to the floor.

ᚢᛃ

The Society of Norsemen had been formed to explore trade opportunities, wind farms and cardboard – but it also supported the translation of literature, the promotion of myth and poetry. The ceremony was held on an auspicious day, following reports of a dark raven and two men seeking renown, in an auditorium a few suburbs from the city.

Jack arrived late and stood at the back of the room. The

Norsemen were tall or bulky, their hair like silver or copper, their eyes full of weather. After a discussion of recent scholarship on the sagas, the provenance of old charts, they moved to their tradition of kenning. A raven was the swan of battle, a battle the quarrel of swords, a sword a blood-snake, blood the drink of ravens: it could go on forever. But they all agreed that Thorn's was a worthy winner. They sat and thought about the soul's sail and sun and all of their handsome faces crinkled together.

There was something pitiable about it, Jack thought, this jamming of words into compounds. It was a language of dwarfs, nothing like the language of angels he'd seen. He couldn't help feeling a shadow of hopelessness over the whole event. He didn't want to be there. The manuscript had never seemed more important or further from his reach. It was powerful beyond his imagination; the Hospitallers and the bombers would do anything to get it back, and his only hope was to translate it first. But he didn't know how.

After the ceremony they gathered in the car park, congratulating each other. Sandy bounced Dev over the asphalt and wedged him into her hip; he looked silently at Jack, holding his fat fingers to his face.

'Good, weren't they?' Sandy said.

'They were all right.'

She lowered her voice. 'But why can't they just say *love*? Don't tell Thorn.'

'No, I agree.'

She brightened. 'I wonder what they'd call a spade.'

'You should enter next year.'

'The ground's woe. The battle-gleam of potatoes.'

A weak sun made the ground steam. A couple of the Norsemen had discovered they were both warrior-poets and were calling each other melting ones and sons of wretchedness. Jack shook his head at all of them and turned back to Sandy.

'Thanks for taking Beth out last night.'

A quizzical look crossed her face. 'That's all right.'

'I just meant, it's good for her to get out.'

'No, it's good for me too. Give this one to Granny and have a few drinks. Even if it's only a quiet night.'

Jack raised his eyebrows. 'What do you call a loud one?'

She smiled bashfully. 'Oh, well, the old me. How was she this morning?'

'All right, I think. I thought she'd be here.'

'They're always changing the shifts around.'

'That's true.'

Ash had done some analysis for a paper on the Vinland map, which showed that the Vikings had discovered America in the eleventh century, but was probably a forgery. He stood talking to Peter under the jacaranda trees. He saw Jack and waved a bandaged hand at him.

'Who's that?' Sandy said.

'I was telling you about him, he's the one I thought you'd like.'

Sandy looked doubtful. 'He doesn't have any hands.'

'Is that a problem?'

'Don't you think it might be?'

'Well, I don't know what you're looking for.'

'Don't you?'

There was a frustration in her voice, and as she swung Dev onto her other hip and looked back at him he saw it in her eyes as well. She put up with a lot from all of them; it would be easy for her to get the wrong idea.

'No, I do,' he said. 'You know I do.'

'I thought you did.'

'Of course I know.'

He looked into her eyes until she believed him, maybe too long. She brushed a strand of hair from her face and turned away.

'They're all gay or taken, that's all,' she said.

Jack tilted his head in Ash's direction. 'Come and meet him.'

'It's all right.' She gave Dev a bounce, and he kept his eyes on Jack. 'I've got a date for the afternoon.'

'You're all right?'

'I'm fine.'

Jack crossed to the line of trees. Thorn stood outside the auditorium doors, talking about love with a group of Norsewomen. They flashed their steely eyes. Peter shot them an impatient glance as he shifted to make room for Jack.

Ash's hands were splinted and loosely bandaged. He held them out at a mechanical angle. Jack didn't know what to do; he offered his own hand and then lowered it.

'Are you all right?' he said.

'It was mostly superficial. I was lucky.'

'How's the lab?'

'It's about to open again. Everyone's dying to work on the bombing but they're sending it out, they think we're all too emotional.'

'We've got warrants out,' Peter said. 'We found out their names and last addresses.'

'Who they are?'

'They're criminals.' Peter shrugged. 'One of them has a conviction for counterfeiting.'

'We don't think that's got anything to do with it, though,' Ash said. 'We were working on a few different things but nothing to do with any documents.'

'Except mine,' Jack said.

'Right. Nothing apart from yours.'

'Did you tell anyone? About mine?'

'Like who?'

'Anyone.'

Ash gave him a strange look. 'Jack, criminals aren't interested in your manuscript. Not for the last few centuries, anyway.'

'Who did you tell?'

'Some technicians did the spectrometry, but other than that it was me.'

'What technicians?'

Ash raised his hands. 'Jack, it's not you. It's not about you.'

It was an unthinking gesture, but the sight of his bandaged palms made Jack pause. Ash might have been careless, but he wasn't part of the conspiracy, he didn't know what Jack knew.

'Sorry.'

'It's all right. Did you find out what it was?'

Jack shook his head. 'I thought I'd tracked down another document that made it all make sense, but it turns out it was burnt.'

Ash gave him a meaningful shrug. 'It happens.'

'Yes, but it's so barbaric. I can't believe people used to burn books.'

'People used to burn people.'

'This was just like that. It was found guilty of having been forged, and condemned to be burnt by the common hangman.'

Ash tilted his head. 'A forgery burnt by the hangman?'

'That's right.' He saw something behind Ash's eyes. 'Why?'

'Nothing, it's something I did for Thorn a few years ago.'

'What was it?'

Ash narrowed his eyes. 'It was ... yes, a fragment from Northumbria, he thought it might have been one of the sources for *Egil's Saga*. Very convincing, an old piece of parchment and the right kind of ink – but no earlier than the seventeenth century, it turned out.'

Jack had forgotten Ash's passion for forgeries; now he felt a ripple of irritation. He didn't care about other documents. They were all too trivial.

'But the interesting thing was, we traced it back and the best suspect for the forgery was the hangman. Who claimed to have taken the document from one of his – one of his clients, I suppose you'd say now. But there was good evidence that the client did have the real fragment, he was a descendant of someone involved.'

'The common hangman?'

'I suppose so. Anyway we found this incredible tradition of forgery among the hangmen of England. Wills and title deeds, but also poems and palimpsests – everything. They were all doing it, and some of them were quite brilliant – much better than they were at killing people, if you believe the stories. So the one who burned your document might have forged it in the first place, or one of his friends.'

'I don't think it really was forged.'

'Well, either way.'

Jack saw a glimmer in the story, though he wasn't sure what it was. He wondered how Ash knew so much about hangmen. Was he part of it after all, was he feeding Jack information? He was trying to imagine what his purpose might be when he saw Beth at the entrance to the car park.

She was wearing her library pants, her library shirt: they must have shifted her shift. There was something wrong with her movements, and a slight bewilderment lay around her eyes, as if she were an angel in a vision, picking her way between the worlds. But she righted herself as she neared Thorn and kissed the cliff of his cheek.

'I'm so sorry, I wanted to be here.'

'It's all right. You'd heard it already.'

She smiled. 'It is the best of all tropes, and you are the best of all poets.'

'That's what my certificate says.'

'Does it?'

'In runes. It is the best of all certificates.'

'It's very good.'

She looked over to Jack, and her eyes suddenly seemed deep and very old. The sun was falling again, a spent red sun, and something made him doubt that she really had been at the library – but he couldn't ask. The moon's sister, low, late-shining, and he couldn't ask a woman where she'd been.

The builders had forgotten to tie the tarpaulin over the church, but it was a mild night with no chance of rain. A soft westerly curled over the gap in the roof. The church-stones looked like the ghosts of stones. Jack thought of the castle where Dee had dug for his chest of books, the ruins of the abbey where Kelley had found his letter, the fields that Cotton had tilled – and now the crypt beneath them, where he had found the manuscript and hidden it again. It was remarkable that any books had survived the fire, the water, the earth – that there had been any ages other than dark ones.

Beth wandered between the lights with the stack of drawings he had collected that morning, the self-portraits in overlapping colours.

'I don't know what I was thinking,' she said.

He thought she was embarrassed, but he looked over and saw her face and felt the weight of the words, and it seemed more like an unadorned admission.

'No?' he said.

'Maybe I was still drunk.'

She worked through the pages, smoothing each against her thigh and shaking her head as she traced the lines with her fingers. She moved the sheets towards and away from her face. She looked up at Jack with hollow eyes.

'You wake up and you know you've had strange dreams. You just don't feel right, you know they were strange. But you can't remember what they were.'

Perhaps she was still drunk. Had she been hiding liquor in coffee mugs and canteens? Her gaze was steady, her movements slow but delicate, and he didn't think she was drunk now or had been when she'd drawn the pictures.

'Really?' he said.

'You think maybe someone you knew was in them,

someone who's dead, but you can't remember because it was just too weird. Like a colour you've never seen before.'

'What kind of colour?'

'Like a sort of – well, exactly.'

He thought again that the angels' language he had almost discovered would have all the words she needed. She held the pictures of the three of her and the four of her; she was looking at the places where her outlines intersected.

'You know everything in the world is made of these colours – or these ones,' she said. 'It's all mixtures of red and green and blue, or of cyan, magenta, yellow and black. But if you lose one of the colours – things disappear, edges aren't right. Do you know what I mean?'

He thought he did. 'If you see an old billboard, or some packaging that's been left in the sun. And everybody's yellow, or they're blue – or cyan, I suppose it is.'

'They're often cyan. Cyan lasts a long time.'

'Why is that?'

'It's just something to do with the ink.'

He felt better. At least they were talking, they were speaking the same language. He wanted to ask what the colours meant. But that was too blunt, it would chase her away. And the ink was already making him think of forgeries, of vitriol and gall, and the tangled pictures reminded him of the way a forger might trace a black line over a yellow one to mimic the separating effects of old ink. They'd done it to the Vinland map, according to Ash. And hangmen had done it to at least some of the documents that came their way – they had made faithful copies, and that gave him hope.

Ketch

Jack arrived at the library before it opened. The days were getting shorter and the sun was still low in the sky, casting the city's spine with a pale yellow. The grass was cool with shadows and dew. He found himself looking around more often than usual, searching for bombers and forgers. The library doors opened and he slipped inside.

Ash had been right: burning books was uncivilised, but burning people – or boiling them, or drawing and quartering them – he could hardly believe it had happened so often and so recently. He read about executions for hundreds of crimes, from translating the Bible to impersonating a pensioner. As far as he could tell, they had all been performed by one Jack Ketch, who seemed impossibly busy until Jack realised that it was a nickname for all the hangmen.

The first Ketch had bungled a series of beheadings, taking four or five hacks to get through the neck and infuriating those of his victims – his clients – who had paid him extra to get it right. His blunt axe, or his weak arm: he wrote a pamphlet denying any drunkenness or malice, but it only cemented his name.

Court records and reports showed that coiners and counterfeiters were burnt at the stake well into the eighteenth century. Mere forgers were treated more humanely, and simply hanged: for stamps and seals, for receipts and bills of exchange. They came from every class of society. Bankers and civil servants, candle-makers, sugar-bakers – and hangmen, or at least one unlucky one, in November of 1786.

599. JACK KETCH was indicted for that he did falsely make, forge, and counterfeit, a certain Pamphlet, intituled, *A Defiance against all arbitrary Userpations or Encroachments, upon the Soveraignty of the Supreame House of Commons, or upon the Rights, Propertyes, and Freedomes of the People in generall, &c.*

2d Count. The same as the first, only concerning a certain Writing, purporting to be by the hand of *John Asgill*; and intituled, *Argument Proving that According to the Covenant of Eternal Life, revealed in the Scriptures, Man may be Translated from Hence into that Eternal Life without Passing through Death.*

3rd Count. The same as the first, only concerning a certain Petition, intutled, *A Petition in Support of the Tolerating of Sports upon the* Lord's-Day.

There were almost a hundred counts, and Jack recognised almost all of the titles and descriptions. Arguments over the Trinity, doubts about Charles's powers, unauthorised translations. He had read about them only days ago. This was the great lost library: a catalogue of heresy, slander and sedition, centuries of objectionable papers condemned to the pyre. Jack wondered for a moment what they were all doing on this charge sheet. He saw the vague shape of their connection an instant before the prosecutor unveiled it for him.

The book-seller *William Beardmore* will testify that he found in the prisoner's lodgings all of the writings I have recited; indeed, that the writings practically over-filled the lodgings, and did for walls and furniture. I do not propose to call any witness to the making of the forgeries; I invite your *Lordship* to take notice that all of the documents I have read out were condemned by this *Court* or by our *Parliament* to be burnt by the hand of the common hangman, and also every copy thereof; and so to conclude that the contents of the prisoner's house cannot be what they purport to be, and must perforce be forgery.

Beardmore gave detailed testimony about the hangman's closets and shelves. He pronounced Ketch's versions excellent and faithful but agreed that they must indeed be forgeries. Jack almost found himself swayed. But he knew how resilient books could be, and his need to find the Glastonbury papers and the key to the manuscript almost seemed strong enough to bend history around it. So he was less surprised by Ketch's defence than the Court was.

Prisoner. Please the Court, there have been forgeries done, but not by me and neither in my possession. All those papers that were meant to be burnt, they were all copied – they were all forged. But it was the copies that were burnt, and the genuine papers kept.
Court. What do you mean? Forged by whom? Kept by whom?
Prisoner. By the others, my Lord. The other hangmen.
Court. What?
Prisoner. Whenever any paper was ordered to be burnt, my *Lord*, the hangman made a good copy of it and burnt that instead, and kept the paper and handed it down. Now we don't burn papers any more, we just hand them down as they were handed down to me. But it was the old hangmen did the forging; they didn'twant to burn the papers.
Court. Didn't want to burn them? Why not?
Prisoner. Well, my *Lord* – it's barbaric, isn't it?

So there it was – a dynasty of hangmen who wouldn't scruple to hack up a fellow man but would work through the night with their quills and lenses to save a pamphlet. It made a perverse kind of sense, Jack thought. The Court didn't believe it. It found Ketch guilty and condemned his forgeries – or whatever they were – to be burnt all over again, and the hangman himself to hanging. But the jury must have been affected by the romance or ingenuity of Ketch's story: they commended him to His Majesty's mercy, and his sentence was commuted to transportation for life in the new colony of New South Wales.

Jack didn't know whether Beth was working that day. He'd seen her pushing the returns trolley, stamping request slips – but he didn't know when that had been. As he read again through the list of burnt documents he was overtaken by the impression that Beth was partly in the library and partly somewhere else. Perhaps it was the red part of her that drifted between the aisles, reflecting the colours of old paper. The blue part was wading into the water of the cove, or sitting between the sky and the sea by Frank's grave. The green part might have been anywhere or nowhere. Was that what the pictures meant? It didn't seem right, necessarily; and it didn't seem useful. It was just an impression.

The charges against Ketch hadn't referred to any letters to abbeys: the Old Bailey hadn't got its hands on Jack's key. But he didn't think it would have mattered. By refusing to credit Ketch's betrayal of the hangmen, the Court had allowed their secret work to continue. Only more forgeries had been burnt by the new Ketch while the old one was waiting for his transportation. The originals had remained untouched. Jack was convinced of it.

He didn't know what the hangman had brought to New Holland: the actual documents, or yet more copies – the notions of forged and authentic now seemed artificial themselves. And he had no better idea why he might have done it. Ketch couldn't have known that one old letter might be the key to an older manuscript, which in the year of his birth had been purchased by a collector from a bankrupt's auction, which had then puzzled London's finest intellects and been sent at last to a monk at Land's End – who had probably learned of the letter, the same way Jack had, just as Ketch was being exiled for its forgery.

And the monk had followed him. Jack felt a shift in his blood: a dark path had finally led him home. He had traced the manuscript from the Knights of Rhodes through its dissolutions and restorations and at last to Constant. It had been torn up and healed, buried and unearthed, and its unriddling had brought it to the crypt beneath their church and into Jack's hands. He had an indistinct memory of another search that the manuscript had touched, another puzzle that it might belong to, but he couldn't remember what that was: all he could think about was the last key.

But he could find no evidence that Ketch had ever arrived in Australia. In May of 1787 he was transferred to the *Friendship* and left for New South Wales with the rest of the First Fleet: eleven ships, eight hundred convicts, five hundred marines and crew, a Bible and a prayer book. The fleet was about forty souls lighter when it reached Sydney Cove after eight months and fifteen thousand miles: there were births, deaths and desertions, and Jack Ketch had vanished. None of the ships' manifests mentioned him, none of the convict musters remembered him. There was no record of his departure or demise, but he hadn't made it.

Now Jack knew that Beth wasn't at the library and hadn't been all day. He had searched for Ketch through each corner of every floor and wing. He walked once more between the rare books and the open access area, but Beth wasn't anywhere to be found. If she wasn't working, he didn't know what she was doing.

The library was curiously empty: a few students, a few amateur genealogists. He felt a sudden loneliness, then fear that he was being watched by tattooed bombers or suspicious volunteers. And if they weren't here, if they had found the church, and Beth was still there – he was torn. But the most important thing was the mystery of Jack Ketch.

He searched diaries and journals in flowing longhand, homesick letters published as pamphlets, watercolours and pencil sketches of the colony. Its illegible terrain, its patchwork animals. He read about the collapsing relations between the settlers and the local Aborigines, beginning with mutual curiosity, ending in the exchange of spears and smallpox. How different might it have been if they'd been able to speak to each other? They built a kind of pidgin, but it wasn't a language. Scurvy loosened the colony's joints and teeth despite the lemon aspen and native cranberry ranging around the harbour.

There was no sign of Ketch in New South Wales, nothing to remind Jack of the hangman. It was too late: whatever had happened to him had been on the voyage here. On each of the transports, at least one marine had kept a diary of the journey, the heat and sickness, the terrifying latitudes. The fleet's convicts hadn't written any journals, and were only mentioned when they sickened or died or committed further crimes. There were only occasional glimpses into their lives below the waterline.

We discovered that unknown convicts had, with great ingenuity and address, passed some quarter dollars which they had coined out of old buckles, buttons belonging to the marines, and pewter spoons. A strict and careful search was made for the apparatus wherewith this was done, but in vain; not the smallest trace or vestige of any thing of the kind was to be found among them.

Jack searched the journal for more evidence of the coiners, but there was nothing. The natural part of the light was fading, leaving only the library's fluorescent strips: the sun was falling behind the skyscrapers. He was running out of time. He returned the diary to the pile and picked another one.

July 6th. Wind still unfavourable, fleet has made scarcely 1° lat. this past week. Now at 6°36'N & ever more eager to cross the Line, which we approach like Achilles after a tortoise. Water allowance reduced to 3 pints per day & sun very constant; some convicts and crew report unexplained sights & sounds, tapping and feminine moans from without the hull, pale lights at the horizon where no land is reckoned to be, &c. One seaman protests that the *Friendship* is making so little headway because she attempts to sail through sand dunes; he has been placed in irons and educated in the nature of winds between the Tropics.

At the desk opposite Jack's, a fluorescent tube stuttered on and off. A pale young man read a magazine by its flickering light. Jack gathered up the journals and moved to another table. The young man kept reading his magazine.

7th. But clap me in irons beside him, for today I have seen stranger things than even heat & doldrums might explain. First light & almost underway on a gasp of wind when a tremendous commotion off starboard. Often shoals of porpoise, flying fish &c., but this morning nothing but a naked man in the water, salty as Lot's wife. When dragged aboard turned out to be a marine from this very brig, said he'd fallen in on Wednesday & been swimming ever since, our old tub just beyond his reach. Poor Tantalus! Nobody believed him one of us, but there he was on the manifest, & when we took him to his bunk all his papers were in order & he was much relieved to be reunited with his case of books. Even I failed to recognise him, abused as he was by the sea, but have spent the day with him & found him as pleasant as he must ever have been, & can scarcely believe we almost lost our dear Private Wm. Fide.

A sudden silence filled the library, and Jack looked up to see that the young man was gone, replaced by the rangy eucalypts, the creek and sloping beaches that had been there when the First Fleet had crossed the equator. The marines hadn't bothered with the ceremonies that usually took place between the hemispheres. The pollywogs among them had become shellbacks, but there had been more significant translations. The forger had been busy at the *Friendship*'s manifests, but his great work had been on himself: he had stripped and salted his body, he had waited for Jack Ketch to wash away and had emerged a new man. A forged man, but that wouldn't make any difference where he was going.

And Jack laughed at the transformation Ketch had undergone, and at the use the hangman had made of his outlawed books and papers. His namesake: another translator, another forger. Jack thumped the table and laughed because he'd spent so long so close to the key. He'd known too much Latin and religion to think about the names and what else they might mean. The answer had been there the whole time.

Ϛυϲυϩι

It was after six by the time Jack arrived, and the *Depositum Fidei* – a Deposit of Faith but also of Fide – had closed for the day. The sun was smearing the clouds with the last of its colours, and the reflected red and orange made the city's glass towers look like the sketches of buildings. The barracks looked new again as he scuffed across the courtyard and hammered on the door, loud enough to wake the convicts in their hammocks.

There was no answer. He knocked again and peered through the window. The night lamps gave a grudging light, and a shadow moved between the shelves – more than one shadow, and he pressed himself against the wall to watch. Drifting through the twilight, joining and dividing in that shadowy way, and he thought again of the Knights Hospitaller and feared they were ahead of him – until he remembered the upcoming auction, the cataloguers brought in to make sense of the Deposit.

Finally Sandy passed the window. He thought he saw a twitch of disappointment as she recognised him, but she gestured towards the front door and gave him an amused nod when he pressed his finger to his lips.

'What are you doing here?'

He kept his voice low. 'I need to find something.'

'Jack, the place is in chaos, we don't know where anything is.'

'Nobody knows where this is.'

'Why don't you come back when it's done?'

'It'll be too late.'

She stood back from the door. 'All right. You're on your own, though.'

He stepped into the building's dusk. 'You haven't seen Beth, have you?'

'What do you mean?'

'She wasn't at the library today.'

'Is she at home?'

'I don't know.'

'Why don't you go and see?'

'I need you to sneak me downstairs.'

She rolled her eyes, but helped him down the staircase to the library that had grown from Ketch's condemned books, from a single case of books and papers – possibly forged, who would ever know? – into Fide's store of faith.

The centuries had bent the Deposit into a labyrinth, full of dead ends. After a few turns he no longer knew where he was. He pulled books halfway from their shelves to remind him of the way; when he retraced his steps he found his signs missing or moved. Perhaps the cataloguers were enemies after all, if not the Hospitallers then in league with them, rivals in his search. There were more of them and they were better organised. They could reshape the library behind them. If he ever found the secret, he'd be buried with it.

On the lower floors the ceilings dropped and the shelves huddled closer together, the aluminium shelving gave way to dark oak and the books grew more esoteric. They snagged his attention as he tried to hurry past. John Dee was there, with his diabolical machine: *a companion of the helhounds, a caller and a conjurer of wicked and damned spirits.* Kabbalists apprehended the world by rearranging the letters of the Torah, first written in black flames on a white fire. The Templars resurfaced among the Freemasons and Rosicrucians, rumours that became true – and even in the Royal Society, where the manuscript had left its mark.

The stairwells took him deeper than he thought possible,

and the shelves must have led him past the barracks' foundations. He'd never have guessed there was so much to the collection, and he wondered why the hangman had become so interested in religion – and what had really brought him here. It couldn't have been bad luck; he must have allowed himself to be discovered and arrested.

Had he found out what the Glastonbury letter meant? Perhaps he'd heard something about the manuscript – from the rumours of prisoners, the confessions of doomed men – and it had terrified him. Ketch knew more about darkness and horror than John Dee and Edward Kelley had when the letter and the manuscript had last brushed together. He might have been the first person to understand what it really was – the first and still the only one. His hangman's vows wouldn't let him destroy the letter, so he had brought it to the bottom of the world and buried it in meditations and devotions, and the collection had grown from that concealing urge. Hidden societies, tattoos and oaths, as the lights flickered and blurred the Deposit's edges.

Now the shelves began to interrupt and overlap each other: Jack had to climb over them, stoop and soon tunnel through them. He thought of Constant exploring the occult and heretical aisles with his own black flame. It was getting warmer, and though he was only a few floors below ground he felt the labyrinth was leading him deep into the earth, below the railway tunnels, the fossils of unimaginable marsupials. He felt dizzied by the alchemists and kabbalists and shadow societies, the layers of light and darkness, truth and rumour, history and fiction, and all the transformations between them.

The cataloguers had multiplied. He could hear them everywhere, saw them in flashes as they disappeared between the shelves. The auction would come with the dawn, like a hanging. No matter what depths he sounded, what narrowing alleys of books he squeezed through, they had been there before him: a whisper, a pattern of dust, messages that told him he was too late.

*

There was a sudden silence, and he realised he was alone. The cataloguers must have finished: it was already tomorrow. He felt the failure in his stomach. He was a long way from the surface and had no idea how to get there, where to begin. He hadn't slept properly for weeks. They said you only had to keep choosing the same direction, to keep faith in the left or the right. Jack chose left. He turned and trailed his left hand along the shelves, gathering dust. He just wanted to get home; he only wanted to sleep.

But after a minute he saw that the books' dust had already been furrowed with his fingerprints – he was walking in circles. He went around again, dragged another stripe of dust. It didn't make sense. Either the maze was some kind of Möbius strip, something with the wrong number of dimensions – or this was the end of the maze, its heart and centre. He walked around again and confirmed that it was a solid rectangle of shelves, a few metres wide, and no way in.

He pulled out an armful of books and was met with another layer, another shelf of books. Darkness behind them. He pushed at the books, and they crashed to the ground in plumes of dust. He poked his head into the gap, then his shoulders, and found himself wriggling through the hole. He stood up on the other side and dusted himself off.

Shelves surrounded him, reaching to the ceiling. He was in a small chamber, the size of his crypt and walled entirely by books. Walled entirely by Bibles, he realised as he scanned the shelves – in Latin and Greek and the various English translations, Catholic and Anglican and the Bibles of every other schism. An inner sanctum made of hundreds of old Bibles, even a Great Bible supported by a wooden lectern. A dim light crept through the space he'd made and glittered in the Bibles' inlays, gold and silver.

Ketch must have built this stronghold – to protect the manuscript's secret from intruders, or was it the other way around? Jack couldn't hear his heart or the blood through his body, only the creak of the leather as he hefted open the

Great Bible. He turned the first few pages: the illuminations, the red letters, the Gothic type. He browsed the Old Testament. He got as far as Psalms.

A hole had been cut in the middle of the Bible, a rectangle half an inch thick, in the dimensions of a small book. It was an old trick, a good place to hide things. He didn't think you were supposed to use the Bible. But someone had carved a hiding place into this Great Bible.

He looked closer and saw that the text of the Bible had been diverted around the hole, the Psalms made way for the hole. The Bible had been printed for the purpose of hiding something.

But there was nothing there.

They'd got there before him. The cataloguers had found the chamber, tunnelled their way in and taken the letter up to the auction. Someone with a tattoo, some Knight of Grace or Justice was bidding for it. Jack had to get back to the surface, or he would never solve anything. Was the manuscript still safe in the crypt, or had they been there too? He should have chosen right: he should have chosen starboard, it was always starboard.

He couldn't seem to leave the chamber.

All these old Bibles. The first fragments that William Tyndale was burnt and strangled for. The Coverdale Bible, full of bugs and treacle. Cranmer and Douay, the exiles in Geneva. The Idle Bible, the Place-Makers' Bible, the Standing fishes and Rebecca's Camels Bibles. There were better places to hide a letter than the Great Bible, on a lectern in the middle of the room.

He scanned the shelves for the less conspicuous Bibles. The small and battered Bibles, the unpopular translations. He pulled them out; they were all complete. He thought perhaps the King James Version in one of its thousand editions, but the letter wasn't there. He tried all the books with blank covers, no inlay or embossing – but they were all ordinary Bibles. He kept looking.

Here was a Bible he recognised, perhaps the only one that meant more to him than the King James Version. It was the

Vulgate, the first translation into vernacular Latin. It was the heroic work of St Jerome, the patron saint of translators and librarians.

It was an old and worn edition, and seemed thinner than it should have been. It could hardly have hidden anything; he wasn't sure what had drawn him to it. But his fingers closed on its cracked binding with the familiar feel of skin, as if he had clasped another hand. He pulled it from the shelf and the cover slipped off it: it was only a cover. The Vulgate was gone, and here was a letter instead.

The pages were coarser than those of his manuscript, parchment instead of vellum. He pressed them open and tilted them to reflect the light of the Bible room. The letter was written in a panicked minuscule. The first page was headed *Epistola ad Johannem abbatem Glastoniensem* and dated *Id. Mai. AD MCCXCI* – halfway through May 1291. It had been sent to Glastonbury from Acre, the last Crusader outpost in the Holy Land.

He heard a soft scratching through the library, muffled by the endless pages but still distinct. He wasn't safe. He stuffed the letter into his jacket and crept back through the wall of books. He knew where he had to go.

υ)

The offshore winds scraped against the rising land with the sounds of the city and suburbs, but in the lee of the light-house the air was still. The lamp seared and faded with a rhythm that suggested the passing of many years. The iron gall ink had eaten into the parchment, and at several points the light shone through the words and onto the next page, as if the letter had been written in fire.

Jack had come here on an instinct. It felt like somewhere the Hospitallers wouldn't follow him: a godless and desolate head-land, safer than the church. He remembered the story he'd told Beth here and felt it might also be a place where particular kinds of truth could rise like the spray of the breakers below. He felt that all the mysteries were converging, all the answers were at hand.

Apostolicus namque Romanae sedis ultra montanas partes quantocius profectus est cum suis archiepiscopis episcopis abbatibus et presbiteris coepitque subtiliter sermocinari et predicare dicens Fratres uos oportet multa pati pro nomine Christi uidelicet miserias paupertates nuditates persecutiones egestates infirmitates fames sites et alia huiusmodi.

He had always struggled with Latin; at best he could piece it together from French and Italian. He picked his way through the first lines, trying to identify the roots and guess at the endings. *Apostolicus Romanae sedis* had something to do with the Pope, *ultra montanas* was beyond the mountains. There were archbishops and bishops and abbots, misery, poverty, nakedness – it wasn't as hard as he'd thought. He remembered Constant's scratched verse, from the Pentecost: *And how heare we euery man in our own tongue, wherein we were born?* The tongues of fire, and then of pure light. It was something like that: Jack could read the letter in his own tongue.

So the Pope set out as quickly as possible beyond the mountains with his archbishops and bishops and abbots and priests to give sermons and preach with great eloquence, saying, 'Brothers, you should endure much suffering in Christ's name: misery, poverty, nakedness, persecution, want, illness, hunger, thirst, and so on.'

Urban's army of one hundred thousand robbers and farmers and several knights suffered much more in the name of Christ than their Pope had thought of, but first Edessa, soon Antioch and finally Jerusalem fell to His bellicose pilgrims, and the Holy Land was restored to Christendom, though briefly.

For the Crusaders quickly learned that they much

preferred to inflict than to endure misery, nakedness and the rest, and the return of Jerusalem to the Mohammedans after only ninety years might have permitted our kings and princes to reflect on their fitness to know or implement God's will.

But far from falling to these tedious heresies they have fortified their convictions and more than redoubled their efforts to liberate Jerusalem from Saladin's tolerant rule. That is why I travelled from our Abbey to Acco as confessor and adviser to his Highness Edward, though not why I have stayed these twenty years.

He might have got the tenses wrong, mistaken the subjects and objects. But he knew what he held: a first-hand report of the Crusades, lost for two hundred years and hidden for much longer. Even if it were an eighteenth-century copy, that would hardly matter: the story was what counted. Even if the story had been invented, it was long enough ago to have attracted its own value. Over the years, all forgeries became genuine. He thought for a moment that whatever happened it would make his name, and perhaps his fortune – but it was only for a moment.

The letter continued. Prince Edward had left England in 1270 with his confessor and a thousand knights, a fraction of the army that had first taken Jerusalem. He planned to meet his cousins at Carthage, but arrived to find Louis dead from plague and Charles already preparing to return home. Edward pressed on with his thirteen ships but could do little to save Acre, let alone Jerusalem.

We saw that what remains of the Kingdom has fallen among the many novel military orders – the Knights of the Temple and the Hospital, of St Thomas and St Lazarus, and of the Teutonic Order – who fight over its scraps like dogs under a table. United they might conquer the Saracens in an afternoon, but they cannot be joined any more than the north and south winds might blow together. And so they build ever more elaborate fortresses and intrigues against each other, and compete lustily in the slaughter of local peasants who, while assuredly infidels, seldom prove significant to the recapture of Jerusalem.

The only Order that has failed to distinguish itself by avarice and bloodshed is that late of Mount Carmel. From the time of the First Temple some power in this mountain has drawn knights to abandon their swords, merchants their spices and bolts, and pilgrims their thoughts of home to live like bees in its caves and cells. Their rule demands poverty and toil, abstinence from meat and gossip, and no ownership except in common. They could hardly have been nearer in spirit to the Pope's exhortation at Clermont, or further from the excesses of the military orders; but now they are gone.

By the time the Saracens again plucked the Holy City like a ripe apple from a low branch, the last Carmelite had left the mountain for England. And many in Acco have confided to me that the Kingdom's fortunes soured exactly then, that free of the Carmelites' influence the Templars and Hospitallers discovered new depths of villainy, and that the quiet hermits' disappearance did not so much anticipate as bring about the loss of Jerusalem and would bring more suffering yet.

Things were shifting at last into place. Here were the Hospitallers, who had dogged the manuscript from the beginning and were still after it – who had dispersed its quires and now wanted them back. And the Carmelites, who George Ripley had followed to England after he had paid off the Knights and rebuilt the manuscript. To search for the key, to find out what the monks remembered, what they'd brought from Mount Carmel centuries ago?

The wind swung around the lighthouse, and Jack felt his pocket of air slipping towards the cliffs. The pages rustled between his fingers, and the city whispered to him in all its languages, its plaintive drunksongs, its bitter plenties. He thought he could hear the Hospitallers' footsteps, the scratch and sear of a flint. The lighthouse beam left their shadows behind, picked out their tattoos – and he could almost read them. They were older secrets than he could have imagined. He had read in one of Frank's magazines that ancient remains had been found in Carmel's caves, older than any surviving story or myth, Gilgamesh, the flood, the trickster gods. The parchment flapped in his hands.

I persuaded seven Hospitallers to postpone their treachery for a few hours and escort me to the mountain. It is a long and narrow ridge, falling steeply towards the sea and Acco though more gently on its far side towards Jerusalem; it is covered in a loose scrub and honeycombed with caves. The monastery was abandoned, and beginning its collapse after thirty years without faith or maintenance. The Prior's cell, the refectory and chapel, the monks' caves had been emptied of their stools and tables, their pulpits and crosses, and the livestock had been killed or freed. Only their books remained: precious copies of Augustine and Anselm and Bede, even the Vulgate lying broken-backed on the cave floor.

As we considered these indignities we heard from some distance a soft sound, which we thought was running water until we saw that the spring that the monks had channelled was now dry. We followed the sound out of the monastery and down a narrow path along the mountain's northern face, where we found a cave away from the others and quite unlike the rest. It was wide and deep but very low: we all had to stoop to look inside. The sun penetrated only a short distance into it, but the walls and ceiling danced with colours, soaring red and gold like shining angels. The colours transpired from a wondrous construction of wood and glass, in which several elixirs bubbled over low flames, and light travelled between crystals and lenses.

This surprising apparatus was tended by an even more extraordinary custodian. He was a large man, fat as a

King of Jerusalem despite his diet of honey and locusts, with a bald head that bulged grotesquely as if it held two or three brains. His skin was as white as St John's vision of Christ, white as wool, white as the snow; but his eyes were not like flames but tiny and sunken and dull, and his clothes more ragged and filthy than those of any vision. He blinked piteously as we surrounded him and asked who he was; he looked at his machine and then at us and seemed unable to speak. Indeed he had no teeth whatsoever, only smooth pink gums like a baby's.

When at last he summoned a few words they were none I had heard before. I do not know whether his language was more like English or Latin or Greek or one of the desert tongues, but it was better and worse than any of them: better because it rose like music from the lunatic's soft lips, it gathered into fluent motives and phrases and never lurched or stuttered like our languages do, and it filled my mind with thoughts and images so limpid that I felt I knew what the man was saying though I understood not a word; worse because these sudden thoughts matched exactly my blackest secrets and most shameful doubts, and told me what I feared most about heaven and earth and our place between them.

He turned to the Hospitallers and spoke to each in turn, and I knew that they understood him as well as I did. To one he spoke of men committing sins of the flesh together, advising that the chance of love was like a fresh fig in the desert and should always be taken and never wasted; that man's face twisted with anger and perhaps, I thought, regret. He warned another that he would never earn the respect of his friends or rivals whatever he did in the Holy Land, and should seek his happiness elsewhere. And so to each of the Knights, in his gentle language, until they could stand no more and, moving as one, began to hack him violently to pieces.

As they reduced him he continued to speak, and though his voice became distorted with pain and fury his language remained as unequivocal as ever. I do not know why he chose my secret for his last curse: perhaps he blamed me most, though I had no sword nor would have raised any; perhaps my shame was the worst of any; or perhaps in the end all of us in the Holy Land shared it. All of your doubts are truth, he seemed to say. There are no gods and no infidels, and we are alone. We are accidents and rumours whose only occupation is to spread. All we can do is build meaning and understanding among ourselves, pretend it like shelter where there is none. And by killing me you destroy all that we are and can be, and for nothing. And then he died, and by no means well.

And how hear we, every man, in our own tongue – wherein we were born? Egyptians and Libyans, Jews and proselytes, Knights Hospitaller from seven *langues*, from France, from Italy, from Germany, and a baffled confessor from Glastonbury Abbey – but Jack could hardly marvel at any of them, he wasn't confounded, because the same thing was happening to him. He could read this medieval Latin, he felt he could read the constellations traced by the lighthouse beam and reflected in the sea – and he could hear his enemies on the wind, and knew they were still looking for his letter. He had to get it back to the Deposit before they realised it was gone.

Having at last dispatched a man who might have posed some small danger to the Pope and Christendom, the Knights exchanged their congratulations and left the cave. They are all since dead, suicides of various sanctified and unsanctified kinds, and only I am left.

Then as now I stayed behind, in the dust and the lunatic's blood and the shards and splinters of his machine, and wondered what we had done. It was then that I noticed that his clawed hand was stained black with ink, and that beside it lay a strange book, a codex in vellum untarnished by the sand and the gore of slaughter, and when I opened it I saw that it was written in an unfamiliar script, somewhat like Arabic or Hebrew or even this Latin, but none of them. It was the lunatic's angelic or diabolical language, and for twenty years I have attempted to decipher it, for I long to hear it again. I have taken the book to the wisest men of every faith and none, but none can help me nor will ever help me now.

For our latest detachment of berserkers and marauders have surpassed even the Templars and Hospitallers in their coarseness and cruelty, and the Mohammedans have had enough of us. The Mamelukes have broken through the outer walls with their catapults and mangonels. They are attacking the Accursed Tower and will soon be upon the city. A few ships wait at the quay, demanding prices that should sail us to the moon, but I will not return to pretend that there is any more sense in the civilised world than there was in the Crusader Kingdoms. I will simply write to tell you what has happened here, and welcome the fate that awaits every Christian and infidel.

Hankin Kirk

Jack folded the letter and returned it to his jacket, stood and climbed to the top of the verge. The lighthouse beams rolled over the city, and he looked down at the paths of light and thought of the manuscript hidden in his crypt. Written by a madman in the storm centre of history's madness, it had driven men mad for eight centuries – but there was a truth at the bottom of it, there was reason under it all. He couldn't quite read it, but he knew enough about it. He knew where it had started, and it would end with him.

ひ

He steered the car down the long road from the lighthouse, wheels barely touching the ground. He'd been right all along

– not exactly, but almost. The manuscript was a perfect language after all: not a philosophical language, not invented by anyone, but perhaps some ancient language of deserts and nomads, of deltas and crescents – the tongue wherein we were all born. It was a language of humans, but it made angels. A language you didn't have to learn; you only had to hear it to know what it meant.

The streetlights swept past, giving him different faces in the rearview mirror. He felt invincible as he drove towards the city. It wasn't just the language, it was what the manuscript did with it, what it described and built. If the lunatic hadn't just guessed luckily, if the machine with its bubbling flasks and precise lenses had somehow shown him the Crusaders' hearts, then his manuscript was worth the carracks of silver Ripley had sent to Rhodes. It was worth an exile to the colonies and all the regret suffered by every pretender to its secrets. With the perfect language Jack could say anything; but with a machine like that he might understand at last.

His mood shattered as he reached the barracks and parked across the road. The wind was howling through the city's canyons. A police car sat outside the Deposit, strobes across the sandstone. The flashing lights made everything happen twice, split the world into unconnected red and blue. For a moment he thought it was for him, they'd discovered his theft. But the barracks were dark, the cataloguers gone. The chill down his back, the cascade. He rapped on the car window.

'What happened?' he said.

The constable shook his head. 'People attacking librarians now. What's the world coming to.'

'Christ. Christ.'

The street tilted beneath him; he took an awkward step to keep from falling. The thoughts of many hearts, truth in the inward parts, and the interpretation of the things. All the secrets, the rustlings, the scratchings in dust. The graze of blood on the library steps – and he had a sudden, terrifying vision of all the dark meanings laid open, the meanings better left unread.

6 Jack ran to the hospital – past the old government buildings, the sandstone bright in the moonlight, the arches and columns thick with shadows, the clawing trees. He ran along the middle of the road, weaving between the last taxis. The hangman had been right: the letter and the manuscript should never have been brought together. Here was the exceeding regret already, and he wished it had fallen to almost anyone other than Sandy.

They said she had some kind of aphasia and couldn't remember the words for things. Her eye was bruised and swollen. She was concussed from a gutter or step. She lay in the hospital bed and frowned as she tried to speak properly. Peter stroked her forehead as if imparting words to her; he looked close to tears. Thorn held Peter's forearm and turned to look at Jack.

'There you are,' he said.

Jack crossed to her. 'Sandy, what happened?'

'The, I. Li – library? Tripped up over.'

He frowned. 'I'm sorry?'

She glared at him. Peter covered the lower half of his face with his hand.

'Me ... jump. A man.'

They exchanged glances; she saw them and furrowed her brow.

'The man, jump ... I.'

'Darling, who was it?' Peter said. 'What did he look like?'

She winced and grasped the air with her hand as if trying

to pluck the word. There weren't enough words to describe people anyway. She grimaced and shook her head.

'They say she'll be all right,' Thorn said. 'It's not permanent.'

'Thank God.'

'Some – swelling, you know? Pressure. But it'll go down.'

'Dev,' she said.

'He's all right,' Peter said. 'Granny's got him. He's fine.'

'Dev.'

Jack clutched her hand, bent and held it to his face. He couldn't think about it. If anything worse had happened to her – if they had been left without her, if Dev had been left without anybody. The blood on the library steps – he couldn't get it out of his mind. And now Sandy, groping for words.

'I'm so sorry,' he said, and felt all their eyes on him.

He didn't know that he knew Beth's footsteps, but he recognised their rhythm now, the heel and toe and occasional scuff. He turned to the door as she appeared.

'Oh my God. What happened?'

'She was attacked,' Peter said. 'Outside the barracks.'

'Who was it, Sandy? Do you know who it was?'

Sandy tilted her head to evaluate the question, then shook it firmly.

'A … strangest.'

'He was a strangest?'

'She's got concussion, aphasia.'

'You poor thing.'

Jack wanted to ask Beth where she had been, what had taken her so long. But of course he couldn't. He felt the unasked questions, knew that she felt them too.

'Outside the library, I can't believe it.'

'You can't tell us anything about him?'

Sandy's eyes brightened. She raised herself up in bed and rubbed her upper arm.

'He had skink.'

'A skink?'

Sandy frowned. 'Skin. Nink.'

'A tattoo?'

'Tattoo, a tattoo.'

Jack slumped. He'd allowed himself the smallest hope that this hadn't been his fault: it was senseless violence, and they wouldn't be back.

'What kind of tattoo?' he said.

She gave Jack a look that said: *come on*. But he ignored the look and all the looks. He rubbed her shoulder where she had indicated the tattoo.

'Sandy, what kind of tattoo was it? What tattoo?'

'Jack.'

It was the first time Beth had spoken to him. The realisation took him aback, and he noticed the others were looking at him and at Beth as if there were something hideous about them both. He saw the reflections in their eyes and didn't recognise himself.

ひ

They were silent in the car on the way home. Sandy had helped him find the letter that revealed the manuscript, and she had been beaten by a strangest with skin-ink. He hoped she was safe in the official hospital, away from the St John brigade – but there were still Maltese crosses everywhere, red if not black. They weren't shadows any more, they had form and fists. He wanted to explain it to Beth, to warn her, but where to start? The headlights were too bright, the gravel too loud as he crawled into the driveway and watched the darkness for movement.

Inside the church, he drew the curtains and twisted the floorlamps away from the squints. He hefted the trapdoor and crept down into the crypt. He was sure that the cataloguers had been there and had spirited the manuscript away – but it was still beneath the stone where he had first found it. He took it back up to the nave.

Beth emerged from the bathroom tying her robe over flannel pyjamas. She had been sleeping in a T-shirt and boxer shorts, or old tracksuit bottoms and a singlet. He didn't know why she swung between such extremes of dress, as she pulled on mismatched socks and a football beanie.

'Are you cold?' he said.

'Not cold, not exactly.'

'I can turn up the heater.'

'Can I watch something?'

'Home movies?'

'No, something else. A video.'

'Of course, anything.'

'I won't disturb you, I'll use the headphones.'

'It's all right.'

She rummaged through the video tapes, and he returned to the desk and pulled Hankin Kirk's letter from his jacket. He wished he'd found a way to return it to the Deposit, but it probably wouldn't have done any good. They already knew it was gone. They'd be coming for him. First Ash, now Sandy – who would be next?

On top of the cliff, with the furling light and the stars and the sea, he'd thought the manuscript some kind of miracle. A language that united the world, and a machine that showed the true nature of things – he had seen what Dee and Kelley had seen, he'd heard the talk of angels. But as he lay the manuscript and the letter side by side for the second time in almost a thousand years, he saw what a mistake that had been. The dupe and the charlatan had no idea; only the hangman knew. The truths Kirk had seen on Mount Carmel were terrible, despairing truths; they had riven the confessor and his escorts. They were the kind of truths Jack had glimpsed in the manuscript from the beginning.

No wonder the Hospitallers were after it. They had seen what it could do, they could guess at the power it would give to anyone who survived it. To see the barren truth, and not look away – what would that make you, what would you become? An angel, perhaps – but an angel of the apocalypse, a destroyer of worlds.

They had searched for centuries, and now they were on his doorstep. Who had betrayed him? Had Ash said something, carelessly or on purpose? Had Thorn, or Peter? Had Sandy been collaborating with the cataloguers, had they beaten his name and his hiding place out of her?

The telephone rang, startling him. The clock said midnight. Beth was lost in her headphones, so he got up and met silence on the line. Or not quite silence: the near-silence that betrayed presence. Then the line went dead.

He turned to tell her about it, and saw what she was watching on television. The rusting ships, the endless dunes, and he remembered the time before the storm, the rain on Thursday that had consumed him. The film was where he had left it. The clouds were thickening, and a few drops of rain fell into the sand, then a few more. Chelovek stood out in the sandy channel as the rain gathered, trying to catch it on his face, while Zhenshchina sheltered beneath the listing hull and wept. Every time the camera cut to her she was crying harder.

Beth sensed him at her shoulder and pulled one headphone from her ear. The Russians argued tinnily, and he strained to listen.

'Where did you find this?' he said.

'The machine.'

'It's not quite finished.'

'Jack, I'm sorry.'

'It's—'

He started to answer, but saw that she was crying as well. He stared at her. She didn't cry often, or hadn't until recently. He looked at the screen, confused.

'I didn't think it was such a tear-jerker.'

'Jack.'

'Maybe you can explain it to me.'

'Look, Jack.'

Chelovek had started to sing. A traditional Russian song; Jack had heard it before. A song about a drunken farmer. Chelovek had a fine singing voice, a forceful baritone. His subtitles appeared in italics to indicate singing.

The subtitles were nonsense. *Jfeef34r werrij4d efij39f*, sang Chelovek. *Leok2er weri$f l8r(rf c* efr*. They appeared a half-second after he opened his mouth, remained on-screen for the right length of time. Only two lines at once, fifty or sixty characters, all nonsense.

Zhenshchina chastised him in the same non-language. *Dijf8oij doewdww 23d @ef8u*, she shouted. *Dew%H weu#(hRr cS&F!*

Jack frowned. 'That's not right, is it?'

She shook her head slowly. 'I don't think so.'

'What's happened?'

'It was fine to start with. Then a couple of spelling mistakes, you know they just sit wrong. Then whole words that didn't make sense, numbers, symbols. It's like this from about twenty minutes in.'

'This is on the tape?'

'I don't know, I suppose.'

He had burned a script's worth of nonsense. He had weighed up every nuance, pondered over synonyms and idioms, and ended up with static.

'The program must be playing up.'

'Yes, it must be.'

He knew that it wasn't. The program would take whatever he typed and record it to the videotape. It would faithfully translate his madness.

'Turn it off,' he said.

He didn't want to think about it. He returned to his fledgling transcription of the manuscript, and found he couldn't read it. He rubbed his forehead but the letters wouldn't resolve. And everything in the church was the same: the posters, piles of unread newspapers. He couldn't read any of it.

'We're a pair, aren't we, Jack?'

'I suppose we are.'

'You spent so long on this ...'

'I don't know what that is.'

'While I end up – I don't even know. Not myself, not sure of anything.'

'You're all right.'

But it was a reflex. She's pretty: yes, pretty. That's a pretty dress: I'll buy you one like it. He didn't know whether he meant it, he didn't know what he meant. He couldn't understand anything. The subtitles he knew to be gibberish, the newspapers that probably weren't: they all looked the same.

The film continued, and the subtitles made no more sense. He heard the tinny dialogue and knew what the translation should have been, and knew that the letters on the screen had nothing to do with any of it. But Beth kept watching, she couldn't look away.

'I went to see Mum tonight,' she said.

'That's where you were?'

'I asked her.'

'You asked her?'

'I asked her if she'd had an affair.'

Jack stared at her. 'What did she say?'

Beth turned from the screen. She looked frayed; she looked like the pictures she had drawn. Her lips trembled.

'She said they had their problems, they didn't see eye to eye on everything. They didn't want to worry me so they kept some parts of their relationship from me.'

'Beth.'

'She said they always loved each other, that was the truest thing.'

The words sounded even less convincing than when Judy had spoken them less than a week ago. Did they sound that way to Beth? Surely she knew how completely she'd been betrayed: that was why she looked so wretched, so torn. Surely she wasn't using her mother's words as proof against him.

'I'm sorry,' he said, not certain she'd know what he meant.

The Russian film had finished, the nonsense subtitles faded at last, and Beth had the headphones around her neck. Her face crinkled with a kind of longing that was something like Zhenshchina's, and a kind of sympathy that was unlike anything that had passed between the Russians. And unlike Zhenshchina she stood and crossed the floor to him, she pressed her palms into his thighs as she leaned forward and kissed him, sadly; and he felt the old waves of tenderness and hope working again at the shoals of his heart, and wished, as he always did, that he had the words to tell her about it.

6 Jack slept deeply for the first time in the three weeks since the hailstorm, an exhausted and dreamless sleep. Even when he woke in the last of the darkness, Beth still huddled against him, he felt for a moment that the world was less threatening and more reasonable than it had seemed. The hole in the roof was striped with new joists, the light through the tarpaulin soft and blue in the dawn. The shadows in the church were just shadows.

Then he heard a small sound from the churchyard, and though it was probably a magpie hopping in the gravel it was enough to remind him it wasn't safe outside: Sandy was lying in hospital, the Hospitallers were closing in on the manuscript. And as Beth rolled away from him he tried to understand what had happened last night. What did she think Judy had told her, and what would she do now? Had she forgiven him for his clumsy help? The night had been a relief, but he had woken to find things as they were.

He lay unmoving in the overcast light until she woke, half an hour later. She prepared slowly, heavy across the floorboards, labouring with her stockings. She bent to kiss him and he heard the tired sound of her bones.

'Don't go to work today,' he said.

'I have to.'

'It's not safe out there.'

'I know, isn't it awful. Poor Sandy.'

'It isn't safe for you either.'

She stepped into her shoes. 'I'll be fine.'

He swallowed. 'There are – what happened to Sandy,' he

said. 'What happened at the forensics centre. They weren't accidents.'

She gave him a concerned look. 'What were they?'

'They were—' He didn't know what to say. Who was it, exactly? The St John Ambulance, some other cult? He knew how either would sound, even to Beth – especially to her. 'They had something to do with the manuscript,' he finished.

She blinked a few times. He didn't like the way she was looking at him, as if he were a zealot on a street corner. 'I have to go,' she said.

He reached for his car keys. 'I'll drive you.'

'No – it's fine.'

There was a weary pity in her eyes. He held his keys and watched her as she buttoned her jacket and clipped up her hair. He flinched as she opened the door, but there was nothing he could do. He couldn't stop her leaving the church.

Perhaps she was safer away from him. The laboratory explosion hadn't been meant for Ash, or the beating for Sandy. Beth should stay as far from the church as she could. They'd find their way here, whoever they were; they'd be coming. And he could only think of one way to defend himself, one weapon against them.

The sun rose higher and the colours of the stained glass drifted across the floor. Max and O'Rourke climbed onto the roof without bothering him. They seemed more hurried than usual. Their shadows passed over the dwindling hole as he pressed open the letter and the manuscript and looked for his salvation, the secret words that would protect him if only he could read them.

Kirk had described the lunatic's speech as fluent and musical; his language would have many of the features Jack had assumed when he thought the manuscript was Wilkins's perfect invention. The notes he had made about plosives and liquids might still apply, the vowels and consonants would still line up. He returned to his notebook and found the passage about Babel and Shinar. It hadn't conjured the images that had moved the Crusaders, but he'd never heard it out loud, and that might have made the difference. Language was natural, but reading was an invention; it used a different part of the brain.

No – he had heard it once. He just hadn't been listening. Dev had spoken a line in the Deposit, and the shapes had begun to rise in his mind – dim and unformed, but it had only been a line. Jack tried to remember what the baby had said: a slight reassortment, a small vowel shift. He tinkered with his correspondences, embarrassed to be taking advice from a baby, but remembering what Kirk had said about his lunatic. His swollen head, his missing teeth. He didn't know what the head meant, but without teeth he couldn't have said *f*; he would have had to make a kind of *ph* with his lips. He copied the passage again.

Ter sholpal tikim pə nashi owal lekim əs owal tokim. Shol mushom pə ekayi bekh epim əs pə ahuki latim is Shinarim əs pə esti əhim. Akim pə ə toki as rapim tizh wim azh atuki eph wim as kultim əs as bergim takh kir kotim namti ukh ostikim əs wim azh tuki eph wim as nipim atiph wim ozh sherte alukh tikir phaltim. Er barakim pə sherti as akim bekh ə shim alukh tikir phaltim əs akim pə khepi as atuka tar kultim. Er kim pə nipe as Babelim tizh re barakim pə əshim babi as shol tikir lekim əs barakim pə bekh əshim sherti as akim alukh tikir phaltim.

He read it aloud as the builders clattered on the roof. He tried to mimic the baby's pronunciation, but he hadn't heard enough of it. And yet his mind was cast back to the silty floodplain, the gathering people, the tower to heaven – it was the half-built tower of the manuscript's front page, but vivid with detail and dimension, like the stereoscopic photograph of the church they'd seen in the library. Constant had marked the page with a reference from Genesis, and the monk wasn't just being allusive: it was more or less a retelling of the biblical account. Jack reached for the King James Version, and the manuscript and the letter and the Bible all seemed to connect in an uncomfortable trinity.

And the whole earth was of one language, and of one speach. And it came to passe as they iourneyed from the East, that they found a plaine in the land of Shinar, and they dwelt there. And they sayd one to another; Goe to, let vs build vs a city and a tower, whose top may *reach* vnto heauen, and let vs make vs a name, lest we be scattered abroad vpon the face of the whole earth.

And the LORD said; Behold, the people *is* one, and they *haue* all one language: and this they begin to doe: and now nothing will be restrained from them, which they haue imagined to doe. Goe to, let vs go downe, and there confound their language, that they may not vnderstand one anothers speech.

So the LORD scattered them abroad from thence, vpon the face of all the earth: and they left off to build the Citie. Therefore is the name of it called Babel, because the LORD did there confound the language of all the earth: and from thence did the LORD scatter them abroad vpon the face of all the earth.

He traced the lines with trembling fingers: first the manuscript, then the Bible. They seemed to align perfectly: *Ter sholpal tikim pə nashi owal lekim əs owal tokim* meant *And the whole earth was of one language and of one speech.* So *owal* meant *one*, and probably *lekim* meant *language* and *tokim* meant *speech.* Nouns seemed to end with *-im*, adjectives with *-al*, so *sholpal tikim* was probably *whole earth.* The rest were more opaque, but he was sure he'd be able to work out the details.

His head spun as he glimpsed the possibilities behind the old story. The explanation in Genesis wasn't literally true, but perhaps the whole earth had once spoken the same language. The Babel tongue had been shattered into six thousand pieces not by a nervous God but by the forces of language change, predictable and chaotic as the weather. And there might have been other kinds of truth in the account. *Now nothing will be restrained from them which they have imagined to do*: what might the world have achieved if everyone could understand each other perfectly?

Someone was climbing the porch steps. The handle rattled against the door. Jack covered the manuscript with the letter, the letter with his notebook, the notebook with the Bible, and hid them all beneath his desk. Someone was fumbling with the lock. It was barely midday; Beth would be at the library for hours. Jack stood and backed towards the oratories, bumping against the pews. The door swung open and Beth stood in the porch.

He didn't have time to calm himself before he saw that she wasn't alone. A middle-aged man – an old man – stood behind her, staring into the church. He had a round head with a tonsure of grey-brown wisps, watery eyes and a smooth, tanned scalp. He wore an old suit that looked like it was made of carpet, a woollen tie with an uncommon knot. He held a tweed cap in one hand, over his heart. He looked nervous, and Beth bit her lip and couldn't stop blinking. Jack's first thought was that the man was holding her hostage; there was a stiffness to her movements that suggested a gun in the back.

'Are you all right?' he said.

'I'm fine,' she said. 'This is Sam. He's an old family friend.'

Jack searched her face for a signal, a shake of the head invisible to anyone else. There was something behind her eyes, but it wasn't what he was looking for. It didn't look like terror; he couldn't tell what it was. The old man took a tentative step into the nave and held out his hand. It felt like paper.

'You're home early,' Jack said to Beth.

'I ran into Sam,' Beth said. 'We've been talking.'

It was hard to imagine; Sam still hadn't said a word. Now the old man cleared his throat and couldn't think of anything. But there was something in the air that convinced Jack, the threads of a long conversation that still hung over them. If Sam really was a family friend, then it must have been about Frank. What had he told her?

There was a heavy thump above them, and a shower of sand fell from the roof. Jack looked up and got sand in his eyes. He blinked and rubbed his face.

'*Izvinite*,' Max called down to them. He spoke Russian after all, and Jack understood him – but everything else was dislocated. He opened his eyes again. Beth was looking up at the roof with the panic he had expected when she first came in. Everything was out of order.

She turned back to Jack. 'Can we take Sam to the lab?'

There was still a grain of sand in his eye. 'What lab?'

'The forensics centre, where your friend works.'

Jack felt an unfolding horror. 'Why?'

'He's got a – he can't really talk about it. He needs some analysis done. We thought perhaps your friend – Ash, isn't it? – might be able to help.'

So that was it. Jack had covered his tracks as well as he could, he'd locked the church against his enemies – and at last they had reached him through Beth. He looked deeper into her eyes for the flicker that told him *don't* or *I'm sorry*, but there was nothing like that. She wasn't being forced against her will, she just didn't know.

Sam saw him hesitating. 'I'm sorry to interrupt your morning,' he said. 'I did rather hope you could help. This – analysis, as Beth says. It's a bit delicate, to be honest, and also quite urgent.'

His voice was mild, his accent gentlemanly. But there was no mistaking the threat behind his pleasantries, the way he said *Beth*. If he didn't get what he wanted, she would suffer for it. If only she knew – but here she was exchanging glances with the old villain, a shared secret. What choice did Jack have? He nodded and went for his keys.

As he followed them from the church he noticed that the heels of Beth's stockings were brushed with sand. It must have come from the roof, but he couldn't see exactly how.

He took the most direct route, since they had already found him. The back streets might have given him more time to think, but he couldn't take any risks with Beth in the car. Why the forensics centre, and not the St John headquarters? Was Ash at the centre of it all, had he almost lost his hands bombing his own building – or allowed himself to be blasted to deflect suspicion? Jack cursed himself for trusting him. The signs had been there: his fascination with old documents, his insistence that the manuscript was a forgery. Peter had sent Jack to him – was he involved as well? Was there anyone he could trust?

The last weeks of autumn had brought restless skies. Twists of cloud passed over the sun, edges gleaming as Jack drove along the main road to the city. The traffic was mercifully bad – Sam couldn't blame him for that – but he still couldn't think quickly enough. If only he'd had more time, if only he'd been able to solve the manuscript. Beads of sweat slid down the back of his neck, and he shifted gears and worked the clutch.

'Nice church you've got there,' Sam said from the back seat.

'You've seen it before, haven't you?' Beth said.

In the rearview mirror, Jack saw Sam glance at Beth. It looked like a question. 'Must have been past it a thousand times, over the years,' Sam said. 'Maybe went inside for a wedding or a funeral, once. I'm not too religious.'

'Me neither,' Beth said.

Perhaps she was doing the right thing – going along with this masquerade, pretending that Sam really was a kindly old man in a fix, even a friend of the family. Jack didn't know how long she'd spent with him: perhaps the whole morning, long enough to work out the safest way to deal with him.

'Do you live around here, Sam?' Jack said, ashamed at the creak in his voice.

'Oh, yes,' Sam said. 'All my life.'

'It must have changed a lot.'

'Yes and no.'

How natural it almost sounded, hardly different from any conversation between two men of different generations who'd just met. You wouldn't know that this old man was silently directing Jack to his probable doom for a thousand-year-old order bent on a powerful manuscript – and Jack felt a sudden doubt. Why hadn't Sam made any effort to bring the manuscript with them? He hadn't even looked for it.

'Sam's got a place down by the water,' Beth said.

Was that a look of gratitude in the mirror? He glanced over to Beth and saw the confused warmth in her expression, the tears in her eyes. Perhaps the old man didn't know anything about the manuscript after all – Jack didn't want to think about it. Because something was going on, and if it wasn't the conspiracy Jack had no idea what it could be.

The laboratory building had almost recovered during the ten days since the explosion. The pathologists and chromatographers would know where the walls had been repaired, where the paint didn't match, but perhaps nobody else would notice. Jack scuffed the grass for any evidence beyond his lingering skullache, his paranoid thoughts. He bent to pick up a sparkling prism of glass and spun it between his fingers. He clenched it in his fist and set his jaw as he followed Sam and Beth into the forensics centre.

Past a new bank of metal detectors and reinforced guards and through the sterilised corridors, he saw the real effects of the explosion. Last time the lights had brightened every corner of the laboratory; now there were shadows and hiding places. Despite the extra security the building felt vulnerable.

Ash didn't look happy to see him, and Jack couldn't blame him. If Sam had nothing to do with the manuscript, then neither did the laboratory, neither did Ash – they only had Jack in common. Ash tried to cover his discomfort with help-fulness. But he was right: whatever was going on here, they were all in danger. If the Hospitallers hadn't caught Jack they couldn't be far away, and he had been lured away from the church and the manuscript.

He agreed reluctantly to leave Sam and Beth to talk to Ash in private. He peered through the tinted front doors before venturing outside; they opened and shut as he waited. The sky was still smudged with clouds, but the light was glossy and bright. Jack crouched with his back against the wall, watching the car and the parkland beyond it. The trees, the buildings and citizens seemed to be hung with billowing paper. There was something deep within them that only Jack could see. They had forgotten their true names, but he would remind them.

When Beth emerged from the laboratory he thought she had closed the door twice, and as her footsteps tripped across the courtyard it looked like there were two of her, each moving in the other's wake like the pictures she'd drawn. Sam followed behind her, looking uncertain around the edges as well.

'How was that?' Jack said.

Sam gave him a blank smile. 'Thanks for that. I'll find out in a few days.'

'I hope it's not serious,' Jack said.

'It's serious,' Sam said. 'But not life-threatening.'

Beth flickered for an instant and was herself again. 'Do you mind taking Sam back? I've got to get to the library.'

'I'll drive you there.'

'It's all right, I'll walk. I could use a walk.'

'I was going to check on Sandy.'

'I'll see her after work. I'll give her your best. You should take Sam back.'

'All right.'

But she'd already set out across the parkland towards the city, the buildings fluttering in the breeze. He turned to Sam.

'Where to?'

'The church is fine. Don't want to trouble.'

Sam still wore a nervous expression, a kind of worry in his pale eyes, but he sounded more relaxed: Ash must have helped him, whatever he'd needed. Jack was bewildered. He didn't have the first idea what had happened, who anyone was. Sam turned to him.

'You do the subtitles, don't you?'

'That's right,' Jack said.

'For foreign movies.'

'Mostly.'

'No, I know that sounds stupid. But did you see that movie, English movie – I mean in English, American movie I think. Where there are subtitles but it's what the character's really thinking. Like, a bloke says, pleased to meet you, ma'am, but the subtitle comes up, mate, that's an enormous arse you've got there!'

He rested his arm on the windowframe and tapped on the Citroën's roof. He tilted his head and stroked the loose skin of his neck. He smelled like cigarettes, though he hadn't smoked any.

'I think I did see that one,' Jack said.

'And so *she's* saying, what do you do, young Johnny? And where did you go to school, and that's very interesting. But it just comes up, there is no way you'll be putting anything in my daughter!'

He was babbling, and Jack could suddenly see everything that he'd been holding back. Where had he come from, this garrulous stranger?

'While poor Johnny's saying, why, I'm, I don't know, a physiotherapist and I went to the World's Finest Finishing School of Physiotherapy, but of course the subtitle is Christ, I can't believe Betty's going to wind up with that arse!'

216

He could hardly say *arse* for cracking himself up; he wiped his eyes and grinned helplessly. Jack found himself liking this new Sam. There was something simple and generous about people who told jokes. He wished he could do it. There were a few translation jokes, but they were all terrible … And Sam had stopped laughing. He gave Jack a sideways glance.

'Anyway, I always thought that'd be pretty handy.'

'Sure.'

'I don't mean for arses. I mean when you're putting on a whole song and dance and all you're really trying to say is, are we all right here? Or I like you, do you like me? Or just, thanks, you know.'

'That would be handy.'

'It just seems that a lot of what people say doesn't boil down to much.'

Jack nodded. 'It's like when Nixon goes to China and tells this really long, rambling joke, it takes about half an hour, and Zhou's translating, he says five words to Mao and all the others and they kill themselves laughing. And Nixon tells Zhou, this is incredible – not only do you guys have a great sense of humour, your language is so efficient. How did you tell that whole thing in five words? And Zhou says, I didn't have time. I just said: *He tell joke. Better laugh.*'

They were back at the church. Jack parked on the street and Sam climbed out and crunched through the gravel. He looked up at the stained glass as if he did remember, as if he'd been there before. And Jack kept wondering who he might have been, until after his last goodbye he rounded the corner and lit up a cigarette with a flinty *ch*, the old affricate, and then Jack knew.

∪)

The church was finished. Max and O'Rourke had replaced the last roofstones and taken the tarpaulin away. The harbour scene was too high to see properly, but it was there:

a pattern surrounded by smoothness, a slight shadow. Apart from that, everything was as it had been. As if nothing had happened, no hailstorm, no crypt or manuscript, no bombing and no forensics centre.

But it had all happened. Two weeks ago he had taken the manuscript to the forensics centre, and he'd just returned with the old man. Sam had nothing to do with the manuscript after all: he was Judy's smoking friend, her old or new lover. Jack had been right all along, heartbreakingly right. Beth had doubted Judy's denial – perhaps it hadn't even been a denial – and had returned in the morning to find Sam in her house. She must have been devastated. But Jack was touched by the way she had helped the old man, the tenderness she'd shown towards him. There had been another emotion between them that he didn't understand. He didn't know what it was, but he knew how he might find out.

He took the manuscript from the bottom of its pile. The Hospitallers hadn't crept in and taken it, O'Rourke hadn't left with it: Jack still had a chance. He had caught sight of how the manuscript might work, just before Beth had come home with Sam. Now he saw that it could solve all of their problems. He opened it again to the Babel story, the first language and the doomed tower. It was a parable in more ways than he'd thought.

Language let you teach and learn and collaborate. It made you smarter than you really were. It wasn't the shoulders of giants, it was their libraries. The language before Babel had expressed everything, it had encompassed all humanity. It was the kind of language that would let you do anything you had imagined to do, and would let you imagine more than you'd thought possible. It had united the world and raised it almost to heaven.

God had toppled the tower and scattered the people, and perhaps he had been right to do it. But thousands of years later, on a cave in a holy mountain, monks had found a lunatic who remembered that first language and everything it contained. He had built the tower again – not of brick and clay on a great plain, but in his cave and of stone and glass. The machine was at most a metre high – but it gave the outlook that the first tower had almost reached. It could see the truth. It showed the world from the vantage of angels. It was built by, and in every important way it *was*, the first, best and only language.

The sketches of the flasks and struts were blurring into the vellum. Night was falling over the nave. Jack called the hospital to see if Beth had been to visit Sandy yet; they told him that Sandy had been discharged. He tried to call Beth at the library, but nobody could find her: she must have been deep in the stacks or on her way home. He worried about her, out in the twilight, but soon it would be all right. With the lunatic's machine he would foresee every attack, he could keep ahead of them forever. He could see their weaknesses. And when he found out everything Beth needed to know, he would know how to tell her.

He returned to his notebook and continued his transcription. Past the tower, through the scenes from different cultures, the sack-people in their vegetable kingdom. As the pages filled he felt he was stripping away the manuscript's skin and looking at its most secret structure, the trusses and buttresses that held it together. New shapes and patterns appeared in his pencilled tangles, a ragged coastline, contour maps of things never seen. When he was sure he had copied a paragraph properly he read it aloud and listened to its echo in the nave.

The church sounded different with its new roof. They weren't quite images in his mind, and they weren't quite sounds. But they were something: a kind of mourning tinted with hope that he recognised as *saudade,* a sudden view of wretchedness he thought was *litost,* and all more translatable emotions. He was putting the language through its paces. It was wonderful, but the feelings were indistinct, and he couldn't hold them. They wouldn't help him build the machine.

It was after eleven, and Beth still wasn't home. He called Sandy's apartment, but there was no answer. He called Peter, who told him that he had taken Sandy to her parents' house: her concussion had passed. Peter agreed to call his police friends to see if the hospitals had reported Beth, but it hadn't been long. He was sure she was fine.

Jack wasn't so sure. The way she had hurried from the forensics centre, the connection she seemed to have with Sam. His shiny scalp, the angle of his neck – and Jack felt a troubling suspicion taking shape. He tried to remember the man in Beth's photographs, the man he didn't believe in. He glanced around the church, but she'd tidied the pictures away. He looked for the cardboard box, but it wasn't in the oratories, or in the kitchen, or under any of the pews.

The fragments of the church, the molester she thought she'd found. Jack had set her straight, and at last she'd confronted Judy and discovered Sam. Now she was involved in his forensics, and her photos were missing. A cold feeling settled in Jack's stomach. He thought she'd given up the imagined man, but she hadn't. She thought the man in the pictures was Sam.

He hadn't understood the emotions that had rolled over her in the church, in the car, at the laboratory. He'd thought she was terrified, or upset, or just overcome. Now he thought it was all of those, but in the end she had just been lost. To herself, and now to him. Was she safe, at least, with a friend or with Judy? It was too late to call them, and too complicated. He wished he had his machine, his lens of truth. His transcription broke over the lines of his notebook, filling the page. He muttered the words into the night air and stone of the church, trying different emphases and accents, and saw new colours and heard otherworldly music, but it wasn't enough.

In the middle of the night he crept from the church and drove through the suburbs. The orange streetlights made everything flat. He took the manuscript with him, and glanced at it as the traffic lights cycled from red to green. He could read it without transcribing it, now. He couldn't understand it, but he could read it.

He parked outside Judy's house. There was a single dim light in one of the bedrooms, perhaps a candle, sinuous shadows moving behind the curtains. Jack felt disturbed but in a small way privileged by this evidence of their secret. Had Sam always been there, invisible to the eye? He didn't know, not yet. And other shadows were gathering in the street, sharper angles and edges. He had to get back to the church.

Beth hadn't come home. The church was empty and cold, it was all crypt. Jack fell into an exhausted sleep, and woke a few hours later with the first light. He searched the oratories again for the box of pictures and photos – it felt like the most important trace of her. If he could only see the pictures again, the enlargements that had convinced her. But the box was gone.

The film projector sat on a pew like it always did. A little grey cube with two arms raised, as if in surrender. He noticed that the film wasn't threaded through the gate, but hung in two parts from the reels: it had been cut in half. Jack held one end up to the light and saw the tiny shapes of Beth and Judy at the beach, each square almost identical to the last.

She'd left him something after all. But she'd taken something too: when he wound the film back through the projector he saw that the severed ends were cut at different angles and didn't match up. She must have snipped out a frame – it couldn't have been much more than a frame, the blink of a mechanical eye – and given it the same treatment as the other pictures, blowing it up until its shapes and colours diverged.

He found scissors and sticky tape and did his best to splice the film together. His fingers were numb and clumsy; it wasn't a convincing restoration. He wound the film through the gate and unrolled the screen in the middle of the nave.

They were back at the beach, Frank and Judy and little Beff, taking turns with the camera. She was six or seven, and her parents were in their late twenties, younger than Jack and Beth were now. The film was old and the camera shuddered. Everything was slightly faster than life-like, the waves lapped and receded too quickly. Beff was keen to swim: she tugged at her parents, jumping in the sand. Other bathers and sunbathers watched her and smiled. It was a sunny day, though the film's colours had faded and dawn light was filling the church. The camera panned the beach and he recognised it now. It was the narrow strip at Camp Cove.

The picture darkened for an instant as the sticky tape slipped through the gate. The projector only rested with the shutter closed, the image couldn't be paused, so he had to watch it forward and back. The whole beach coordinated in a shaky and repetitive dance, a step, a reconsideration, a step back, as he scanned the crowds, the blurry observers, until he found Sam.

It could have been him. Something about the angle of his limbs, the way he stretched his neck. He had hair, but it was already thinning. There was a moment when he looked straight into the camera, a moment that lasted longer than all the others. It was an unreliable image, never quite in focus. Sam had rescued her that day; he had been there all her life. It could have been anybody, but it was probably him, and that had been enough for her.

The sky was heavy and overcast; it gave nothing but twilight. They drove all day, Jack at the wheel, Judy beside him, Sam leaning from the back seat. It felt pointless but they had to keep moving, slowing for every shadowed park, every huddle of smokers, and home to check for lights or movement. They travelled further every time but always returned to graze the church, a long orbit through the suburbs.

Sam and Judy had said nothing to each other. Judy kept her gaze locked to her part of the view, her mouth set in an expression of sadness but not surprise – as if something she had always known would happen finally had, and at least it was no worse than she had imagined. Sam moved restlessly behind them, trying to catch Judy's eye in the rearview mirror, holding the top of her seat so he could brush her shoulder with his fingers.

It seemed to Jack an oddly familiar arrangement, the man and the woman, and he thought he understood both the mood of the car and other tensions that had puzzled him long ago. Sam had done what he'd needed to, and could be only partly sorry. Judy was angry, but she was also in love, and had been for a long time; and although she didn't look back she leaned into Sam's fingers, into his touch.

When she spoke at last it was to Jack. She looked at him almost defiantly.

'I suppose you think I'm terrible.'

And she was, in the way that everything that turned out to be more flawed and complicated than it should have been was terrible: ruined cities, drunken gods, frail parents. She sat there with her terrible lusts, and she was terrible. Jack had never felt more tender towards her. But he looked away from her, back out into the twilight and the road.

'I just want to find Beth.'

They had all spent most of their lives on this sloping headland, wedged between the harbour and the ocean. Even in his three years with Beth they had covered most of its ground together, strolling its parks, trying to find its parties. Everywhere he looked held a memory of her. It must have been worse for Judy – and even for Sam, if he'd been appended to their lives for so long.

He turned back to Judy and saw that she was still watching him. He glanced past her and through her window, trying to prompt her, but she wouldn't look away. His eyes flickered back to her.

'I don't think you're terrible.'

'You do. You think I'm insensitive, that I've just rushed into this.'

'No – not at all. The opposite.'

She raised an eyebrow. 'Or that I was just waiting until Frank was gone. That I could hardly wait.'

'Not even that.'

'You don't think I did wait. But I did, and I would have waited a lot longer. Not for Frank to die. I was waiting for him to come back.'

Jack glanced at Sam in the rearview mirror. The old man allowed his mouth the smallest twist. Judy noticed Jack's look, as she seemed to notice everything, and shot him an irritated sideways glance.

'Ten years he pretended to build that damned church. Ten years, while I got old and wrinkled and he wouldn't believe there was nothing going on, that we were only having lunch. As if I wouldn't have lunch with him after what happened.'

In the mirror, Sam lowered his eyes. 'You don't have to—'

Judy waved him into silence. 'Sam says somebody else

ould have rescued her, that day. And I would have had
nch with whoever did, whoever it was. Lunch, and that's
ll. But Frank felt so guilty, he thought I must have been
nfaithful. He almost wanted it, he thought he deserved it.
He was an idiot sometimes.'

There was such a chord of tired affection in her voice that
or a moment Jack believed her: everything had been fine
ntil one day Frank had gone for ice-cream and wasn't there
o rescue his daughter, and his pride had banished him to the
church. Not a loss of faith but a lack of it, a mean appraisal
f a wife's love. That might have been part or even most of
, but Frank deserved more.

'He didn't know?'

'Know what?'

'What Sam was doing there, at the beach, in the first
ace.'

She gave him the look that he always thought of first,
henever he thought of her. It was a look that promised to
e dismissive if it could muster the interest, a drawbridge
ok. But now it softened, and she looked away.

'No, he didn't know.'

'Because Beth worked it out from the photos and the film.
nd he had all that there with him, in the church, and a lot
f time.'

'Beth didn't work it out. Sam told her.' She gave the mirror
sharp glance, and Sam sat back in his seat and stared out of
e window. 'I told him it was my husband's; it wasn't his,'
e went on. 'As soon as I found out. A woman knows, I just
new. It was an irresponsible, an utterly thoughtless thing, it
most ended my marriage before it had started. But it wasn't
bad as it could have been.'

He watched Sam's face as Judy spoke, but the old man just
oked at the mirror with a blank resignation. He'd had thirty
ars to think about all of this, years of lurking, of keeping an
e, and then years of lunches and waiting: nothing would
rprise him. Only Judy felt there was any more to talk about.

'And I would have told Frank, if he'd been anybody else. Told him and waited until he forgave me. But I knew he wouldn't. Because of his church, and his family – everything I was so afraid of in the first place. So instead I pretended it hadn't happened. I forgot that it had happened, until that day on the beach.'

Sam gave a sad smile. 'You can't blame me for wondering, though.'

'I told you.'

'You told me, but I couldn't know like you knew. I always wondered, what if. How it could have been. One week and you spend the rest of your life wondering.'

It was a lot of talk and didn't amount to much, like Nixon's joke. All they were saying was *understand me*, like everyone else: *understand me and love me anyway*. Jack knew he'd failed Beth – he understood that much – but was only beginning to see the depths and chasms of his failure, how he'd kept so many things to himself, how he'd left her alone to discover the paper and wire of her family, and what lay behind it. There were answers in the manuscript, but not the kind she'd wanted.

At the clifftop cemetery, in the sudden calm above the twilit sea, he thought they might find her draped over Frank's grave. Tracing the crisp chisellings with her fingers, husband of Judy, father of Beth, neither of them as true as she'd thought. He thought he understood her pictures, now; he understood the colours. But she wasn't there.

ᴗ)

The twilight wouldn't shift. The headlights looked feeble as the road rose and the land narrowed. The inevitability of driving in the east, the way it eased you in the one direction. Judy looked around and turned to him uncertainly.

'Where is this, where are we going now?'

'Not much further.'

'It isn't – you can't possibly think she'd—'

'No, it's not that.'

North and east, the pull of the cliffs. The encouraging stairs, the acquiescent barriers. The stations of heartbreak. He didn't think she'd – he hadn't thought she'd.

'Oh, it's the lighthouse. You gave me a fright.'

'You've given me one.'

He left the car running and thumped across the road and the wet grass. The lighthouse beam swept overhead, still pale. The hill was slippery and sent his feet skidding. They called after him as he reached the crest and stumbled down the slope, over the last fence and towards the edge. She wouldn't jump from the Gap, with all the suicide tourists: she would jump here.

'Jack!'

'It's not safe!'

He couldn't see anything. No broken body embracing the rockshelf. No library blouse snagged on a tree, no library shoe rolling in the surf. But he couldn't see through the spray, and she could have been sucked out by the sea already.

'For God's sake, Jack!'

They were leaning over the fence. He listened to the waves for echoes of her scream. The beams flinging across the horizon, firming as the darkness fell. He stared out to sea, and a new doubt appeared like a distant tanker. This was where she brought boyfriends. She wasn't here, and yet, and yet. He had assumed she would want to be alone, but what if she had run to someone else?

'Jack, what are you doing?'

'She isn't here!'

His clothes were wet from the undergrowth; his hands were muddy and cold. He was scratched by rocks and branches and had bruised his knees. He felt suddenly heavy. Who had she run to? Who had she met?

She had been gone for a day and a half. Jack had hoped to find her before this. They all must have hoped it. They hadn't tried the most obvious place first, the place that connected them all.

The sea was grey before them, almost black. There was not much wind, not much rain. The sand was cold and cratered, a wet crust that collapsed under their feet. A few last birds were circling. On one side the harbour, on the other the sea. Red and green beacons drifted towards home.

Two decades ago they had all been here. Something had happened, though there was disagreement. A rescue or sabotage, everyone crying into the sand. A reunion without a parting, a confused combination of beginnings and ends.

Now they were back. Frank had gone missing for a moment and now for good. They had saved Beth once, but lost her again. He thought there might have been a confrontation. But instead they sat in the sand, at some distance from each other; they sat in the sand and said nothing. They stared out to sea, and drew patterns or let the sand run through their fists. They sat there as dusk and then night fell at last, and Jack sat a way off and watched them. They were all old, and none of them understood anything.

Jack spent the night at the edge of delirium. Drops of sweat shattered off him like dropped crystal. Time owed forwards and back. He dreamed or knew or imagined er return a thousand times. She set him riddles in different nguages. She was at the window, the church door. She came ome all night, but never came home. He was alone with irits and whispers that made him believe anything. First uild an impossible machine. First defeat a conspiracy of adows. He was suffocating with the weight of them. Some oor of his mind banged on its hinges. Where had she gone? ho had she met? When would she come back, and when ould she stop coming back?

He got up at the sky's first rumour of dawn, the moon still , the stars still out. He clasped his hands to his skull to ep it closed, and returned to the only thing that could keep m together, the only thing that could still save them.

is head filled with dark suggestions as he read the manu- ript from the beginning – as if he were watching a film rough thick glass, listening to a whispered story. People re divided and spoke many languages: that was the broken d abandoned tower, but perhaps it was something else as ll. The next sections showed all the world's cultures, and scribed their languages and writing systems, their hand gnals. Then – he wasn't quite as sure – the universe's other nguages, everything that could be read: the rings of tree- inks, the paths of stars and planets, and the chemical gnatures whose replication was life. *Accidents and rumours*

whose only occupation is to spread, the lunatic had told Kirk
It sounded like DNA, and Jack found a page full of the same
four letters repeated in different combinations. Earth, air, fire
and water; or whatever A, C, G and T stood for – he couldn'
tell, but the point was clear: it was all a mess. The seventy
two languages after Babel didn't begin to describe it.

But there was a way out – a machine that could interpret
all of these languages and more, a universal translator, a lens
of truth. It would make sense of every mystery. You could
direct it at people and see their past and potential. You could
point it at the world and find your lover illuminated.

Instructions for the machine took up the largest part of the
manuscript, starting with the ingredients, the plants and
minerals. The images in Jack's head weren't clear enough, but
Wilkins had marked them with his alphabet: lapis lazuli
madder and woad, trubs which were truffles, spunge or
asparagus root. Constant had referred to the Book of
Revelation, and Jack looked up the verse: *The first foundation was Iasper, the second Saphir, the third a Chalcedony
the fourth an Emerald.* The alchemists had added their
symbols for lead and gold and mercury. There were a few he
couldn't identify, outlandish crystals in colours he wasn't sure
he'd seen before. But he only had to work out enough to
build the machine, enough to find her.

Each group of ingredients surrounded a flask or barrel or
bottle. Each container found its place in the apparatus
described in the last part. They were held by wooden claws
raised by levers, heated over flames, poured into prisms
They were penetrated by arrows and bathed in light, and the
machine glowed with their colours. The instructions were
barely comprehensible, they forced the roots into every part
of speech – *woad the galled sponge, saffronly engold the
myrrhing mercury* – but he would read them perfectly, soon
enough.

The end of the manuscript escaped him. The fiery tower
the rain that had led him astray. There were drawings he

hadn't noticed before: a woman emerging from a book, two pictures that seemed identical but were on inspection completely different. There were bottles of wine and carvings in stone, storms and music and a city's tallest towers poking through the desert. It didn't matter. He knew what the machine was for and had at least crude instructions to build it. He wanted to start right away, to scour worksites for timber, laboratories and nurseries for ingredients. But he was torn between going to look for her and waiting for her to come home.

He could usually sense her about to arrive, or thought he could: some disturbance in the air that announced her. But he felt nothing as the morning heaved past. She seemed ever further as he searched the dense end of the manuscript and caught the glint of light off secrets but could make nothing out. She seemed impossibly far, as if she had escaped to other dimensions.

The manuscript was breaking its own rules, drifting from its now-familiar alphabet and introducing new characters: a picnic table, a beer glass. They didn't quite fit, weren't part of the perfect alphabet. He should have paid more attention.

Because here was one that he must have skipped or looked at wrong, which he was certain he hadn't seen before: he would have remembered it. He hadn't seen it before – or not in the manuscript. It was a simple letter, two lines meeting at an angle. It was drawn casually; it fitted in with the rest of the text, easy to miss. But its single angle was unmistakable.

It was Beth's tattoo.

$$\upsilon]$$

He thought a thousand things at once. The tattooed bombers, the blackened laboratory, the secret Hospitallers. Sandy wordless in hospital, the blood on the steps. The path was dropping away from him, a sheer slope. If she was one of them and had always been – wait a minute. If she knew what the machine was, if she had seen its – wait a minute. If everything she had said, everything he had tried to understand about her – wait, wait. He tried to stop himself but couldn't.

The church was cluttered already. The oratories were packed with plastic bags and cardboard boxes. The kitchen overflowed with items they had forgotten they had and kept buying. He rifled through the piles, lifting a flap, examining a shoebox. He kept having to remind himself he was awake.

Ash had told him that everything left a trace. A note, a receipt, hotel shampoo, a bus ticket. Any clue that might tell him where she was. He searched all afternoon and into the night. The crypt only held wine; there was nothing new under the flagstone. Judy rang with no news. He called the library and each of the librarians. He called the police and – cautiously – the hospitals. He called the coast guard. There had been no sign of her.

Had they taken her to punish him, to warn him off? Or had they persuaded her to join them, or had she always been with them? None of it made any sense. She'd had the tattoo for years, since long before he'd read the manuscript – or he thought she had. Was the manuscript changing beneath him? He felt it pressing against his head from inside and out, turning his skull to paper.

Of course it was always in the last place you looked. When you found it, you stopped looking. Under the bed, pushed behind boxes and books: a folded piece of paper in the last place. He unfolded it and thought it was blank. But it was scratched, like the manuscript. Something had been written against it. It belonged to the phone pad, a strip of gum at one edge. It wasn't Beth's handwriting; it wasn't her message. It looked like the handwriting of a child, or someone writing with effort. It was a scratched address.

He drove south and west for almost an hour, away from the harbour and the ocean, through the failing light. The streets grew wider, the buildings larger and further apart. Whose address was it, and when had it been scratched? Why had they lured her out here? He had brought the manuscript with him. Let them do what they wanted with it, as long as they gave her back.

The house looked just like its neighbours, except that it had been abandoned. He could tell as soon as he pulled up outside it. The drawn blinds, the unraked leaves, no footprints or tyre tracks, too much junk mail. And a silence inside, expanding where the echoes of occupation had faded.

He knocked and tried to peer through the cloaked windows. He pulled a wad of catalogues and looked through the mail slot, but couldn't see anything. He clambered over a gate and walked down the side of the house, searching for squints. There wasn't much in the kitchen: bare walls, an unconvincing table. There was a toolbox on the table, gathering dust, and a cardboard box on the floor.

The yard was covered with leaves, brown and crimson with the early winter and slimy with the rain. Bare trees stood clawing each other. Between them, a bulky shape covered with tarpaulin and sacking. The coverings flapped in the wind, and he saw a flash of sand. He pulled off the tarpaulin and was doused with its collected rain.

She was life-size and carved in sandstone. She looked like she had at the beach, soaked in the ocean, coated with sand. She lay on her back with one knee in the air, head tipped backwards, stone hair falling. Stone breasts, curves of thigh, a nude's stone cleft. He felt her abrasive skin and watched her through tears. He blinked and swallowed. He took a step backwards, but the ground was not where he expected it to be.

The mat of leaves sighed and embraced him as he fell. He sat in the leaves and watched her. It was an arresting sculpture, and clearly Beth. He recognised her angles and attitudes, the taper of her calves, the way she crossed one leg behind the other. But there were things he hadn't seen before.

He dug through the leaves and found sand. A suburban beach or desert covered with dead leaves, lined with bare trees. How long had Max taken to carve this statue? He was fast, but there was so much stone and sand. Had she lain naked in the back yard, had leaves fallen on her as she lay? Had she posed for him first, fucked him first? When had the lie begun?

The pile of catalogues he had pulled from the mail slot sat in the leaves beside him; they had fallen with him. But they weren't all catalogues. He flicked through them and found among them a letter to Beth, a computer-generated label to her. The envelope was printed with the logo and details of the forensics centre, stickered and barcoded by a courier company. They hadn't wasted any time. The eye and magnifying glass, and the winged heel.

Out here the houses were churches, shrines to some great dream. But this was more, a temple to Beth. As night fell he sat in the leaves, hands full of sand, surrounded by her. He stared at the statues and wondered who she really was, who she had been.

6 Jack could barely keep to the road as he drove back to the city. O'Rourke must have seen the manuscript all those years ago, and now Max was involved as well. He must have had a tattoo somewhere. After Malta the Knights had gone to St Petersburg, perhaps even Vladivostok. His house in the suburbs, the headquarters of their secret committee, where they met to – but he couldn't keep it up.

She wasn't involved in the conspiracy, she was fucking a builder. He'd waited too long to tell her what Judy had told him, he'd let her think terrible things had happened in the church. He'd done everything else wrong, and Max had been there with his pale eyes and empty stare, and there was infidelity in her blood.

All these secrets, all these uncovered truths. He knew too much already. He could only hope for a better truth beneath it all, something ancient that would bring all these setbacks into the great redemption. He parked in the driveway and locked himself into the church. He checked and double-checked his ingredients. He made lists of everything he needed: wood, clamps, bottles, lenses, plants, minerals. He followed the diagrams and tried to guess the verbs for mix, blend, boil. He tried not to think about her.

He hadn't paid attention, he hadn't understood her quickly enough. The light that saw through you: he didn't have that. He'd caught glimpses of her, the small and unique thing that was truly and only her, but only for an instant. Maybe Max had done better with his searchlight eyes, his flameless gaze. Max had looked down from the roof and seen her in bed: he'd seen her tattoo and known she was one of them. No – he'd just seen her body and wanted it. That day or the next he had pressed his address to her hand. The machine would need bolts and a drill, slow and fierce flames. He wondered how important the shapes of the flasks were, and where he was going to find Job's tears.

Then she came home late, and wore clothes to bed. Her days were naked enough; she was naked for Max and not for him, posing and fucking, perhaps fucking on the sand and leaves as the statue of herself took shape. There was no library, no overtime or filing, no drinks with Sandy. There was only sand and stone and skin and leaves and fucking. She wore clothes because otherwise he would know, he would see the mud and sand and handprints on her skin, the new tattoos – and he would know.

But he still had his manuscript, and whatever it would bring him. It seemed like less, now, but soon it would be more, it would be everything. It wasn't safe outside. The shadows were gathering, the Knights were tracking him down. He'd stay here and build the machine, and nothing would be restrained from him.

ᕦ)

It was dark in the crypt with the trapdoor closed; he hammered and tied by lamplight. Wine cases splintered for their wood, jars and bottles for flasks and lenses. The front door was bolted, the back door latched, the squints covered with blankets. The film projector fused to wood and string at one end, at the other a flat glass plate prepared to catch the final image. The light would reflect and refract through the mirrors and lenses and prisms, and would be transformed by the elixirs he would mix.

The telephone rang, and he ignored it until he remembered Beth. But nobody spoke. It wasn't even breathing, only the faint sound of lurking. Splinters of daylight fell onto the loorboards, and he heard echoes of his thoughts on the phone. Everything in the church reminded him of Beth. He aw the carved roofstone high above him and hoped for nother hailstorm. He hung up and crept back underground.

Day and night passed without distinction. Whenever he vas too tired to focus he slept for an hour or two with a blanket in one of the recesses. Whenever he emerged into the ave he was surprised at the time, the angles of light and darkness. He didn't know how long he had spent building the nachine. It had felt like no time at all, but he looked at the omplexity of the apparatus he had constructed and knew it ad been days. It had expanded, growing new arms and legs, illing the crypt.

He broke the quicksilver from a thermometer and watched scurry around the bottom of his jar. He found coloured halk, and burned a wooden spoon for charcoal: it was lready half-burnt from the Cajun fish. Cornelian was a kind f chalcedony, which was a kind of quartz, and there was uartz in his watch. He unscrewed it with a knife and pulled ut its crystal. He had some lead sinkers from a rare attempt t fishing – they had swum in the moonlight instead. A strand f fuse wire, the verdigris from bathroom pipes, all their ours of baths. Beth had given him a gold ring. He rolled it etween his fingers and remembered three or four things bout her at once.

υ)

horn and Peter rang to ask whether he'd heard from Beth. hey sounded worried, but he couldn't bear to tell them nything. Judy rang to see how he was, and to tell him she as sure Beth would be all right, she just needed time. More hantom calls, and calls he ignored or missed. He wished they ould leave him alone. He just wanted to finish the machine.

On the third or fourth day there was a timid knock on the oor; for a moment he thought it was Beth and felt all the untranslatable emotions. But he opened the door to the daylight and found Sandy standing on the porch steps among the mail and newspapers. Her face was still bruised with painful colours, purple and black against her dark skin. She wore make-up and had done her hair. She wore a tight jumper and he noticed the curve and shadow of her breasts, felt guilty and then defiant.

'Hi, Jack.'

'Are you all right?'

'Are you?'

She looked concerned but also remorseful. He knew what it meant, and why she had come. She touched his arm and he shrugged her off.

'You knew,' he said.

He saw her weighing denials and recognising his resolve. She shifted into a resigned posture. 'I thought it was just a phase, she was confused, best if she just – I don't know. Got it out, her flirting-with-builders. I didn't think it was serious.'

'Not serious.'

'I'm sorry, Jack. I begged her not to do it, I actually begged. I feel so bad, it's a disaster for us all. You know you were my last best hope.'

'You should have told me.'

'I'm devastated.'

She did look devastated. She held her face with the heel of her hand and looked at him with anguish and tears. He felt his anger ebbing, and took her by the arm.

'It's not safe out here.'

She gave him the look the rest of them had given him at the hospital. 'Not safe?'

'I can't tell you anything, it's too dangerous. They've got tattoos, Sandy. You've – you've been attacked already, and it was my fault, I know who it was.'

'What do you mean?'

'The stranger, the tattooed stranger.'

She looked at the ground and he couldn't read her expression. The understanding had suddenly slipped, and he couldn't see what she was hiding.

'Remember?' he said.

Her voice was soft and reluctant. 'It wasn't a stranger.'

'You said—'

'It was a date, he was my date. I'd seen him a couple of times before. I was late, I'd forgotten – the auction. We got into a fight. He did this.'

Why was she lying for them? They must have threatened her with more violence – they must have threatened her baby. Fury and shame flooded over him. Little Dev, who'd taught him so much – he couldn't stand it.

'Come inside,' he told her. 'They'll be back any minute.'

She looked at him as if he were crazy. 'Jack, I'm trying to explain—'

'I know – I know what's going on.'

She looked into his eyes. 'I would have told you. But I was ashamed, to get myself into – he wasn't a good person. None of you would understand why I'd get involved with someone like that.'

'Come inside.'

'No – it's fine, Jack.'

She held his gaze and he almost believed her. Shadows flicked past the squints, disturbing the nave's light. It wasn't safe, not even here. He couldn't do anything for her; he had to let her go. They would all have to look after themselves.

He locked the church door and returned to the crypt. Small piles of minerals and dried plants lay on the rocky floor, charcoal and chalcedony, fuzball and trubs, grouped with the manuscript's instructions. He lit candles and knelt to mix the ingredients, scraping with razorblades, grinding with a mortar and pestle. Some of them combined into coloured dust, others into thick paste. The alloyed quicksilver slowed and darkened, shimmering green. He worked patiently, feeling new power in his fingers. He didn't have any lapis lazuli, no madder or malachite. But he hoped it would be close enough.

The chemicals began to react immediately, foaming, smells and vapours through the crypt. The jars sat in a row, like the bottles Beth had picked her blues from, and their clouds mixed and intertwined. He felt a part of his brain fill with sparkles, like champagne behind his eyes. He knew he was at the threshold.

Rumours of lost languages, the dream of a perfect language, translations abandoned, mysterious regrets. All the things he had hoped the manuscript to be, and what he now knew it to be. A universal translator, an eye of truth, a keyhole to the heart and true nature of things.

A steady rhythm echoed through the crypt, sending the plumes and vapours twisting together. The jars quivered as he lowered them onto their platforms; the candleflames danced as he secured them beneath his flasks. The rising heat, the rolling colours. Some of the mixtures dissolved and brightened. Some held a gritty residue beneath a contrasting fluid. He tightened strings and added struts to bear the new weight.

He was dizzied by the possibilities of his machine. The Russian film translated, a unified field theory described on a napkin. The intractable mess of Beth and her parents, the romantic tragedies: if it happened again, he would be prepared. He could point the machine at himself and invite others to look; he would know and be known. The thought bombarded him as he watched the machine warming to life.

The elixirs bubbled, producing mauve or cobalt ripples of gas. Intoxicating smells wafted through the crypt. He switched on the film projector and a flickering light bounced between the jars and mirrors. The elixirs bent or tinged the beams, and the prisms split and recombined them. The machine was a tangle of light in the crypt's darkness. He passed his hand through the beams and felt them warm him.

But the light was dull and inconstant, and the beams stuttered. Perhaps it was the fragile nature of truth, but he knew he had done something wrong. He had skimped on ingredients. He adjusted the apparatus, stirred the elixirs. But no matter where he pointed the mirrors and prisms, how near or far he moved the lenses, how many candles he added beneath the flasks, he could not coax the beam to the glass plate. It sat dark and dirty, waiting. The machine was incomplete.

ℿ

The telephone rang through the church. It had rung half a dozen times and nobody was ever there. He wondered if it was the Hospitallers making sure he hadn't left, waiting for him to finish their machine. If Beth had been involved, she was no longer here to protect him. If she had never been involved, there was no protection. The presence on the line, the almost-breathing terrified him; he felt it down his neck. But he had to answer it.

'Hello?'

His voice felt rusty and thin. He couldn't remember the last time he had spoken. Perhaps they hadn't heard him.

'Who's there?'

It was someone. He wondered what they were listening for. The bubble of the potions, perhaps; the sound of the light. He felt sweat at his neck.

'Look, if you want me you can come in here, all right? And if you want the machine then for fuck's sake stop calling and let me get on with it.'

The rage felt good. All his rage, his disappointment. He was being defeated at every turn, but he had his rage.

'Then we'll see, all right? Then we'll see what happens. Fuck.'

He hit the phone against the wall and listened again. There was an interruption in the silence, a drawing of breath – like on a record, the imminent singing. But nothing came; there was a slow exhalation, and then nothing.

And then the flint of a cigarette, the telltale sound.

'Sam?' he said.

There was silence on the line, and it was the same silence, the quiet sounds of lurking that he had heard before, many times before. Things matching up, things just beyond his grasp. The phone seemed to be heating up.

'Why are you calling? How long have you been calling?'

'I'm sorry.' And Sam hung up, a snap of static and then real silence.

Jack pulled the phone out of the wall and threw it to the ground. He belted the computer keyboard against his desk until the letters came free and sprayed across the floor. He took a crate of wine and smashed every bottle against the wall, showering himself with glass and wine. It seemed to help, the wrecking. He stooped and listened to the crashing of his heart as the wine coursed down him.

Another percussion, a knocking at the door. They had come for him at last. He lowered the bottle. The knocking stopped and then continued, a strange rhythm. He crept across the floorboards, careful not to creak, remembering the artillery of the hail, the crashing stone that had started it all. Or had it all started a thousand years ago, had everything and even this been illegibly described in the manuscript from the beginning?

'Jack?'

They were using Thorn's voice. Jack clutched the manuscript as he approached the porch door. He looked at its concluding sections, the pages where he couldn't read anything. There were pictures of cloaked and hooded shadows with bright letters on their foreheads. A church with a crooked and blank headstone. And dense horizontal lines, like darkness or fog, in which he was sure he saw a man hiding from enemies.

'You in there?'

The porch door was old and some of its boards had shrunk from each other. He saw daylight between the cracks, and the shift of flesh, and a glint of silver. It really looked like

Thorn. He pressed his face against the door, then opened it cautiously.

'There you are,' Thorn said. 'What's happened to you?'

Jack stared at him. 'What's happened to you?'

Thorn looked like somebody different. A deep furrow of anguish ruined his equable features, and the silver of his hair and eyes and skin seemed tarnished and dull.

'Is Beth back?' he asked.

'Not yet.' Jack couldn't say that he no longer thought she would come back, or that he wouldn't know what to do if she did. Thorn looked worried, but Jack didn't think it was about Beth.

'I didn't know where else to go,' Thorn said.

'What's the matter?'

Thorn followed Jack inside and looked around the nave, the hurled clothes and smashed equipment, shards of green glass. He stared at the blackout curtains over the squints and then nervously at Jack.

'Peter's gone,' he said.

'Gone where?'

'He's met someone else.'

'Who?'

His face folded along its new lines. 'It's Sandy.'

'What?'

'They've been spending all this time together, dancing, you know. And now since the attack, and he's been staying with her, in case the guy comes back.'

'What guy?' Jack said.

'The guy she was seeing, the one who hit her.'

Jack stared blankly. More conspiracies, more tattoos. Or had Sandy been telling the truth after all? It was more elaborate than he'd ever thought, or perhaps much simpler. Thorn looked away.

'He said – he just said he'd fallen in – fallen for her.'

So Peter and Sandy had found a new tragedy, the kind of tearful union that Jack only partly understood. He supposed it made sense: she had only wanted someone to love her and her baby, and Peter had always been there. But they would be torn, barely able to comfort each other.

'I mean, he's never – he's always. He says it shouldn't matter because she's a woman. How am I supposed to – what am I supposed to do?'

And Jack realised that for all his restraint Thorn was probably the more devoted, the more passionate of their couple, and that beneath all his layers was something inexpressible and daunting. His wounds would fester and not heal.

'I can help you,' Jack said. 'I know what will help. But I need some things.'

'What things?'

'Madder, I need malachite. Madder and malachite.'

'I don't know what you're talking about.'

'Do you have any lapis lazuli?'

'Any what?'

'I'm trying to help you, I need lapis lazuli.'

Thorn frowned. 'Like in manuscripts?'

Jack's heart pounded. 'What do you know about my manuscript?'

'What do you mean?'

'Do you have any or not?'

'Jack, you're insane.'

'I'm trying to help.'

'What's the matter with you?'

Jack didn't know. He looked down and saw that he was holding Thorn by his collar. He unclenched his fists. 'Sorry.'

But Thorn had already turned and left.

უ

All the regret that had followed the manuscript – the lunatic butchered, Kirk lost, Constant exiled. Sandy had been bruised, Ash burned, Thorn heartbroken. Jack had been pursued by shadows, threatened by silences and finally abandoned. It didn't matter whether the manuscript's secret cult had done all or any of it. It didn't matter whether there was a cult or not. The manuscript was still responsible, one way or another.

Lapis lazuli, madder and malachite. He checked and double-checked the pages to make sure he needed them. All the names were there, and the stones and plants were illustrated with their exact colours. The brilliant ultramarine, the bright green, the red-purple tincture. They were exactly right. The words were all there, the pictures were there: there was no getting around it.

He stared at the manuscript's colours as they flickered in the candlelight. They were exactly right; they were perfect, and he suddenly realised why. *Like in manuscripts?* They were all dyes, used before synthetics. The Book of Kells, all the illuminated Bibles, all the old books. The vellum's pigments didn't just mimic the ingredients – they *were* the ingredients. The red-purple really was madder, the bright green malachite, the ultramarine lapis lazuli. And the last mineral, the one he couldn't identify – it didn't matter, because it was there on the page.

He razored grains of colour from the page, trying not to nick the vellum. He felt sweat bubbling at his forehead, running into his eyes. But he managed a tiny pile of each of the missing ingredients.

The potions responded instantly to the new pigments. They flared into colour, amplifying the light from the candles and the projector. One bubbled a bright blue, one a clear blood red, one a dragon's green. One was clear and almost invisible. The final flask contained a colour he'd never seen before; he couldn't begin to describe it, couldn't say whether it was closer to red or blue or green.

He watched as the crypt flickered with all possible colours, and beyond the visible spectrum into shades of infrared and ultraviolet. The stars had returned to the walls, stretching into the distance, and they were joined by new planets and galaxies. They fooled his depth perception again, and he felt he was floating with his machine in the middle of the universe.

The last glass plate began to lighten, gathering a bright white. He stared as it shone like the moon through thinning clouds. He couldn't believe it, but the machine was working – the eye was opening.

He waved his hand in front of the projector, absorbing and interrupting its light. A darkness appeared in the first elixir and travelled along the beams, infecting each flask with a new colour. The green became redder, the red bluer, the invisible potion more golden, and each by degrees, as if the machine were slowing down the light.

Then the shadow connected with the final plate and he saw everything that was his hand: the loops and whorls, all of his futures in creases and folds, the layers of his skin, the rips and currents of blood. He saw the cell walls shift and make way for the endless combinations of his DNA. He snatched his hand back and the shadow ran out slowly, and the image remained for seconds.

He noticed that Beth's home movie was still dangling from its reel, held by the projector's arm. He threaded it past the bulb and set the motor running.

ʊ)

They were all at the beach, waves lapping too quickly, and he remembered the first time he and Beth had seen the movie, when it had played against her. Judy was filming while the others made sandcastles and buried each other. It was a typical home movie. The machine magnified the celluloid, overlaid the picture with its veins and grains, but otherwise the movie looked like it always had, a small but faithful image unfolding in the glass.

Then a blurry figure appeared in the middle distance. A balding head, the tilt of the neck. As Jack watched, it split into two figures: one that kept its distance, another that grew larger and more distinct as it approached the camera. It was Sam, and as he drew closer the whole scene blurred and doubled, like crossed eyes. One of the eyes left its place and followed Sam up the beach. Jack had the sensation of being torn in two. Frank didn't notice anything, continued as always. But the image of Beff reached for Jack's attention. As she stuck a shovel in the sand an outline faded over her, a sweep of charcoal: it was the face of anguish she had drawn, the flipper arms holding her body, the slants of pain. The half-Sam kept looking and smiling into the other exposure as they walked along the beach, and finally Frank noticed that Judy was half-gone, and what looked like his spirit melted from his body and sank into the sand.

ᴜ⊓

The film ran out and its white tail flicked over the reel as the broken image of Beth faded from the glass. Jack pressed his hand to his forehead, his aching brain. The machine had seen through the blur of the beach and into the tunnel of the future – it had seen the truth. It was a verifiable truth, a truth he knew and should have known all along.

So the machine worked. The manuscript had kept its obscure promise, the promise he had wrung from it with sweat and regret. The interpretation of tongues, the window opened and curtain set aside. There were shadows and tattoos circling him, gathering around the church, but he had the corroborated truth. He had cobalt and vermilion and emerald potions, invisible and indescribable colours, and he had the truth in his cellar. He was in terrible danger, they couldn't be far, but now he might defend himself.

But the machine had only been tested on things he already knew; there were mysteries that had waited a thousand years. The test – the real test was the manuscript. Everything the lunatic had written, the secrets of the universe, its forgotten languages, its wild idioms. A language that could build anything. He had decoded enough to cobble together the machine, and that much had cost him everything; but it was a crude, a functional translation. Now he would truly read it. The message lost for centuries, resurrected and read at last – he would read it at last.

The manuscript was already glowing with the light of the candles and potions. It trembled as he carried it to the first lens and placed it in front of the projector. The beams darkened into a palette of deep golds and browns.

He chose a page at random, dense with text and no pictures. He scurried to the glass, careful not to knock the apparatus. His heart pounded and his breath rasped; the vapours were thickening. He clasped his hands to stop them from shaking. He waited at the glass as the image emerged.

It was blank.

The writing had disappeared. All of the loops and curls, the headless snakes were gone. No sign of the gall and vitriol. The annotations shone in the ultraviolet light: Constant's references, Wilkins's real character, the marks of alchemists, the under-linings and question marks. But they weren't annotating anything, they weren't underlining anything. There was nothing there.

He returned to the manuscript itself, and the page was as full of the lunatic's script as it had always been. He flipped through the last pages and found a picture of a man surrounded by colours, found the words for madder and woad. He pressed the vellum flat and angled it in the projector's light.

In the glass there was no picture. There was nothing but the cracked and stained vellum. He could see possibilities, shapes that might suggest a hand or an eyebrow, the mast of a ship, a dress blown by the wind. Like patterns in clouds, the weasel and whale, like the man or rabbit in the moon. But it wasn't a picture, it wasn't anything.

The colours had vanished; the text had vanished. He flicked back through the manuscript and waited for the glass to fill.

Dense marginalia, nothing else. He tried to remember what he had seen there before: a woman emerging from a book, conspirators, a miraculous machine. Now there was nothing.

He tried to remember what Ash had said about the manuscript and its decaying isotopes. The lunatic's ink hadn't bitten into the vellum like the gall and vitriol were supposed to. And everybody else's writing had faded from view. He wondered what it all meant, what had produced this illusion in the last lens.

But in some part of his mind beyond instinct and reason he knew that the machine had worked, and that he was seeing the truth.

The manuscript – the true manuscript was empty.

His extinct language, his perfect language, his universal translator – there was nothing there. He had taken what he wanted. The manuscript could have been anything; he could have extracted from it any meaning he wanted. It could have been anything, and what did that mean? It meant it was nothing.

He told himself it couldn't be true, it didn't make sense. If the machine worked then the manuscript had no meaning – but then how had he built the machine, how had he made it work? But an answer pulsed in a small corner of his mind. The blueprint had been his own invention, like everything else; and he hadn't needed the machine to tell him the manuscript was empty, not really. He'd only needed to be prepared for the truth.

He leafed through the manuscript and read its silvery annotations, the obsession of many lifetimes. Annotating nothing, or each other – underlining each other. In the cold and true light he recognised the mysterious regret he had been warned about. There was no conspiracy of shadows, no secret sect. Organised criminals had bombed the forensics centre, people had tattoos for their own reasons, and the St John Ambulance was a fine charitable organisation. The regret was the bewitchment, the curse of needing to understand. It had distracted him from Beth and he had been unable to help her, and everything tumbled from that: her confusion, her affair. He remembered Constant's scratchings, his Revelations. *And I tooke the little booke out of the Angels hand, and ate it vp, and it was in my mouth sweet as honie: and as soone as I had eaten it, my belly was bitter.* That was the regret, and all his fault.

He fell against the crypt wall and slid to the floor. He had tried so hard, but he had obtained nothing and destroyed everything. He scanned the manuscript in desperation, looking for something to cling to. But all he found was the madness of centuries, the misled obsessives he had joined. He wished he could blame anyone but himself.

The candles were guttering and the elixirs slowing, losing their colour. The last light of the machine showed a picture. There was something there after all. He couldn't think what it was doing there. Then he realised someone must have traced over it, doubled its tentative lines; the ink had faded into the vellum and been revived by the light.

The tower topped by fire. People had written *Babel?* and *Pharos* next to it, and Constant had scratched *Sgs 3.* And underneath it: Beth's handwriting, her efficient library script

It said: *Find me.*

うﾉ

Jack stumbled out of the church and blinked in the sudden light of the graveyard. The sun was directly overhead. Constant's grave tilted at its usual angle, and he crouched by it and knew that it could have been anyone's grave. He crunched to the front of the church. A week's worth of newspapers piled on the porch, maybe more. It had been a month since the hail storm, two months since Frank's death. The church was locked, the squints covered. He bundled the manuscript back into the satchel with Johnson's letter and Kirk's letter. He remembered the monk's last Bible reference as he slammed the car door. *By faith Enoch was translated that he should not see death; and was not found, because God had translated him.*

Uchuni

The world seemed infinite. After the crypt and the church and the city, the horizon belonged to some other geometry. There were no landmarks in the distance. Fields of long and dry grass blurred past, hay like needles. The highway a steady rumble below.

He was bearing north and west, inland to the far corner of the state. He had clattered with semi-trailers, climbed through the blue and ochre layers of the mountains, droplets of mist stretching across the glass. After Bathurst he no longer recognised the towns or the landscapes. He only had his sense of direction to guide him through the mountains and down into the plains.

Wind hissed through the windows, ruffling the manuscript's pages. He glared at the vellum as he drove. He didn't know how he had been fooled. He had been blinded by promises, thought the manuscript to be what he needed most. It was no excuse.

The straight roads like landing strips for the sun. He drove all day past satellite dishes of every size, mobile phone towers in the middle of nowhere. There were billboards whose colours had faded to cyan or magenta. The road was hypnotic, and hours of momentum pressed at him; when he stopped to stretch he found himself leaning forward as if into the wind. The grasses flattened and broke into patches, revealing pale sand. The clouds divided and the sun overtook him. There was usually another road beside the highway, worn asphalt punctuated by shocks of weed. There were towns on the old roads. There were towns for no reason. He drove faster than the speed limit, as fast as he could.

He spent the night in the only hotel. It was a mining town, or had been once. Its main street was shattered into floes and had no footpaths. Its other streets were dirt; most of the town was dirt. A steady wind piled red drifts into corners. He didn't have a suitcase to unpack, didn't have a toothbrush or a change of clothes. He slid the manuscript under the bed, not sure why he had brought it, and stood in his room as the desert pressed against the window. There was a picture of the hotel taken a hundred years ago, horses and carriages in the street.

Truck drivers lined the bar, old miners and travelling salesmen. A young couple parked their campervan and came in for beer and showers. He sat and ate a tough steak. The bartenders were married: he could see it in their wrinkles and in the way they made room for each other. The young couple sat at a table in the corner. The only sounds were cutlery and glass.

Nobody could help him.

'Never heard of anything like that.'

'Where'd you get that idea?'

His old paranoia surged, and he scanned their foreheads for tattoos. But all that was behind him. He was a translator from the city, looking for something that didn't exist.

'Just wondering,' he said.

'Not the strangest thing we've heard, is it?'

'Couple of blokes a while back, after an inland sea.'

'Died, didn't they?'

'Long dead.'

He wanted to ask them if they had seen Beth. But places like this had no memory for people. Even a tall and slender woman with astonishing skin would pass through like so many others, the hit men and lunatics, the gypsies and drunkards and miracle healers whose paths crossed at the edge of the desert and left nothing but eddies of dust, soon disappearing into the sand's slow tides.

n the morning he gathered up the manuscript, bought coffee
and petrol, and drove on. North and west, and the sand
dunes rose around him, and the car pitched and yawed
against the road. The dunes looked like the bodies of giants.
He imagined he saw Beth lying there, her shin or the crook of
her elbow, red dust spilling from its folds.

He drove on bitumen and asphalt, on dirt roads stiff with
gravel or weeping from his tyres. The dunes rose and fell in
mathematic curves. Fences enclosed three sides of nothing.
There were road signs so riddled with buckshot that they
couldn't be read. Salt lakes and dry lakes and claypans, and
blond and red sand marbling together.

Sometimes he stopped and walked a few metres, knowing
that if he lost the car behind a dune he might never find it
again. He crouched by the spinifex and kerosene grass and
felt the earth.

He felt that at any moment he might recognise a landmark
and know where he was. He scanned the dunes and the old
shadows disappeared from his periphery. He returned to the
car, sweating as he drove, soaking his clothes to the seat.

He stared at the manuscript, frowned through what he
thought he knew until the true nonsense emerged again. He was
training himself to see it as it was. But he wasn't really thinking
about it. He was thinking about Kirk's letter, almost as old, and
what the toothless lunatic had told him. No purpose or plan,
but meaning and understanding like shelter where there is none.
That was it, that had to be the barest truth.

The crossroads all looked the same. He looked for the sun
and tried to find north, and rehearsed each intersection so
that he would know it again. He didn't think he had driven
the same road twice. It no longer mattered much where he
was going, as long as he kept covering the ground.

People were becoming surprised to see him as the towns dwindled and stretched from each other, as the dunes rose higher and the salt lakes spread. He sat in corners eating stale sandwiches or drinking strong beer, counting out the last of his money. He chewed and listened and dropped hints.

'An inland sea? Wonder what gave them that idea.'

'The desert's full of mirages. Water at the horizon, but you never get there.'

'What if there was one, once? Wouldn't there be anything left? Some, I don't know, wharf or slipway, some breakwater.'

'City folk.'

They had legends of their own. The way test pilots panicked and thought they were upside down, about to crash into the ocean – so they rolled and crashed into sandy clouds instead. Men had drilled an oil well dry and gone down to look at it, the dripping and glittering cathedral of the emptied earth – and now wandered the desert, eating sand. It hadn't rained for a thousand Thursdays. They couldn't tell him what he wanted to know.

'You've come a long way for nothing.'

'Knew you were crazy, moment I saw you.'

He looked crazy. He could feel his eyes becoming wild, his hair thickening with sweat and dust. His skin was tight and burning, pricked with days of stubble. His clothes were sopping at night and stiff in the morning. He stared too deep into their eyes and asked impossible questions. He was as conspicuous as it was possible to be in this huge and anonymous land.

The stones of creek beds were rubbed smooth by the wind and had desert air trapped inside them; if you left them in campfires they would burst into arrowheads. He scraped salt from the lakes and wondered at their traces of pink. Legends of massacres, the blood of explorers. He searched the shores for ruins. He stopped at the dingo fence and swung open the gate. Every point was a point of no return.

There were whispers surrounding the deaths of Robert O'Hara Burke and William John Wills, whose search for an inland sea left them blanching in the desert, skin peeling like the most delicate paper. Nineteenth-century forensics were too primitive to test these hushed theories, which in any case were never taken seriously in the city. But in the desert it was maintained, and some still maintain, that the explorers had died by drowning.

5

He found it at last, after days or weeks of driving. The sun was setting as he came to a chain-link fence that only extended ten metres either side of the road, an open gate. The asphalt was worn, but only by the wind and sand. The access road didn't go far enough; it surrendered to dirt a few hundred metres after the gate. He felt the wheels sinking and pressed the accelerator carefully.

It had looked like a derrick or well-head in the distance. But it was the wrong shape, and now the wrong colour, glowing with the purpling orange of the sky. He kept the accelerator down; night was falling and he couldn't wait until morning. But the road was softening and the tyres were spraying great wakes of sand behind him – and then he stopped.

He climbed onto the roof and looked around at the falling darkness. The horizon was almost featureless, a perfect curve. The road behind him, collared by the gate, the interrupted sunset in front of him. He saw himself as if from a great height – the blank desert, the gate, the road, the car. The sky's smooth shift from gold to darkness.

It rose twenty or thirty metres into the air, a skeleton thumb. The wind had stripped its whitewash to the thinnest layer, and its raw stone showed through in patches. The dome's glass was unbroken, the lens frozen above him. It stood on a rocky outcrop that rose gently out of the desert. Cliffs curved like a coastline, and fell a few metres to a sea of soft dunes stretching into the west. The sand of the dunes was as pale as beach sand.

The lighthouse leaned a few degrees off true, as if the rocky shelf had tilted. A metal door rusted in its base: it was padlocked, but came off its hinges when he felt its handle. The generator at the bottom of the lighthouse had rusted, as if the air were salt spray. Numbers punched into the rust said 1976.

He climbed with difficulty, clutching the satchel, unsettled by the lighthouse's tilt. The stairs were unworn, as if nobody had climbed them before. He thought of the smooth and rounded ledges in the crypt and oratories of his church, their church. He no longer felt thirsty or fatigued. It was as if he hadn't driven days and weeks through the desert. His heart hammered as he climbed, but not from the effort.

The stairs rose through a rusted trap door and into the lamp room. The lens rippled with magnification before the thick bulb. The room was glass on all sides. He looked out at the sea of dunes as the sun set. The sand spilled with orange light and looked like waves. It was a trick of perspective or the shifting sunset that set them alive and made him think they were rolling towards him.

५

He couldn't believe he had found the lighthouse. The dunes lapping against the cliff, the sound of waves in the desert wind. He gathered dead wood and dry scrub and hauled them up the stairs, hurrying as the light faded and the sky returned to a darkening blue. Most of it was too sandlogged to burn. He cleared an expanding semicircle around the lighthouse, working his way back towards the car.

The sun had set, but the horizon was still tinged with gold. He climbed to the lamp room: a room without corners or walls. He moved the satchel to the far side, sat on the stone floor with his back to the glass and touched a match to his pyramid of tinder. The fire burned quickly in the desert air. He had to keep it small and feed it continuously with twigs, daggers of spinifex. The stars were coming out behind him, and reflections of the fire played in the glass. It cast the sand dunes with a faint, flickering orange.

The lamp room felt like a space capsule passing into the earth's cold shadow, drifting with no hope of landfall. Perhaps it was the anti-climax: he'd found the lighthouse, now what? The emptiness in all directions, the silence, the landscape waiting patiently to overtake and forget you. Secrets and calumnies, things seen or imagined. There should have been some light, somewhere: the mirage of a distant town, Christmas trucks on the highway. But there was nothing, a perfect horizon of darkness as the last memories faded from the sky.

He felt the pull of the manuscript, the comfort and distraction. He reached for it again, he took it from the satchel. It made sense, even though he was seeing pictures that couldn't have been there. Satellite dishes, infinite fences. A man in a lantern in the desert, asleep as the sun warped the horizon. A woman with astonishing skin: a dream.

On the third night he realised he wasn't alone. There were shadowed figures out there, skimming across the sea of dunes. The fire sent soft boundaries of light and darkness across the desert, and the figures weaved in and out. At first he thought it a trick of the light. But they were always there, and he began to learn their patterns, to know where to look. Hooded figures waiting in the desert, heads bowed, arms hidden in the folds of their robes.

They were after the manuscript: they were still after it. They'd followed him even to the desert and this lighthouse. Was Beth among them? Would a habit drop to reveal her pale skin, the astonishing skin he knew best? He frowned and tried to remember what he'd decided, the conviction he'd tried to bring with him – but he could only think of the manuscript's promises. Thoughts of many hearts, the interpretation of things. *Who will haue all men to bee saued, and to come vnto the knowledge of the trueth.*

Imagine if he built the machine again – here, in his lighthouse in the desert. The unbroken horizon, the outlook in all directions. The old lighthouse at Pharos held a mirror so powerful that it could spy on Constantinople, its curved and inverted treacheries. With a new eye of truth, this lighthouse could see into the heart and many hearts of the universe. He would spend his days and nights immersed in truth. He'd be immune to shadows. What would that make him? An angel, and perhaps a god.

The machine, the elixirs, the plants and minerals. Where would he find them in the desert? Chalk and quicksilver, fuzball and trubs, chalcedony and cornelian. Would he be able to fix the generator? He remembered the eye's colours, the beautiful colours. Madder and malachite, lapis lazuli ...

He wrenched awake. Heart pounding, covered in cold sweat – how had he fallen asleep? He blinked and couldn't see properly, couldn't wipe the darkness from his eyes.

The fire was going out.

He scrambled to it: a pile of embers. The pool of light had shrunk around the lighthouse, like a shawl gathered against the cold. The darkness was closing in, and all it held – the shadows, the manuscript's secret sect.

He knelt and blew into the fire, and it flared for a few seconds. He thought he saw himself in the embers, a wild figure kneeling, warm light at his beard, tiny bloodshot fires in his eyes. An infinite desert around him, crammed with enemies, the fire guttering already.

He looked around for tinder, but there was nothing left. The moon had set, but the stars shone bright and cold: the dawn was hours away. He'd already cleared a huge tract around the lighthouse, far beyond the diminished circle of light. He'd never find anything more to burn, or not before the light went out. He shuddered at the thought. The fire failing, the darkness sweeping in. The night would tear his mind from him, and the tattooed shadows would crash over him. He had to keep the light burning.

But there was nothing left to burn.

There was only the manuscript.

He couldn't do it. He read it again in the fading glow. Hearts, truths, interpretations. All the world's secrets open to him. All of its promises, everything he wanted.

A disturbance in the light at his shoulder. He whirled and saw the darkness folding into a menacing shape behind him, a robe, a tattoo, a cross, the glint of a knife. The figure looked back and seemed to be gesturing to the shadows behind. Jack lunged to blow on the fire, the last of his breath, and the shadow flickered and threw up its arms. His chest and neck thumped as it faded into the wall. He knew they'd be back.

He had to keep the fire burning. But it wasn't just the tattooed strangers, there was more. Why had he come here in the first place? It wasn't the eye of truth. There was no eye of truth. But there were other reasons.

The manuscript was covered in sand and sweat. He opened it and brushed it off and the pages shifted in the fire-light, catching colours in their fibres. He remembered Kirk's lunatic and what he had said. There *was* no truth – there was so rarely a truth to be known, even under it all. But there might be a something else, another order of truth. You strug-gled to comfort and comprehend, you could build meaning and understanding. There might be no truth in the universe, no drifting galaxies of truth. But there might yet be small pockets of truth that people built together, huddled around like fires.

He peeled a page from the manuscript and held it over the dying fire. He was suddenly afraid the vellum would prove indestructible. And for a moment the flames slid along its surface, embracing it without touching. It took an instant for the fire to take hold, and then the edges flared. He dropped the page, and relief spread from the back of his neck and warmed him in the desert night.

There was plenty, and it burned slowly; he could burn it

for days. He dealt a few more leaves and watched the flames change colour with the burning pigments, green and blue and gold, bursting as the chemicals caught and the fire cast the desert with new colours.

ᴜ)

Chelovek was dancing outside in the desert. At the periphery of light, a little jig. He was looking right at Jack, dancing for him. Soon Jack began to hear music in his head – a Russian folk song, something about the rain.

He looked up and saw that the glass was glistening with Chelovek's colours, the ruddy brown of Soviet film stock. They came from the fire, the manuscript's pigments – the colours were playing out into the desert, and some trick had combined them into Chelovek, dancing patiently in the desert.

The manuscript sparked and the glass changed colours. They weren't Chelovek's colours any more, and it wasn't him dancing. They were Beth's colours. The colours of the home movies, the beaches and barbecues, her skin tanning and paling again, her hair darkening. He scanned the desert for her, but there was nothing outside – only her outline in the glass, reflecting the fire's colours. She was swimming at Camp Cove, girl and woman. She was red and blue and green, she was cyan and magenta and yellow and black. She knelt, flickering, to blow across the top of wine bottles, and the desert howled with breathy notes.

He knew what it meant. He reached to touch her, and his hand caught edges of the coloured light, and his shadow fell across her and blocked his view. On the horizon, a flash of lightning gave the silhouette of a small stone church with a broken roof and a single headstone. His fingertips knocked against the glass and he knew what it all meant, he knew what everything meant. But now it was too late. He slumped in the lamp room and watched the lightning in the distance, tall ships collapsing into the

esert, dunes crashing against the cliffs and sending sprays
f sand high into the air.

ŋ

haros was the world's first lighthouse, built to guide ships
to Alexandria. It rose from the island in three stages and
as topped by an octagonal chamber where a great fire was
ollected in a curved mirror and reflected around the harbour.
he mirror could see to Constantinople; it could gather
nough of the sun's rays to set fire to passing ships.

Ptolemy II locked seventy-two scholars in cells or oratories
n the island until they had finished the Septuagint, their
anslation of the Old Testament into Greek, for his great
orary across the harbour. He ordered the architect to dedi-
te the lighthouse to him – but the architect carved his own
ame into the rock before covering his disobedience with soft
aster and writing *Ptolemy* into that. The king was long
ead by the time the plaster crumbled to reveal its first
scription: *Sostrates, son of Dexiphanes of Knidos, on
half of all mariners to the saviour gods.*

The king was dead, but the architect lived on. He sat in the
acon room and watched his beams sweep across the harbour.
he plaster crumbled, revealing his name, and the saviour gods
warded him with an eternity of watching: they remade him in
eir image. He watched as the tides rose and fell, as the delta's
t clogged the sea. He watched the sandstorms in the desert,
ing like great waves behind the city, clouds of sand raining
nd over sandy seas.

As the library burned across the water, he saw the words
d letters carried on the flames. He looked around at a
rker world. The seventy-two scholars floated from their
lls and pointed out the letters of the Torah, first written in
ack flames on a white fire, written again as they rushed
om the burning Septuagint and into the Alexandrian air.
he universe was spelled out in their rearrangement, and the

seventy-two nodded as if many things they had taken for granted had just been confirmed.

He looked down and saw that his hands were covered in writing; he tore off his clothes and his whole skin was etched with writing. He caught a handful of sprayed sand and rubbed his skin away. But his veins still ran with writing; he pulled them away and they hung from the beacon room like streamers. And his bones were burnt with writing, seared with black characters he didn't recognise, dots and whorls and loops. He collapsed against the wall and kept watching as the lighthouse showed empires collapsing, knights on crusade, watching like a god or angel.

After fifteen centuries an earthquake rocked the lighthouse and sent it tumbling to the harbour's floor. He kept watching as the mirror grew dull and encrusted, as weeds entangled his bones, as his name was wiped clean by the sand and the tides. He only saw fish for a long time. Then scuba divers came to investigate the ruins and let out triumphant bubbles as they recognised his lighthouse. The library at Alexandria was being rebuilt at last, but he didn't know that – and at any rate it would soon sink again, because its architect had forgotten to consider the weight of the books.

უ]

He dreamed he had found a lighthouse in the middle of the desert. They said, or someone said, that people came from miles around and parked their cars and went fucking in the sand and loved each other forever. There was a light so bright that it shone through you, a light to know yourself and others by. He felt certain that someone had said that, once.

When he found it, it was deserted and broken. He sat in the lamp room with sandstone at his back and watched the sun setting over a sea of dunes. He lit a fire as the wind picked up and the air was filled with sand. He watched storms at the horizon, the loneliest man in the world. He

stened to the sounds of the ocean and thought he might stay
ere forever.

'Jack.'

He dreamed that Beth came to see him, which seemed to
ave been the whole point, once. She looked good, tanned by
e desert. She wore shorts and a singlet, hiking boots. Her
in was brown and smooth and astonishing, and she smiled
him.

'Jack, wake up.'

He struggled to open his eyes, but everything was the
me. The lighthouse, the crashing dunes. The fire was dying
ain; it was still dark outside. Beth was pulling him by the
llar, staring into his eyes.

'Thank God. How long have you been here?'

He tried to speak, but his voice stuck in his throat. He
lped like a fish, trying to breathe out. His mouth felt like
alk. He shook his head apologetically at the dream of Beth.
didn't matter much.

'Here, drink this. You look terrible.'

The water was cold and wetter than he could have imag-
ed. It shocked him out of his stupor. It wasn't a dream. It
as Beth, glorious, beautiful, astonishing.

'You came.'

Her eyes filled with tears. 'I can't believe you're here. I
n't believe I found this place and you're here.'

'You – you found it all right?'

'I started out, I didn't know where I was going. And then
ollowed the rumours.'

'There were rumours?'

'Everywhere, people were talking about it everywhere. A
hthouse in the desert, built by mistake. Just like you said.
meone had discovered it. Every pub I went to they were
king about it, every truck stop. first they were just rumours
rumours, nobody knew much. Then some of them had
tually met the guy, whoever he was, the one who found it.
ey all said he was crazy, he was absolutely insane.'

'Me?'

She grinned. 'You fit the description.'

'How did you find me in the dark?'

'You're in a lighthouse.'

He nodded. 'I've got something of yours.'

The envelope from the forensics centre, Beth's name and Max's address. It was smudged with sweat and creased from his pocket. She took it and lowered her eyes.

'Where did you get this?'

He didn't look at her. The fire was dying, so he pulled more pages from the manuscript and crumpled them onto the pyre. They caught and sent new colours through the flames. She didn't say anything else. He met her gaze and saw warm tears.

'Where is he?'

She wiped her eyes. 'It wasn't anything, Jack. I was so upset, I was lost and I just – liked the way he looked at me. I needed someone to look at me like that. I'm so sorry. But I sent him back a long time ago. We couldn't communicate, of course. He was worse than you.'

'Beth, I'm sorry, I—'

'It's all right, Jack. I'm sorry too. But here we are.'

'Thank God you came.'

She glanced around at the lighthouse walls, the glass opening to the desert, the flickering sand dunes. 'Did you make this?'

'Maybe, I don't know. I think we both made it.'

'It's nice.'

She held the envelope in both hands and read the address, looked at the magnifying glass and forensic eye. He stared at her and saw many things passing across her face. Her skin was tanned and brown, and it suited her. She dropped the letter into the fire, and it caught and blackened and curled.

'You're sure?'

She watched as the envelope opened and the letter unfolded within it, an official blue wrapping into origami

264

etals. The edges glowed and he saw the words *Beth* and *laughter* overtaken by darkness. He averted his eyes but didn't need to; the fire had already consumed it.

She turned to him. 'Can we go downstairs now?'

'One minute.'

He dumped the rest of the manuscript onto the fire, rips and currents of spark and ash. He was afraid he had extinguished it, but it soon reappeared around the pages, flickering and crackling. The vellum curled and bubbled, and the fire burned with new colours. Its leaves were separating and it seemed to melt as it burned. It smelled terrible, like skin.

⌣

The sand got everywhere. It wrapped their sweating skin and scratched them as they rolled across it. It drifted over them and blew into their mouths as they kissed. His hands trembled against her breasts. She clasped his buttocks and scratched sand from his back. The dunes crashed against them and tried to pull them under, but they struggled to the surface and climbed over each other and shook the sand from their hair.

There wasn't enough fire for the lens to produce a beam, but the lamp room glowed and sent warm colours across the dunes and their bodies, electric greens and blues, orange like rain at sunset. He looked up at her as she sat up and ran her hands across her body. Her perfect skin, dark nipples, the angle of their hair. The coloured flames. They weren't bright enough to shine through her, but were bright enough to see her by. He looked past her skin and saw her, the part of her that remained when everything else had been stripped; he looked with the same part of him. He looked into her widening eyes and understood.

The manuscript burned until morning.

Jack's manuscript is based on the unreadabl manuscript discovered by Wilfryd Micha Habdank-Wojnicz in the library of the Villa Mondragone i the Alban Hills near Rome in 1911, and now held in th Beinecke Rare Book and Manuscript Library at Ya University. It has been claimed over the years to be a code c cipher, a natural language, an artificial language and a hoa but has never been convincingly translated.

Quotations are taken or adapted from the anonymous L *Gesta Francorum et aliorum Hierosolimitanorum* (c. 1100 John Dee's *Mysteriorum Liber Primus* (c. 1581); the King Jam Version of the Bible (1611); John Wilkins's *Mercury, or, th Secret and Swift Messenger* (1641) and *An Essay towards Real Character, and a Philosophical Language* (1668); Mér Casaubon's *A True & Faithful Relation of What passed fc many Yeers between Dr John Dee (A Mathematician of Gre Fame in Q. Eliz. and King James their Reignes) and some spiri* (1659); Thomas Fuller's *The History of the Worthies England* (1662); John White's *Journal of a Voyage to Ne South Wales* (1790); and Jorge Luis Borges's 'El idiom Analítico de John Wilkins' in *Otras inquisiciones* (1952). Mar other sources have been invaluable, not least David Kahn's *Th Codebreakers: The Story of Secret Writing* (1967) and Umber Eco's *The Search for the Perfect Language* (1995).

Thanks to all at sci.lang.translation, particularly Ray Stein and Andy Gronski for the Russian idioms; to Joe Regal, for h helpful comments on an early draft; to Jenny Darling for ever thing; to Michael Heyward and Michael Williams; Madeleine Shaw and especially to Joni Henry.